A BROKEN SOUL

A PEMBROOKE NOVEL

JESSICA PRINCE

PROLOGUE

QUINN

"So, what? You're not talking to me now?"

At the sound of Addison's soft, sad voice I felt my white-knuckle grip on the steering wheel begin to loosen. Tonight was supposed to be special, memorable. But instead of a romantic dinner with my wife, we ended up arguing. I went silent, turning into the brooding, moody asshole I knew I could be when I was upset, and in return, she got upset, never liking it when I lost myself in my own head.

"How long are you going to give me the silent treatment this time, Quinn?"

I sighed and took my eyes off the dark, rain-slick road for just a moment. Addison's gorgeous blue eyes glimmered in the lights coming off the dashboard, and just like every goddamn time I looked at her, a rush of undeniable love enveloped me. "I'm not giving you the silent treatment, baby. I just don't understand why you won't even think about it."

"Because I'm not ready," she stated, turning her beautiful face away and staring out the windshield. "I love you, Quinn, you know that. You're the love of my life—"

"And you're mine," I interrupted. "That's why I want to try for another baby. Sophia's getting older now. Don't you think she'd want a little brother or sister?" Taking one hand off the wheel, I reached over and laid my palm on top of Addy's clenched fist. As always, the tension melted away and her grip loosened, allowing me to thread my fingers through hers and hold her hand tightly. That was just one of the many great things about our marriage. Even when we were arguing, we couldn't help but show each other unconditional love. "We've always talked about having a big family. I thought that's what you wanted."

"I do! I want a big family like we talked about. Just... maybe not right at this minute," she stated hesitantly. "We're still young, Quinn. We have years ahead of us. Can't we just enjoy what we've got right now?"

My shoulders tensed and my back went straight as I stared out the windshield, the headlights casting a glow along the dark, tree-lined road. Anxiety began to claw at my insides at the thought that Addison could possibly have any regrets in our life together. "What are you saying?" My voice was hard when I spoke. "Do you wish we'd waited?"

"No!" From the corner of my eye I saw Addy turn in her seat, fully facing me as she held on to my hand with both of hers. "No, not at all! Quinn, I *love* our life. I love you and Sophia more than anything. But we're still young. I want to enjoy our time together, just the three of us, for a little while longer before we start filling our house full of kids. That's all. But I *do* want to fill our house full of kids, I swear."

Even though her words helped to ease my worries, I still needed to be positive. "You sure?"

Her voice went low as she leaned across the console and pressed her lips against my ear. "Absolutely." Christ, I loved when her voice got husky like that. I felt myself getting hard behind the zipper of my slacks as thoughts of what I'd do to her when we got home began to run through my mind. "And in the meantime, I think we should practice..." Her teeth grazed my neck, sending

2

sparks of pleasure through my body. "*A lot.* Starting tonight. Sophia's with my parents and we have the whole house to ourselves. I think we should *practice* in as many rooms as possible. Starting with the kitchen."

I groaned, struggling to stop my eyes from rolling back in my head as her hand slid down my chest and between my thighs. "Christ, I love you," I grunted.

She giggled into my ear. "I love you too, Quinn. More than anything. Drive faster."

I didn't have to be told twice. My foot began to press on the accelerator, and I warned, "As much as I love what you're doing baby, you want to make it home in one piece to live out that kitchen fantasy, I suggest you stop."

Addy's laughter when she sat back in her seat warmed my chest. I loved when she laughed, it was one of the best sounds in the world. Second only to the sound of our daughter calling me *Daddy*. For the millionth time since Addison came into my life, I thought to myself that I was the luckiest bastard in the world.

Glad that we'd moved past the tense conversation from earlier and we were back to normal, I turned and smiled at my wife. "Love you, sweetheart." Grabbing her hand again, I lifted it and pressed a kiss to her knuckles. She smiled brightly back at me.

"Love you too." Her gaze turned back to the windshield and her eyes got big just seconds before she shouted, "Quinn, watch out!"

I jerked back just in time to see a deer standing in the middle of the road. On instinct, I slammed on the brakes. Addison's scream echoed through my head as the car began to spin out on the slick roads.

Time seemed to slow down to a crawl as we spun out of control. The screams were replaced by the sound of crunching metal as the car came to such a bone-jarring halt that my head bashed into the driver-side window, causing stars to burst before my eyes.

It felt like an eternity passed before my cloudy vision cleared and the ringing in my ears finally stopped. "Addy, baby..." I groaned in pain, the sound of my own voice ricocheting through my skull, making it feel like my head was about to explode.

She didn't answer. Pain gave way to hysteria when I looked toward the passenger seat at my wife's unmoving body. "Addison! Addy, baby, wake up!"

Ignoring the bolts of agony slicing through my body, I struggled against the seatbelt, futilely. "Addy! *WAKE UP!*" I screamed at the top of my lungs, fighting in vain to try and get to her. "Help! Somebody help us! Baby, please wake up. Don't leave me, Addy! Please, don't leave me!" I turned my head, frantically, hoping to see the headlights of an oncoming car while I continued to shout. "Someone help us! Please!"

My screams gave way to sobs as I tried so desperately to get to my wife. "Please, baby. Please." My voice cracked and I reached out, straining with all my strength, but I couldn't get to her.

People say that your life flashes before your eyes in near death experiences, but that wasn't what happened to me.

Time slowed to a crawl. An unbearable, anguished crawl, until it finally...

Just stopped.

1

LILLY

*S*TARING UP AT the ceiling fan, I counted each rotation of the blades as I watched them go round and round, hoping the repeated motion would help to shut my tired brain down. Sadly, it was pointless. There wasn't anything that could calm my mind enough for sleep to take hold.

I couldn't turn any of it off. And what was worse, there was no one I could talk to about it. My best friend, the one and only real friend I ever had, was with her husband in Denver where they had their second home during the football season so they could be together while he played.

I missed her like crazy during the months she was gone, but that did nothing to take away from the happiness I felt that she was finally with the only man she'd ever loved.

Unfortunately for me, I was going through something in my life. Something so heavy I wasn't sure I could bear the weight all on my own, and the only sounding board I'd ever had was gone. And telling Eliza over the phone that my father was dying and there was nothing that could be done about it wouldn't have done me any good. Not when I needed someone to lean on when I broke down in tears, not when I needed a designated driver to make a store run when I drowned my sorrows in every bottle of wine I owned and was in desperate need of more.

No, I couldn't have that conversation over the phone. And even though I knew she'd be a rock for me, I couldn't bring myself to pour out the painful emotions rolling around inside of me on my mother. She was suffering enough as it was, knowing she only had, at best, a handful of months with the man she'd loved for as long as she could remember.

I finally gave up on sleep, but once I did, the conversation I'd had with my parents earlier that day wormed its way to the forefront of my mind.

I thought it was business as usual when my mother called asking me to make the drive from Pembrooke to Jackson Hole for dinner. It wasn't a far drive, honestly, but I was usually so busy with the dance studio that it was hard finding the time to see them on a regular basis. That was why we scheduled dinner together at their house at least twice a month.

I should have known something was wrong when my mother called a week early and requested I come, claiming that she and my father had something they needed to discuss with me. But I was so wrapped up in everything I still needed to do before I began gearing up for the Winter Showcase, I didn't stop to think how odd of a request it really was.

They knew how time consuming running my own business was, and weren't ones to ever make requests like that. I should have known. I should have paid attention to something other than myself. I shouldn't have been so selfish. Maybe if I'd have been around more, paid more attention to my father's declining health, I could have done *something*, like force him to stop being so stubborn and go to the doctor before it was too late.

But I didn't. And now I had to suffer the consequences.

"PROSTATE CANCER? *What are you talking about? You can't have* cancer," I declared in disbelief. There was no way my father was sick. Cancer was something that happened to other families, not mine. And with the exception of the past six months or so, my father had always been the epitome of good health.

My mother made a soft noise, but I couldn't tear my eyes off my father's earnest expression. If I saw my mother crying, I knew I'd lose it. And it wasn't true. It couldn't be.

"Sweetheart—" he started, but I wouldn't let him finish. I couldn't. Because that would make what he was saying a reality.

"No. No! You don't have cancer. That's not possible. You need to go get a second opinion."

Dad's hand came to rest on top of my clenched fist where it was resting on the wooden table and squeezed. "Lilly Flower, I've already been to three different doctors. I'm so sorry, sweetheart, but it's true."

I pulled in a large breath and worked to get a hold of the tears that wanted to fall. "Okay," I finally replied on an exhale. "All right. So we'll talk to them about treatment. Maybe you can do chemotherapy or radiation or something. There has to be something they can do. You can beat this, right?"

"Oh honey." My mom's voice broke as she pushed her chair back and came toward me, leaning down and wrapping her arms around me from behind to hold me as Dad shook his head in defeat.

"I'm sorry," he whispered.

"Don't say that!" I shouted, finally losing the battle and letting the tears slide down my cheeks. "You can fight this, Daddy. You're the strongest man I know!"

My father's eyes grew red-rimmed as he swallowed audibly. Mom's hold loosened as she moved around me and crouched beside my chair. "The cancer had already spread by the time they found it. Treatment would give your father a little more time, honey, but that's it, maybe a few extra months if we were lucky. The quality of life wouldn't be worth it. The chemo would be intense and would make him so sick most of the time those few extra months wouldn't count for much anyway."

"But—" I had to force that one word past the golf-ball-sized lump in my throat.

"I don't want you to remember me like that, Lilly Flower. I don't want your last memory of me being this sickly, bedridden man with no hair. I want to go out like I've lived. On my own terms. Please tell me you understand."

What could I possibly say to that? My father looked resigned to his fate, but still scared at the same time. I wasn't lying when I said he was the strongest man I knew. He was. But I could see the fear in his eyes. And I refused to do or say anything that could cause him any more pain.

Just as he had my entire life, Dad realized what I was about to do before I did it and stood, braced for impact as I moved from my chair and launched myself into his waiting arms. "I understand," I cried into his chest, because I did. I understood him not wanting to go through a grueling treatment for a chance at a few short measly months that wasn't even a guarantee.

I didn't like it, but I understood.

And as I stood there, letting my father's button-down shirt soak up my tears and I memorized his spicy, woodsy scent, a scent I'd known since childhood, I let reality wash over me.

I was going to lose my father far too soon.

SQUEEZING my eyes closed against the fresh onslaught of tears that threatened, I inhaled deeply through my nose then blew it out slowly before sitting up in my bed. It was only four in the morning, but I knew of only one thing that would temporarily allow my mind to stop swirling around. It had been my escape since I was a little girl. And now, more than ever, I needed to lose myself.

Letting the light of the moon shining through my bedroom window guide me, I brushed my teeth and threw my hair up in a messy bun on the top of my head before dressing in a pair of black dance shorts and a tight burgundy cami. With my iPhone in hand, I crept through my dark apartment and took the stairs that would lead to my dance studio below.

I needed my music. I needed dancing to wash away the sadness that filled my veins.

Hooking my phone up to the dock I kept down in the main studio, I scrolled through my playlists. When the opening beat of Kaleo's "Way Down We Go" started playing, I began to move, letting my body take over. I danced until one song bled into another, until sweat poured down my face and my muscles screamed from the exertion. I danced until the minutes ticked into hours and my mind cleared of every thought except executing the next turn or leap; until the darkness outside the window of the main studio was forced from the sky by the early morning sun.

My mind remained calm for the first time in twelve hours, but the reminder of everything that was happening was still there, and the dull ache in my chest hadn't disappeared completely. As the song on my iPhone changed, the music becoming softer and sadder, I finally allowed myself to let it all out. I cried for my father and what he was going through. I cried for myself at what I was going to lose. I cried because for the first time in a really long time I was reminded of just how lonely I was. I cried because there was no one I could lean on to share my burden.

Music and dancing was all I really had, so as long as my body allowed it, I was going to pour my anger and frustrations and pain out the only way I knew how.

2

QUINN

I WOKE WITH a start, jolted out of my recurring nightmare when all the air whooshed from my lungs. It took several seconds for the lingering dregs of the nightmare to let go of my conscious and for sleep to leave me all together, but once it did, I realized it wasn't the dream that rendered me breathless.

That was courtesy of my daughter and her flailing limbs.

Once the nightmare finally released me all together, the pained sound of Addy's voice was no longer at the forefront of my mind. I let out a heavy sigh and turned my head on the pillow to stare at my daughter as she slept next to me. I managed to find a smile as I watched her for a while. The only time I ever got to smile genuinely in the past three and a half years was when I looked at her. There was no sorrow on her soft, sleeping face, and there were times I couldn't help but envy that. Some days I would have given anything to be free of the pain that always lingered in the recesses of my mind.

That familiar ache in my heart, along with the lingering pain in my body thanks to the accident, was a constant reminder of everything I'd lost. It was a reminder that my world had stopped, and to this day still hadn't fully started back up again.

More than my body broke the night I lost Addy. My heart, my mind, and my soul were still in tatters, and if it hadn't been for the sleeping girl next to me, I had no doubt I would have let the pain swallow me whole.

Sophia rolled again in her sleep and I barely managed to catch her arm before she caught me in the jaw. One of the downsides of having a six-year-old who crawled into your bed in the middle of the night was the physical beating I took on a regular basis. My girl tossed and turned like nobody's business.

A glance at the clock on the bedside table showed I had enough time to get a quick shower in before having to get Soph up and ready for school. I flung the covers back and threw my legs over the side of the bed, resting my elbows on my knees and scrubbing the last bit of sleep from my face. Just as I did every morning, I gave myself a few extra moments to gaze at the picture sitting on my nightstand, reaching over and running the tip of my finger along the cool glass that set over Addison's smiling face. "Morning, baby," I whispered into the silent room before forcing myself from the bed and into the bathroom.

Showering and dressing in my PFD uniform in record time, I opened the bathroom door and reentered the bedroom.

I flipped on the overhead light and pulled the covers to the foot of the bed. "All right, Sleeping Beauty. Time to wake up."

Sophia let out a small mewl of protest and pulled one of the pillows over her head to block out the light.

"Uh uh," I chuckled, coming to sit on the mattress next to her. "None of that now." I moved the pillow off her head and tossed it far enough away she couldn't reach it. "Ten minutes, squirt, or you go to school without breakfast."

She let out a grunt but sat up, her mass of blonde hair in tangles all around her head, standing on end. Like a zombie, she climbed off the bed and moved toward the bathroom off the hallway. When I heard the sink cut on, I took that cue and headed into the kitchen to start breakfast.

Sophia joined me ten minutes later, dressed for school. She climbed onto one of the barstools at the kitchen island just as I slid the last pancake onto her plate.

"Teeth brushed?"

"Uh huh," she mumbled, still not fully awake.

One corner of my mouth kicked up in a grin as she rested her elbow on the counter, propped her chin in her hand, and watched as I cut up her pancakes and slathered them in syrup. "You do a good job or just run the brush over them a few times?"

"I did good," she answered, then forked a heaping bite of pancakes into her mouth. "Wanna smell my breath?" she asked around the food.

"I'll pass. And don't talk with your mouth full."

"You asked," she shrugged before turning back to her food. There weren't many dishes I could cook well —Addy was always the cook in our household — but my girl loved her old man's pancakes. It was one of the few meals I didn't have to bribe her into eating. It was either bribe her with a few extra minutes on her iPad or a knockdown drag-out fight, and on the evenings I was home from the fire department, I was usually too exhausted to fight. Needless to say, my daughter was better at using her iPad than I was, and we ate a *lot* of pancakes. Much to my own mother's displeasure.

"Daddy?"

I finished my sip of coffee and looked up from the news site I was scrolling through on my phone as I stood across from her. "Yeah, Angel?"

"Can I be a ballerina?"

My brow quirked up as I studied my little girl. "A ballerina?"

"Uh huh," she nodded enthusiastically. "Yesterday, at school, Missy Davenport was talkin' about how she takes classes to be a ballerina. She said she gets to wear pink tutus and dance around on her tippy toes in these special shoes with ribbons on 'em. I wanna wear tutus and ribbons. Can I, Daddy? *Pleeeeeease?*"

Fuck, but I was screwed. Telling my daughter no was never something I'd been good at. When Addison was alive, she'd been the firm one, while I was wrapped around my little girl's finger. Now that I didn't have Addy to run interference, it had only gotten worse.

"But I thought you wanted to be a firefighter like your dad?"

Her little face scrunched up like she smelled something bad. "That's for boys, Daddy."

My eyes went wide as I stared down at the little girl who, just last week, declared she wanted to fight fires like her old man. "That's not what you said a few days ago." Why I felt the need to argue with a six-year-old was beyond me, but her sudden change of tune made me feel somewhat less important. It was ridiculous, really, but knowing I was my daughter's hero, to the point where she wanted to be just like me, was a huge ego boost. Losing that — for something as girly as *ballet*, felt like a slap in the face.

She shrugged casually as she ate the last bite of her breakfast. "I changed my mind. Now I wanna be a ballerina. Can I? Pretty please?"

Christ, those blue puppy-dog eyes, combined with the way her bottom lip jutted out in a pout just about did me in.

"We can go to the dance school next to where we always eat dinner! You can sign me up and I can start tomorrow!"

After draining the last of my coffee, I put the cup in the sink and circled around the island, reaching out to ruffle her hair. "I'll think about it. Now go get your backpack. We're going to be late."

Sophia hopped off the stool and bolted from the kitchen.

A ballerina. Addy would have been ecstatic. When we found out we were having a little girl, she went on and on about putting her in dance class and gymnastics, and all those girly things.

It was times like this that I missed her the most. Not only

because I loved her and wanted her back, but because she wasn't there to teach our daughter how to grow up into a woman.

And just like every day for the past three and a half years, I was eaten up by the overwhelming fear that I was going to do something that would irreparably damage the only person I had left.

Most days I didn't have a goddamned clue what I was doing. I was alone and drowning.

All I could do was hold on to the hope that I'd find my footing. I'd eventually wade out of the murky waters and feel that confidence as a father I had when I was part of a team.

Until that day came, all I could do was fake it and hope I didn't screw up along the way.

WITH SOPHIA AT school and thirty minutes before my shift was set to start, I pointed my truck toward Sinful Sweets, the town bakery-turned-restaurant that was co-owned by Eliza, my buddy Ethan's wife, and her step mother Chloe. The place served great food, even better pastries, and out of this world coffee. The latter of the three being what I was needing the most.

"Morning, Quinn," Chloe called out once I stepped inside. She ran the bakery side of Sinful Sweets and had been the original owner when it first opened back when I was a teenager.

"Chloe," I greeted, tipping my chin in her direction as I made my way to the counter.

"The usual?" she asked, marker poised against a paper cup, ready to write my name on it as I made my way up to the counter.

"Please. And a chocolate croissant to go as well."

"You got it." Chloe set my cup under the espresso machine and began hitting buttons so it could work its magic, then moved to the pastry case for my breakfast. "So how's sweet Sophia doing?"

One corner of my mouth quirked up at the mention of my little girl. "She's great. She just informed me this morning she wants to be a ballerina."

Chloe's face lit up as she slid the bag with my croissant across the bar. "That's adorable! You know, Lilly runs the studio next door." At her words my gut clenched. But unbeknownst to the sudden turmoil I was suffering, she continued. "I have my girls enrolled there. She really is a fantastic teacher. You should think about signing Sophia up. I bet she'd love it."

I had no doubt she would. That wasn't the problem. The problem was that dance teacher in particular. I'd been back in Pembrooke for a little over two years now, and in that time I'd probably said a handful of words to Lilly Mathewson. And for good reason.

The very first time I'd laid eyes on her was like getting hit by a truck. She'd been crossing Main Street as I drove down it, and at that very first glimpse I could have sworn I was seeing Addy. It took everything I had not to wreck my truck as my entire body turned to stone. It wasn't until she turned and laughed at something someone on the sidewalk said to her that I realized I wasn't staring at my wife. Where Addy's eyes shimmered the brightest blue, this woman's were a soft brown, and her left cheek dimpled as she smiled brightly.

That initial sighting was a pre-cursor to what I'd felt each time I saw her. She was just too big a reminder of what I'd lost, and I had no clue how to act around her. The thought of having to have a one-on-one conversation with Lilly set me on edge in the most uncomfortable way. Unfortunately, it was either sign Sophia up with her or make the drive to Jackson Hole a half hour away every damn time she had a class.

"Yeah," I finally stated once I realized I'd been silent for too long. "I'll be sure to check that out." Reaching for my wallet in my back pocket, I pulled out a few bills and tossed them on the bar top just as Chloe placed my coffee down in front of me. "Thanks for this." I lifted the cup in my hand in indication. "Have a great day."

"You too," she returned with a smile just as I turned and headed for the door with coffee and pastry in hand. I reached my truck parked along the curb and set the cup on the hood so I could pull my keys out of my jacket when something from the corner of my eye caught my attention.

It was still early enough that the sidewalks along Main weren't crowded, giving me a perfect view into the studio next to Sinful Sweets, and what I saw through the window stole the breath right out of my lungs. Lilly was on the other side of the glass, dancing to a song I couldn't hear.

But it wasn't the way she moved, her body as fluid as water, that captured my attention and held it for several long, painful seconds.

No. It was the shattered expression on her face as she danced that called to me the most. It was the very same expression I wore daily for the past three and a half years. In that very instant I felt a kinship to the woman behind the glass, dancing like it was the only thing keeping her going.

Jerking my gaze away from the window, I hit the button on the remote to unlock the door, grabbed my coffee, and climbed in, slamming the door behind me. I threw my truck in reverse with far more aggression than necessary and peeled out as fast as I could, because it was that feeling of kinship that scared me more than anything.

3

QUINN

"*D*ADDY! *DADDYDADDYDADDYDADDY!*"

I spun around on the sidewalk just as my heart dropped to the ground thinking that something terrible had happened to Sophia in the millisecond of time that had passed since we exited Sinful Sweets. That was the *only* reasonable explanation she'd have for screaming at the top of her lungs when I was a foot and a half away from her.

"What?!" I shouted back frantically as I crouched down low to her level, my eyes scanning for injury. "What happened? What is it? Are you okay?"

"Daddy, I wanna be a ballerina," she stated casually, all the hysteria in her voice gone.

"*What?!*" I barked, feeling like I'd just lost ten years off my life, all for nothing.

She threw her thumb over her shoulder in the direction of the dance school right next door. "Please, Daddy? *Pleeeeease*! It's all I want in the whole wide world."

Fuck me, if she was already starting with the female melodramatics at age six, I was screwed as she got older. Standing tall and running a hand through my hair with a heavy sigh, I looked in the direction she was pointing. My heart rate kicked up to an uncomfortable level at the thought of having to go in there and have an actual talk to Lilly — something I'd avoided for two long years — but when I looked down into my little girl's pleading eyes, I knew I couldn't say no.

It was totally irrational, this fear I had, but just looking at Lilly stirred something inside me that I would have rather left untapped.

"All right," I finally relented, earning a shrill scream of excitement as she jumped up and down, clapping her hands.

"Let's go! Let's do it now!" Wrapping her little fingers around mine, she gave me a pull, and on slow feet, as though I was being dragged through wet cement, I followed after.

The bell over the door chimed, announcing our presence, and the very first thing my eyes landed on was the pretty blonde standing at the front desk. She was wearing what I could only assume was standard dancing clothes. Unfortunately, the short, tight shorts and spaghetti strap top that clung to her like a second skin made me all too aware of just how amazing her body was.

"Quinn," Lilly started, her face a mask of surprise to see me standing before her. "Hi. What are you doing here?"

I struggled to keep my expression blank, all the while, unwanted images of the woman before me filtered through my head on warp speed. I wanted to ask her what had her so upset last week, I wanted to know what had made those whiskey-colored eyes look so desolate as she danced that morning with tears streaking down her beautiful face. I wanted to push to find out what had happened in her life that made her look as broken as I felt.

But I wouldn't do any of that. We weren't friends, and despite feeling a kindred spirit in her the other morning, I knew staying back was my only option. Because I was drawn to her in a way that was wrong on so many levels.

Luckily, Sophia was so amped up she answered for me. "I wanna be a ballerina!"

With one last quizzical glance in my direction, Lilly turned her sights on Sophia, bending forward and placing her hands on her knees. "You do?" she asked with a brilliant smile that made my stomach tighten. Sophia nodded eagerly. "Well you're in luck. You've come to the right place, because I *love* turning pretty little girls into ballerinas."

Sophia looked at her in wide-eyed wonder and asked on a breath, "You do?"

"Uh huh. Tell you what, why don't you peek through that window right over there," she pointed to one of the closed doors off the main corridor, "and watch that class for a bit while I talk to your dad about getting you all signed up."

"Is that a ballerina class?"

Lilly gave a light giggle and I swear to fucking God, I felt it in my gut. "No. That's a hip-hop class. My girl Samantha teaches it."

Sophia took off in that direction, and the much needed buffer between me and Lilly disappeared.

"How have you been?" she turned back to me and asked, like we were long-time friends. I couldn't really blame her, we knew each other by association considering our friends were married to each other.

I opened my mouth to reply but stopped myself, thinking the best option was to keep my answers short and sweet, to the point to move this along so I could get the hell out of there, I simply stated, "Good. Busy."

One of her eyebrows quirked up. "Have you talked to Ethan lately? Eliza said it's been a pretty brutal season so far."

"Nope." That was a lie. I'd talked to Ethan just the other night, but she didn't need to know that.

"Uh..." She looked off to the side like she was trying to think of something, *anything* she could say to break through my animatronic behavior. "How are things at the fire department?"

"Fine."

She let out a small, defeated sigh, and I knew she'd finally given up on small-talk and was resigned to getting down to business. Christ, why did she have to be so goddamn pretty? And why the fuck did she have to remind me of Addison? "So, has Sophia ever been in dance class before?"

"No." And I was willing to admit that my tone came out gruffer than I had intended.

Her head jerked back just a bit, and I knew she read the tension in my voice. "Well that's all right. We have beginner, intermediate, and advanced level classes for every style. We could put Sophia in the beginner class to start with to gauge her skill level. If need be, she'll stay there until it's time for her to advance to the next class. We have three teachers here. I handle the Classic Style classes. Samantha teaches the Street Style ones, and Kyle handles our Latin Ballroom and Jazz."

It was like she was speaking in a different language. "I don't know what any of that means. I just need to enroll her in the beginner's ballet class. I don't really care about any of the other stuff." Yes, I sounded like an asshole. I was well aware of that, but I couldn't help it. It was like I didn't know how to fucking function around her. I forgot how to behave like a normal member of society.

"Uh... okay," she dragged out, her face pinched in confusion and a little bit of anger. "I'm sorry, but... have I done something to offend you?"

"Nope." I stuffed my hands in my pockets, keeping my tone flat as I added, "Just got things to do is all."

She looked like she wanted to push, possibly go off on me for being a dick. Instead, she sighed and walked around the back of the front desk, taking a seat in the chair before pulling open a drawer and grabbing a packet of papers. "Fine. Just fill this out and we'll get you on your way, since you're *so* busy." There was no missing the sarcasm in her tone, she made it loud and clear, and a large part of me respected the hell out of her for letting me know she wasn't happy to be taking my shit. "The class schedules and payment information is all listed on the last page. You can leave it on the ledge when you're done."

With that, she stood and headed down the hallway, only pausing long enough to touch Sophia's shoulder and say something that made my little girl laugh. Then she was gone, leaving me feeling guilty for how I'd acted and relieved all at the same time.

What the fuck was wrong with me?

4

LILLY

ELL THAT WENT well, I thought sarcastically as I collapsed down into my office chair, all the while wondering what the hell Quinn Mallick's problem was. We'd been living in the same town for two years now, and that was probably the first conversation we'd ever had. And I was pretty sure it was safe to say it hadn't gone all that well.

It was like talking to a robot. He remained completely emotionless the entire time he looked at me. Dull, lifeless, like he wanted to be anywhere else at that very moment, and having to speak to me in order to enroll his daughter in dance classes was about as much fun for him as a root canal. The only good part of the entire thing was getting to talk with his lively daughter, Sophia. She was absolutely adorable. So unlike her father.

When I wasn't rambling, I was trying to think of anything I could have possibly done to offend the guy, to the point I was almost obsessing over it.

Hell, who was I kidding? I *was* obsessing over it. That was why, ten minutes after Quinn left, I was still wracking my brain trying to figure out what wrong I'd done to him in the very limited contact we'd had over the years.

I was so deep in thought that when my cellphone rang on my desk the sound caused me to jump. Rolling my eyes at my own ridiculousness, I snatched my phone up and smiled when I saw the name on the screen.

"Bestie!" I cried out. "I miss you so much!" More than she probably could imagine. Struggling with the knowledge of what was happening to my father all by myself was driving me out of my mind. I was bouncing back and forth between crying my eyes out and being mad at the world at the flip of a switch.

"I miss you too!" Eliza shouted in return. "What are you doing right now? You busy?"

I leaned back in my chair and crossed my ankles on the scarred wooden top of my desk. "Not unless sitting in my office with my feet kicked up counts as being busy."

Her laughter rang through the line and made me smile. "It doesn't. But it's good you're sitting down. I have some news."

I shot up straight, dropping my feet to the floor. "Oh my God. You're pregnant!"

"How the hell did you guess that from me saying I had news? Good Lord! You're like a mind-reading ninja!"

"So it's true?" I squealed loudly. "You're preggers?" I began dancing around the office excitedly. If there'd been anyone out in the lobby to witness, they probably would have thought I was having a seizure. "How far along are you?"

"Well..." she dragged out. "I'm actually thirteen weeks."

"Thirteen *weeks*?!" I shouted, my voice echoing off the walls. "And I'm just finding out now?!"

"Calm down, crazy," she chuckled. "You were my first phone call. I haven't even called my dad yet. We wanted to wait until we were firmly in the safe zone. It's our first baby, you know? We talked about it and decided to wait until I was out of the first trimester."

I stopped and gave that some thought. "Okay, I can see your

point. And the fact that I was the very first call means you're totally forgiven."

"Just don't tell my dad you found out first."

I crossed my heart and held my index and middle finger in the air. Even though she couldn't see me, I knew she knew I was doing it. "Swear on my life. God, Eliza, I can't believe you're gonna have a baby! I'm so happy for you. I wish I was there to celebrate."

"Well, that just means you're going to have to get your tight little butt to Denver so you can see the bump I'm already sporting!"

I giggled happily. It was amazing how just one call from my best friend could shine a light on my world when it started growing darker. "You got a deal. I'll look at my calendar and see when I'm available to come up for a weekend."

"And I can take you to one of Ethan's games. Maybe we can get you hooked up with one of his hot teammates. And stop rolling your eyes," she finished on a scold, knowing damn good and well that was what I was doing at that very moment.

"Yes to the game, no to any blind dates you might be considering in my future."

"Oh come on!" she whined. "These guys are hot, Lil! I mean like, seriously *hot*—"

All of a sudden Ethan's voice could be heard in the background. "Standing right here, baby."

"Oh, you know what I mean. They're seriously hot for guys *not* as good looking as my husband."

I burst into laughter before saying, "Nice save."

"I'm clever like a fox," she giggled. "So you'll plan to come up here soon?"

"Definitely. I'll call you as soon as I know what weekend is best."

"I can't wait. So, what are you up to for the rest of the evening?"

"I don't know." I shrugged as I sat back down in my chair, thinking that my lack of plans for the evening was more than a little pathetic for a woman my age. "I'll probably pick up some wine from Mabel's and make myself dinner. I found one of your recipes the other day and it sounded really good. Figured I'd give it a shot."

"Oh no," Eliza groaned from the other end. "Stay out of the kitchen, unless you're planning on using the microwave."

"What's that supposed to mean?" I asked in affront.

"It means you're a terrible cook, and don't pretend it's not true."

She might have had a point. I wouldn't be joining the ranks of Master Chef anytime soon, but that didn't mean I couldn't figure my way out around a kitchen. "I'm not that bad," I argued. "I can follow a damn recipe, Eliza. How hard can it be? Besides, there's no way I'm as terrible as Harlow."

"No. You're worse. Harlow's the one that will make meals that'll give people dysentery, but *you're* the one who'll burn the house to the ground."

"That's not true!" It might have been a little true. "That one time was an accident! And the fire wasn't that big. You're exaggerating."

"Stay out of the kitchen," she answered dryly.

I didn't make any promises before ending the phone call. I was going to make dinner for myself, and once I *successfully* finished, I was going to text her pictures to rub it in her face.

I'd show her.

———

OKAY SO MAYBE I wasn't going to show her after all.

Coughing to clear some of the smoke from my lungs, I watched on in embarrassment as the firefighters began descending the stairs that led from my apartment into the back alley behind the café and my dance school.

Honestly, I probably could have gotten the fire out myself, it wasn't that big, but I'd freaked when I saw the flames and immediately called 911.

"Well, the fire's out. It was small so there was no real damage, just some nasty smoke. You'll probably have to air the place out for a while." Quinn stated as he propped his hands on his hips, staring me down. I tried not to notice how sexy he looked in his tight navy fire department t-shirt and bunker pants, but damn it, it was hard! The man might be an android, but he was still fine as hell. Even with that disapproving scowl on his face.

"Thanks," I offered in a small voice.

"You got lucky. It could have been a lot worse."

Rolling my eyes indignantly at his tone of voice, a tone my own father had used on me many times, the embarrassment of my situation started to wear off, and I started to get pissed. "You know, the term *self-cleaning oven* is really misleading," I stated in an effort to defend myself. "Calling something self-cleaning when you're *actually* supposed to clean it first is just asking for trouble! I have half a mind to write a nasty letter to Maytag and express my displeasure. Oh! And while we're on the subject—"

"We're on a subject? I thought you were just ranting."

I ignored Quinn's dig and carried on, because yes, I was ranting. And once I started there was no stopping it. "What's the deal with dishwashers, huh? Dish. Washer. You'd think that would mean it cleans your dishes, right? But *noooo*. You actually have to scrub *all* food particles off first or they come out with dried-up crud on them. I'm better off just hiring a person to clean my oven and dishes since the thousand dollar machines meant to clean stuff don't actually clean!"

I may have been a little out of breath by the time I finished, and I may have garnered an audience from the other firefighters standing in the alley, but the only thing I could focus on at that very moment was the fact that Quinn was watching me, his arms crossed over his chest, with a tiny smirk playing on his lips.

"You finished?" he asked a few seconds later.

I looked up at the dark sky and gave it some thought. "Yes. Since washing machines and dryers actually do what they claim to do, I think I'm finished."

And then he went and shocked the hell out of me by throwing his head back with a loud bark of laughter.

"Holy shit," I breathed out, watching the magnificence that was Quinn laughing. The man was hot as sin on any given day, but add in a laugh and panties all over Pembrooke were at risk of combusting.

"What?" he asked once he was finished, a smile still tilting his full lips upward. It was a great smile, even if it didn't quite meet his eyes.

"You just laughed."

"Yeah," he chuckled. "I tend to do that when something's funny or totally ridiculous."

"I don't think I want to know which one of those I am," I cringed.

That smile of his inched a bit closer to his eyes. "You're funny."

"Oh," I drew out sarcastically. "You see, I was confused, because earlier today I thought you were a robot. You know, devoid of all facial expressions other than complete disinterest?" I crossed my own arms over my chest, mimicking his stance. "I'm sure you could understand my confusion."

He at least had the decency to look ashamed as he rubbed at the back of his neck uncomfortably. "Yeah, I wasn't really at my best earlier. I'm sorry about that."

At least he apologized, I thought to myself. "Well, you're forgiven... *if* you promise me that you'll keep tonight's little..." I waved my hand in the direction of my smoky apartment, "...*acci-*

dent from Eliza. I swear to God, that woman lives to tell me *I told you so.*"

Quinn chuckled again, and the sound of it sent a zing of pleasure through me. "Scout's honor," he returned, holding up three fingers.

"Thanks." I smiled and reached a hand out in front of me for him to shake. "I think we might have gotten off on the wrong foot earlier. I know we've technically known each other for a couple years now, but we haven't actually talked. I'm Lilly Mathewson. It's nice to *officially* meet you... in spite of the circumstances."

"Quinn Mallick." His large hand engulfed mine, sending a shot of warmth up my arm. Oh, this man was potent. "Nice to meet you as well."

We both went silent as we stared at each other, hands still clasped together in a slow shake. My heart kicked up at what I could have sworn was a moment between us, but before I could be sure a loud voice called out, breaking through whatever was happening. "Yo, Mallick!" We both turned to see that the rest of the crew was loaded up. "We gotta go, man."

"Coming." Quinn turned back to me and gave me that chin lift that only guys were capable of pulling off. "You should be good to go back inside, just open up the windows." He said it so casually that I suddenly got the sense that the fizzle I'd just felt between us was all in my head. "Be safe, Lilly."

"Yeah... you too."

"And maybe no more cooking for... well, forever," he called over his shoulder as he reached the fire engine, shooting me a wink before he climbed in and shut the door.

Yep. Definitely potent.

5

QUINN

"*M*ORNING," I ANNOUNCED as I pushed through the back door of my parents' house. The welcoming smell of coffee a pleasant hit to my senses. They sat at the kitchen table eating breakfast as I beelined for the coffee machine. I stopped to pat my dad's shoulder and give Mom a kiss on the cheek, but if I didn't get some caffeine in my system soon, I was going to pass out where I stood.

"Long night?" Dad asked, as I took my first fortifying sip.

I gave him a bland look that was all the answer he needed. "Nothing too serious, but enough to keep us from getting any sleep."

Mom stood up and patted my cheek. "My poor boy. Why don't you let me make you something to eat really quick?" I was just about to tell her it wasn't necessary as she started fussing around, but before I could get the words out, my stomach let loose a loud rumble.

"Sophia awake yet?" I asked, as I finished off my coffee and poured myself another.

"Yep," Mom answered. "She's getting a shower."

That gave me about ten minutes to caffeinate and get some food in my belly before I had to take her to school. "How was she? She behave all right?"

"Perfect little angel," Dad replied with a smile on his face. As far as my father was concerned, Sophia could burn the house to the ground and she'd still be perfect in his eyes. She had her Papaw wrapped around her little finger. She could do no wrong. It was hilarious to see Bill Mallick, the man who'd been known as a powerhouse within the Pembrooke Fire Department, brought to heel by a tiny slip of a girl, but my father wouldn't have it any other way.

Knowing that about him, I turned to my mother for an *honest* answer. She gave me a knowing grin. "She was fine, dear." She set two slices of French toast and a side of bacon in front of me and took her seat once again. "But she woke up in the middle of the night again." *Here we go,* I thought, knowing exactly what was coming. "Sweetheart. You really need to stop letting her get into bed with you." I gave her a look that screamed *I don't want to hear it.*

"Eve," my father spoke in a warning tone, but my mother wouldn't be deterred.

"What?" she shrugged innocently. "I'm just saying, a child her age should be sleeping in her own bed through the night. There's no reason for her to—"

I dropped my fork against the plate, causing a loud clang that startled my mother into stopping. Frustration began to course through me at the familiar, and unwanted, conversation. I knew she meant well, my mother didn't have a cruel or vindictive bone in her body, but well-meaning or not, I was getting tired of being told how to parent my own daughter.

It was times like these that made me miss Addy even more. The constant ache that lingered in every bone grew more acute. She always knew what to do when it came to being a parent. In the three years she had with Sophia, never once did I see her doubt herself, or question her parenting methods. She was so strong, so self-assured. Christ, I missed her. Living without her was like missing a limb. And days like this one, days that seemed to call out my inadequacies as a parent, only made me angrier at life for what it had taken away from me.

"She's six years old," I snapped. "She's lost her mother and has nightmares that wake her up in the middle of the night. I really don't give a shit what a child her age should or shouldn't be doing. If it helps her to climb in bed with me, then everyone else can just fuck right the hell off."

"Quinn!" Mom shot back at the same time my father turned that warning tone on me. "Watch how you speak to your mother, son."

I propped my elbows on the table and dropped my head in my hands, giving my face a good scrub before looking back at my mother. Guilt at having taken my anger out on her rested heavy on me when I saw the disappointment in their eyes. "I'm sorry," I sighed, reaching over to place my hand on top of hers.

She turned her palm over and wrapped her fingers around mine. "It's okay. I'm sorry for upsetting you."

That was just one of the many thing I loved about my parents, one of the many things that made the decision to move Sophia back to Pembrooke so easy. They were two of the most forgiving people I'd ever met.

"So," she released my hand and went back to her coffee mug, "Soph tells us that you signed her up for ballet classes?"

I shoveled the last bit of breakfast in my mouth and chased it with a gulp of coffee as I nodded my head, all the while thinking that I'd be seeing Lilly again. I wasn't sure how I felt about that, mainly because a part of me — too large a part — was excited about the thought of it.

Just remembering back to the look on her face that day at the dance school made my chest tighten painfully. I'd acted like such an asshole, and I hated that I put that look on her face. My head was so twisted when it came to Lilly, because I knew I should have just taken that as my opportunity to keep my distance, but when we'd been called to her apartment later that night, I couldn't help but laugh when she'd rambled on about self-cleaning ovens and dishwashers. I knew I was walking a fine line, but the way she had smiled when I laughed made it impossible to act like a dick.

"Yep, last week," I answered casually, pushing the way my stomach flipped at just the thought of her to the back of my mind. "First class is this afternoon."

"That Lilly Mathewson," she continues in a conversational tone, "she's quite pretty, isn't she?"

"Ah, hell," I groaned. "Mom, come on."

"I'm just saying—" Oh, I knew damn good and well what she was *just saying*. Luckily, Sophia chose that moment to come barreling into the kitchen.

"*Daddy!*"

"Hey there, Angel!" I stood and scooped her up, pulling her tight against my chest. I might not be getting the Father of the Year award any time soon, and I may question whether my choices are right, but there was no doubt my little girl loved me, and when she wrapped her arms around my neck and squeezed so tightly, I got the sense that I was at least doing *something* right.

"You wash behind your ears?" I asked, as I lowered her back down to the ground.

"Yep."

"You use actual soap?" Who knew those were questions I'd be asking one day?

"Uh huh."

"You brush your teeth?" And by the dejected look that spread across her face, I knew she hadn't. "Go brush. Then it's breakfast and school.

She stomped her little foot. "But I just brushed 'em yesterday!"

"Oh my God, miracles really do happen!" I declared to the ceiling before looking back at my daughter. "Then we're going for a new record and make it two days in a row."

Dad laughed. Mom covered her mouth to hide her smile. Sophia glared at me like she was trying to melt the skin off my face, but she turned and headed back up the stairs, so I'd take that as a win for the morning.

It was probably the only one I'd get.

———

"DADDY, I DON'T think my hair is right."

We stood inside the studio door, hand in hand, watching all the other little girls with their hair in perfect little buns on the top of their heads. Yeah, it was safe to say Sophia's didn't look right, seeing as I had no fucking clue how to do a bun.

"It'll be fine, sweetheart. It's just..." I trailed off and looked at the knotted mass of tangles that sat slightly cock-eyed on her head, "...slightly different is all."

I could see sympathetic looks from the moms that were still milling about and wondered if 'How to Make a Proper Bun' was something I could find on Google.

"Hey guys." Lilly's cheerful voice cut through my musings, and I turned just in time to see her closing the distance between us. She was wearing another one of those outfits that damn near bordered on indecent, and I had to fight my body's reaction to seeing it.

"Hi, Ms. Lilly!" Sophia shouted. "Look it! Daddy and me went to the store and bought a whole bunch of ballet clothes." She pointed down at the bright pink leotard she was wearing that declared her a *DIVA* in fuchsia rhinestones. She didn't have the first clue what a diva was, but the thing was pink on pink so she just *had* to have it... along with about a million others that looked just like it. I swear to God, I could feel by balls retreating back up into my stomach when the cashier was ringing up all the pepto-colored spandex.

"Do you like it?"

She bent down to Sophia's level, the smile on her face like a punch to the chest. "I love it! You look like a professional ballerina!"

I hadn't thought it was possible for Soph to beam any prouder than she had when we first purchased the ugly leotard, but I was wrong. Her face glowed like she'd just gotten the world's best compliment. And to Lilly's credit, she didn't say a damn word about that disaster of a bun on top of my daughter's head.

"We're about to get started, so why don't you go join the rest of the class?"

"Okay!" Sophia took off without a backward glance, leaving me alone with the woman I'd been struggling to get out of my head.

"Thanks for not saying anything about the…" I trailed off and pointed to my head, causing Lilly to laugh.

"Hey, I've seen worse, I promise."

I rubbed at the back of my neck, my skin tingled with aware-ness at her close proximity. Jesus, I really was a fucking mess. "Yeah, well, I never was much of a stylist."

She placed her hand on my arm and sparks lit beneath her palm. "Hey, the fact that you even tried speaks volumes. Most dads wouldn't have even bothered."

Christ, her compliment was exactly what I needed to hear. I'd been questioning whether or not I was doing right by my daughter for so long, that hearing another person validate my efforts was a shot right to the gut. There was no question about it. I needed to get the hell out of there. The guilt inside of me was quickly snuffing out the excitement I felt at Lilly's declaration.

I pulled my keys from my front pocket and began to move back. "Well, I guess I'll let you get to it."

Her brows pinched in confusion at my retreating demeanor. "Yeah. We'll see you after class."

"Yep." I turned on my heels and headed for the door without looking back.

6

LILLY

"*H*ELLO?" I CALLED out as I walked through my parents' front door. No one greeted me, but I could hear soft music and the sound of hushed voices coming from the living room at back of the house.

I walked on quiet feet down the hallway and stopped just in the doorway of the living room. The sight before me made me smile happily in spite of the painfully bittersweet feeling tying my insides in knots. It was absolutely beautiful and heartbreakingly sad all at the same time, and I felt tears prick the backs of my eyes as I watched my father hold my mom in his arms as he led her around, dancing to the crooning voice of Eric Clapton.

"Wonderful Tonight" had been one of my mother's favorite songs for as long as I could remember, and watching the two of them dance in a tight embrace transported me right back to my childhood. I could remember how seeing them, so in love, so enamored with each other, used to embarrass me when I was much younger. Now, well, I'd have given anything to make sure my parents had years more of this.

My own tears finally spilled over onto my cheeks when I saw my mother's eyes well up as Dad sang softly into her ear, and I thought to myself, *God, to be so lucky as to have a love like theirs.* And for some reason, the image of Quinn popped into my head at that very moment. I wasn't naive enough to think I might possibly love the guy. I barely knew him. And his mercurial personality made it to where I wanted to sometimes punch him in the face, but I couldn't deny feeling a pull between us. There was something there... like a shared pain that made me feel closer to him than anyone else I knew. It was strange, really, but I just couldn't get the guy out of my head.

"Oh, sweetheart! We didn't hear you come in." The sound of my mom's voice pulled me back into the present, and I moved quickly to dash the tears off my cheeks.

"I didn't mean to interrupt."

Mom stepped back and ran her hands down her cream-colored pants to straighten them. "Nonsense." She gazed at her watch before moving toward the kitchen. "Actually, I need to finish dinner. Thank goodness you showed up when you did or I would have overcooked the roast." She bolted from the room, and I understood not to follow. She needed a few minutes alone to compose herself. My father's illness was even harder on her than it was on me.

"You mind dancing with your old man, Lilly Flower?"

I beamed at my father and pushed off the doorway, stepping into his loving, familiar embrace. "Not at all." Up close, I could tell he wasn't feeling as well as he pretended. It had only been weeks since he told me he was dying, and already his body was starting to show signs. He was thinner than he'd been, almost frail. His complexion was sallow, dark purple smudges rested beneath his eyes. But he still smiled just like he always had.

"How are you feeling, Dad?"

He moved me around the room with such grace. "Couldn't be better, sweetie. But right now I have the two most beautiful women in the world under one roof. What more could a man ask for?"

We grew quiet, and I rested my head on my father's chest as we danced to Clapton's "Change the World."

"How's the dance school?" he asked a few minutes later.

"It's good." I thought back to the classes I'd instructed earlier in the week, and Sophia came to mind. Such an animated, energetic little girl. "I have a new student, Sophia. She's…" I stopped and laughed. "She's a handful in the best way."

He chuckled beneath my cheek. "Sounds familiar. I bet she runs her parents ragged."

My smile faded a bit. "It's just her dad. His wife died in a car accident a few years ago."

"I'm very sorry to hear that." The song came to an end and Dad sucked in a breath. It hurt to see him so weak, but I maintained a neutral expression as I helped him over to the couch, taking a seat next to him.

"Yeah," I continued, knowing not to question how he was feeling. He hated being treated like an invalid. "It's really sad. But you should see him with her, Dad. He took her and bought all of these bright-colored leotards because that's what she wanted. He's just so… big and rugged. I can't picture him going into a dance shop and loading up on all these sparkly tutus and leotards." Dad gave a small laugh. "Oh! And he even put her hair in a bun for her first class." Now it was my turn to laugh. "It was a disaster. Like, *really* bad, but you could tell he tried his hardest."

Dad's face grew thoughtful as he studied me. "Sounds like his daughter's not the only one who's caught your attention."

"Oh, no. It's nothing like that," I argued, even though it was a lie. Quinn had done more than catch my attention, but it was pointless. I knew that much. "There's nothing going on there. He's… he's a good guy. I don't know him all that well, but I can tell."

Dad's lips quirked up in a tiny grin. "Sure doesn't sound like there's nothing there."

I shook my head and whispered in a defeated voice. "Daddy, he still wears his wedding ring."

I watched as his face grew sympathetic. Reaching over, he patted my hand. "I'm sorry, sweetheart."

"What? No words of wisdom? No advice for me?" I asked in a joking tone while really, I was hoping my father would have some sage wisdom when it came to Quinn.

His head shook just slightly. "No, honey. I'm sorry. When it comes to matters of the heart like that there's no one that can help the person move past that kind of loss. It's something that has to come from within. All you can do for someone like that is be his friend. Give him a shoulder to lean on, an outlet for his pain. That's the very best gift you can give that man."

I leaned against him, letting myself enjoy the warmth as he looped his arm around my shoulders and held me. "How'd you get to be so smart?"

"Trial and error, baby girl," he chuckled. "When you've lived as long as I have, you experience *a lot* of trial and error."

A wave of sadness crashed over me. It wasn't fair. He should have had years left.

As if reading my thoughts, Dad's arm around me gave a tiny squeeze. "I know what's going on in that head of yours, and I want you to stop it right now." I pulled in a stuttered breath and clenched my eyes closed as he continued on. "I've had a good life, Lilly Flower. An *amazing* life. I'm sad that it's being cut short, but I got you and your mother so I can't regret a single day. I don't want you to be sad for me. When I'm gone, I want you and your mother to remember all the good times."

I sniffled as a few stray tears broke loose as I sat up to look at him. Anger starting to push to the forefront. "You make it sound so easy. It's not, Dad. I can't just smile and pretend it's all okay. I'm going to miss you too much. I don't want to lose you."

His rough, weathered hands cupped my cheeks. He used his thumbs to brush my tears away as his eyes shimmered with his own. His voice sounded ragged as he spoke. "I know, sweetheart. I know. And I'm going to miss you, too. I know it won't be easy, but you're not losing me. I'll *always* be with you. Never doubt that. It'll be sad, but I need you to remember something for me. I need you to remember that I was able to let go with peace in my heart because of you and your mother. You two gave me more than I could have ever imagined. My time on Earth was so full, so miraculous, *because of you.*

"Be sad, baby girl, it's okay to be sad. But then, let it go. Live your life and search for the person who makes you complete. Strive to get what you and your mother gave to me. Never settle for less than that. You understand?"

I nodded, unable to speak past the mass of emotion that was clogging my throat.

"Good. Now, you know your mom's roast is my favorite so let's eat. I'm not dead yet, and I plan on rolling through those pearly gates fat and happy."

I couldn't hold in my watery laugh, even as I smacked my father's arm and stated, "Too soon, Dad. Too soon."

He grinned back at me and gave me a wink as I helped him from the couch. "Fine, no more death jokes."

"Much appreciated," I deadpanned.

We made it to the dining room just as my mother set the platter in the center of the table. "Just in time. Let's eat."

Dad patted his belly and took his chair at the head of the table. "Great! Oh, and Elizabeth, your daughter's gone all moon-eyed over a young man."

My eyes went wide as my head shot in my father's direction. Leave it to my father to lighten the mood by throwing me right under the bus.

And I couldn't even be mad at him for it.

7

QUINN

"**S**MELLS GOOD," I said as I entered my parents' house through the back door just off the kitchen. Mom was standing at the counter, peeling potatoes as I made my way to her and placed a kiss on her cheek.

"You here for dinner?" she asked, as I pulled the fridge door open and grabbed a beer.

I took a gulp and leaned back against the wall, crossing my ankles. "Yeah. Soph's at a sleepover again tonight. Figured I'd hang with you and Dad for a while. Speaking of…" I peeked around the doorway into the hall. "Where's Dad?"

"He had to run to the hardware store. The garbage disposal's been acting up. He's finally going to get around to replacing it."

I laughed as I picked up a piece of potato and popped it in my mouth, earning a smack on the hand from my mother. "About time. It's only been what? Two months?"

"Three," she added dryly. "That man's convinced he can fix anything. I was this close to shoving one of his tools down inside and turning it on."

"Glad you didn't. He'd probably have a heart attack if you ruined one of his wrenches."

"Yes, well, it would serve him right," she muttered, as she picked up a knife and began chopping. "I'm surprised you didn't have other plans for this evening." She tried her best to come off conversational, but I knew exactly what she was doing. She was in the mood to push. Every so often my mother got it in her head that I wasn't happy with my life, that I needed more. Those conversations never tended to go well. "I figured you'd want a night out since Sophia's not home. You know, with friends... or maybe a nice young lady."

I dropped my head back on a groan. "Christ, Mom. Not this again."

"What? Can't a mother inquire about her son's life?"

I set my beer down and placed my hands on the island that separated us. "You're not inquiring, you're trying to have another one of your goddamn interventions. I'm telling you now, just stop."

"Watch your language," she scolded.

"I'll watch my language if you tell me you understand," I threw back.

Dropping the knife with an exasperated huff, she threw her hands up in the air. "I just want what's best for you, Quinn. I want you to be happy."

That familiar prickling sensation on my skin I got every time I got angry began to nag at me. "You keep saying that! What makes you think I'm not happy, huh? I'm perfectly fine with my life, Mom."

"Perfectly fine is *not* happy," she argued back. "I know you loved her, sweetheart. We all did. Addy was a wonderful person. But it's been three years. You need to start living again."

"I am living," I ground out, my jaw ticking with the effort to not lose my cool.

"There's this lovely new Sunday School teacher at the church. Why don't you just—"

"Jesus Christ, Mom!" I shouted, running my hands through

my hair in frustration. "Stop! Just stop. I'm not dating some Sunday School teacher."

"Well what about the—"

"Enough!" Her mouth snapped closed at the same time her eyes began to shine with pain, making me feel like a complete asshole. I hated fighting with my mom, but I couldn't handle another conversation like this. Turning on my booted heels, I started for the back door.

"Where are you going?" she called out after me. "I thought you were staying for dinner."

"Lost my appetite," I grunted, shoving the screen door open. "Tell Dad I'll see him later. Good night." I slammed the door shut on the sound of her protest, letting my feet carry me back to my truck. Once inside, I dropped my forehead against the steering wheel and worked to control my breathing. I felt like shit for how I acted. I hated that whenever the conversation involved Addy, even indirectly, I instantly closed off to anyone and everyone. But I couldn't help it. Addy was still there every time I closed my eyes.

It wasn't just the death of my wife that kept me from moving on, it was the weight of the guilt I carried with me every fucking day. If I hadn't taken my eyes off the road, if I hadn't gotten distracted, she'd still be here. Living with the knowledge that my wife was gone because of me was something I struggled with every single goddamned day. No woman deserved to tie herself to a man with that kind of baggage. Why couldn't my mother see that?

A large part of me died in that car with Addison that night, and there was no fixing that. I was too broken to be any good to another woman, and the sooner my family came to grips with that, the better off everyone would be.

Because this was as happy as I was ever going to get. It was all I deserved.

HALFWAY HOME, MY stomach protested the decision not to eat dinner with my folks. I decided my best bet was to stop off at Sinful Sweets and order something for carryout. I wasn't the best company, and subjecting the other diners in the café to my foul mood wouldn't have been fair.

I'd just put my order in and was waiting at the counter when I heard someone calling my name.

"Quinn?"

Looking over my shoulder, I found Lilly standing there with a carryout bag of her own. Damn, she looked good. She always looked good, that was part of the reason I'd stayed away from her for so long. There was an undeniable attraction there that shouldn't have been. Even wearing shapeless sweats that left everything to the imagination, her hair thrown up in a messy bun, and her face clean of makeup, she was beautiful enough to have most of the men in the restaurant doing a double take. I wasn't immune to her appeal, even if I wanted to be.

"Hey."

She cocked her head to the side and frowned. "You okay?"

I let out a tired sigh and scrubbed a hand over my face. "Yeah. I'm just... it's been a rough night."

She glanced down at her watch then back to me, her light brown eyes dancing with a mixture of confusion and humor. "It's eight-fifteen."

I shrugged. "Rough evening then."

She took a step closer, placing a tiny hand on my arm. I tried to ignore the way her touch ignited sparks of electricity beneath my skin, but damn, it was hard. "You want to talk about it? I've been told I kick ass at listening. Watch." She shut her mouth and maintained eye contact for several seconds, her brow furrowing in what looked like intense concentration. "See? Hardcore listener right here." She pointed at herself, and there was no holding back the grin that tugged at my lips. The woman was a nut. It was surprisingly refreshing.

"I appreciate the offer, but—"

Before I could refuse, the waitress came back and dropped my bag on the counter. "Here you go, Quinn."

"Thanks." I pulled my wallet out and tossed some bills on the counter, then picked up my bag and turned to face Lilly, geared up to turn her offer down as politely as possible.

"Look," she started, "It would appear that both of us are eating alone tonight." She lifted her bag as proof and continued. "Might as well keep each other company. I just hit up Mabel's and stocked up on wine. And I won't push you to talk about your rough evening if you don't want, I promise. There's no reason for either of us to go home alone tonight, right?" As soon as the words passed her lips, her eyes went big. "That came out wrong! What I meant was we can just... hang out. Not, like, sexual." She whispered *sexual* as her eyes frantically darted around to make sure no one heard. "I wasn't propositioning you, I swear. I mean, not that you aren't good looking. Because you are! Oh my God, please say something to shut me up, already!"

I burst into laughter as her cheeks burned a bright, humiliated red. "It's not funny!" She smacked my arm, but I could hear the playfulness in her tone as she scolded. "Oh, God. That's so embarrassing. Just pretend I didn't say anything. I'm going to go upstairs and shove my head in my newly clean oven. Excuse me."

Without thinking about what I was doing, I reached out and grabbed her arm. "Wait, wait..." I took a deep breath to get my laughter under control. "I understood what you meant."

She narrowed her eyes in a mock glare. "Then why'd you let me keep going like that? You could have stopped me before I dug the hole any deeper."

"And miss the show? Hell, no. That was the most entertainment I've had—"

She held up her hand to stop me. "So help me God, Quinn

Mallick, if you say it's the most entertainment since I set my kitchen on fire, I'm going to punch you right in the throat."

My mouth snapped closed so fast my teeth clanked together, because that was *exactly* what I was about to say. I cleared my throat and fought to keep from grinning as my fingers involuntarily squeezed around her arm. "You know what? I think I changed my mind. Company sounds great."

Her face broke into a beautiful smile that caused my insides to heat. "Really?"

If I were smart, I would have turned and run. I had no business being around this woman, especially with the way she affected me, but she just looked so damn happy about the prospect of us having dinner together, I couldn't bring myself to tell her no.

"Yeah. But I don't drink wine, so I hope you have beer."

She glanced back over her shoulder as she began moving to the back of the restaurant to get to the stairs. "I got you covered."

TWO HOURS LATER we were both sitting on the floor around Lilly's coffee table, and I couldn't remember the last time I'd enjoyed myself so much. Dinner had been eaten, she drank her wine, and I was on my third beer. True to her word, Lilly hadn't pushed, so the conversation had been comfortable.

"So what made you want to be a firefighter?" she asked, as she poured more wine into her glass. She'd had just enough to give her cheeks a nice, pink glow. Her brown eyes were just a touch glassy, but she wasn't slurring her words. We were both totally at ease, which surprised the hell out of me.

It was... *nice* being here, talking with her. Really fucking nice.

"It's what I've wanted to be for as long as I can remember." Lifting my beer bottle to my lips, I finished the last of it before continuing. "My father's retired PFD, so is my grandfather. It's in the blood, I guess. Growing up, I wanted to be exactly like him. It scared the shit out of my mom that I wanted to make a career out of running into burning buildings, but my dad talked her around." I laughed as a memory from my childhood popped into my head. "He used to bring his bunker gear home from the station to wash it. Hated using the machines at work. It drove my mom crazy, because it always stunk the mud room up, but I loved it. I'd sneak in there and put it on every chance I got."

Lilly's soft giggle caused my chest to expand. "Oh, I bet your mom loved that."

"She'd be pissed," I grinned. "Always going on about how I was ruining my clothes putting that nasty, smelly stuff on, but Dad loved it. And she might have bitched, but I'm pretty sure she'd got an entire photo album of me in my dad's gear."

"I bet you were adorable!" she cried.

"I was rugged," I answered with a glare. "I've never been *adorable.*"

"Oh yeah," she snorted. "You came out of the womb like that, all… lumber sexual and stuff."

"Lumber *what*?" I let out a bewildered laugh.

"Lumber sexual. It's like metro sexual, but manly, you know?"

"No, I don't know. I have no clue what you're talking about."

She waved me off and took another gulp of her wine. "Eh, you don't need to know the meaning. Just take my word for it."

"If you say so," I grinned. "So what about you? Have you always wanted to dance?"

Her voice went soft, her expression wistful. "Yeah. I've been dancing since I was about eight. I started a little later than most, but once my mom put me in classes, I was hooked."

"You're amazing," I found myself admitting. "Why didn't you go to New York or something like that?"

Her face flushed, and something told me it wasn't from the wine this time. "You've seen me dance?"

"Yeah. Last week. I was getting in my truck after grabbing a coffee. The blinds to the studio were open and you were in there by yourself." I stopped, thinking back to the sadness on her face that morning. "You were…"

"Crying," she whispered, and although she still wore a smile, I could see the sadness had returned. "Yeah. You kind of caught me on a bad day."

Suddenly I was aware of what I must have been putting my loved ones through, because even though I knew it wasn't fair, I wanted to push her to talk about whatever was bothering her. Instead, I ignored that curious niggling in my gut and said, "You know, I might not be as good a listener as you are, but if you ever need to talk…"

"Thanks," she smiled. "It's okay. I'm okay. I just got some bad news the day before." She stopped long enough to inhale deeply before she continued. "My dad's sick. Cancer. I found out about it the day before."

"Christ," I hissed. "Lilly, I'm so sorry."

"It's all right. I was struggling with how to cope, you know? I couldn't imagine…" Her voice cracked and her throat moved as she swallowed. "I still *can't* imagine not having him, and knowing he's going to die… it really fucking sucks." When she let out a self-deprecating laugh, it took everything I had not to jump across the table and wrap my arms around her. I'd never felt more out of my element with a person before, yet, at the same time, I could relate to her better than most.

"I went down to the studio before it opened and put on the music and just… escaped for a little while. I've always used dancing as a way to escape. When I was little, I had trouble in school. I'm dyslexic and it took a while for the doctors to be able to diagnose it. I know it's not really a big deal, but when you're in elementary school and have trouble reading, well, let's just say the kids can be real assholes.

"My mom enrolled me in dance classes and I discovered that when I was moving, when the music was playing, all the mean things those kids said about me just... disappeared. It was my escape, to this day it still is. So, to answer your question, that's why I never wanted to pursue something like New York. It might sound weird, but what I do now, when I dance, even when I teach my kids, it's all for me. If I tried to join a company, everything I did would be for them. Doing what I do now, I don't have to answer to anybody. I don't have to worry about the routines becoming monotonous. I get to leave my head for a while and not worry about the outcome. Does that make any sense?"

I hardly recognized my voice, the sound rougher, almost jagged as I said, "It makes perfect sense." I had no clue what was coming over me, why I was reacting the way I was, but I couldn't stand to see that heartache in her eyes any longer. Standing from my place on the floor, I held my hand out to her. "Come on. I want to watch you dance."

"What? Now?" she asked incredulously. "You want to watch me dance *right now?*"

I gave a casual shrug and let my lips curl up in a grin. "Why not? You got other plans at the moment?"

"Well... no, but—"

"Perfect, so nothing's stopping you." She didn't seem convinced, and for reasons beyond my comprehension, I wanted nothing more than to see this gorgeous woman dance. So, I pushed.

"Come escape with me for a little while."

8

LILLY

"*COME ESCAPE WITH me for a little while.*"

He couldn't have possibly known how much those words meant to me just then. After finally opening up and telling someone about my father, the need for an escape was beyond intoxicating.

And Quinn realizing that and giving me exactly what I needed meant the world to me. I couldn't have denied his request, even if I wanted to.

Taking his hand, I let him pull me off the floor. Once I had my feet firmly beneath me, he broke the connection, shoving his hands in the pockets of his faded jeans. My skin still tingled from the contact, and my heart squeezed at the loss of it, but I pushed forward, heading to the door that led to the internal stairs, grabbing my keys and phone off the counter on the way.

"This is really convenient," Quinn spoke up from behind me as we headed down the stairs. "No commute, no having to worry about traffic."

I looked back at him and smiled as I flipped the switch that would light the lobby area and moved to the main studio door to unlock it. "It's pretty great. The place used to be smaller when

Chloe lived in it. She had the apartment built when she opened the bakery, but when they expanded and I decided to open a dance school, they gutted the place and made it stretch over both businesses. I love the apartment, but I have to admit, I'd like a house one day."

"Really?" He looked at me quizzically.

"Well, yeah." I shrugged. "I know it's a lot of maintenance, and it's not as simple as just calling the landlord when something breaks, but I'd like my own yard one day, you know? Something that's totally mine that I can do whatever I want with. And preferably something with no stairs."

He chuckled as I hit the lights for the studio, making the entire space bright. "I can see the appeal of no stairs."

"Tell me about it," I groaned. "You spend an entire day dancing, wearing your body out, and then have to climb an entire flight up and down. It's murder on your knees. Some days I feel like a seventy-year-old lady in need of a walker."

I turned back just in time to catch him doing a sweep of my entire body. His green eyes seemed to darken, and I could have sworn I heard "sure as hell aren't built like a seventy-year old," under his breath.

My body gave an involuntary shiver and I was suddenly hit with a bout of stage fright, something I hadn't experienced in years.

"So…" I dragged out. "I'm not really sure which song I should play." My attention darted to my phone clutched tightly in my hands as I scrolled through my different play lists. Normally, dancing was as familiar as breathing, but I was so aware of Quinn standing in front of me that I had trouble concentrating. "Uh… there's—"

All of a sudden the phone was snatched from my grasp and Quinn's large, solid body was only inches away. "How about I pick? You just do your thing."

QUINN

I WAS GOING TO HELL. There was no doubt about it.

As I scrolled through Lilly's phone, I started questioning how I'd ended up in the situation I was currently in. But the only answer I could come up with was: my own stupidity. There was no denying that something about the woman tugged at me, but I should have ignored the pull, not fallen into it.

Too late to turn back now, I thought, swiping my thumb along the screen until I came across a playlist that caught my eye. It didn't take a fucking genius to see she had her music organized by how each song made her feel, that was why the list titled *Seductive* seemed so goddamned appealing.

Like I said, I was going to Hell.

I didn't recognize any of the songs, so going on one with the coolest name, I picked "Gods and Monsters" By Lana Del Ray. "Okay, got it."

"All right. Just plug it in over there." She pointed to where she normally docked her iPhone. I followed her instructions and set the phone up. As soon as I looked back up, all the blood in my body rushed straight to my dick.

"What are you doing?"

Lilly looked at me like I was an idiot. "I can't dance in sweats," she stated like that was obvious to everyone but me. Her pants fell to the floor, revealing a pair of black shorts that left absolutely *nothing* to the imagination. Seconds later, her baggy sweater disappeared, showing the tight teal sports bra she'd been wearing underneath.

I was so busy staring at all her luscious curves I hadn't even realized she said something. "Huh?" I asked, jerking my gaze up to meet hers.

"Can you push play?" she asked with a hint of laughter in her voice.

"Oh, yeah. Sure. Got it." Needing to focus on anything other than the disturbing fact my dick was stirring behind my fly at the sight of my daughter's dance teacher, I leaned back against the wall, crossing my ankles and shoving my hands in my pockets. As soon as the music kicked in, I knew I'd made an epic fucking mistake in my song selection, because *fuck me*, the woman moved like a wet dream to the sinful beat.

I was mesmerized as I watched Lilly dance, her skin tinged pink as she was taken over by the music. I was lost, just like the morning I'd watched her through the window, only this time there was a seductiveness to the song and the way she moved that made me want to bury myself as deep as I could go and lose myself inside her completely. It was a terrifying thought. My mind shouted that it was wrong, but my body wouldn't get on board, and as she lifted one leg straight up into the air, parallel to her body, the ache grew even stronger.

The beat kicked up and her body flowed like water across the floor. Guilt at feeling such an intense attraction to another woman flooded through me, and I knew I needed to move, but I was stuck, transfixed. She hadn't been exaggerating when she said dancing was an escape for her. It was written in the way she moved, the expression on her face. The sadness and pain were gone, having melted away to a serenity I envied.

As the final notes of the song began to fade and the song came to an end, I was finally able to come unglued from the floor. I needed to get the hell out of there.

For no other reason than I didn't *want* to leave her.

LILLY

• • •

THE SECOND THE song started playing that nervousness in my belly erupted in a swarm of butterflies. It felt like my whole body burned red, but, as always, the instant I began dancing, the rest of the world disappeared. There was nothing but the steady thrum of the music and Lana Del Rey's sultry voice. Every fiber in my body moved as if on autopilot, my feet carrying me across the floor as though they had a mind of their own.

My head cleared of absolutely everything. There was no pain or heartache, no stage fright, no nerves. I was in my own world where I ruled over everything. I made the rules here, and the number one rule was that all the heaviness in life was left at the door.

The last few lines of the song played, and I let my eyes drift closed, not needing my sense of sight to finish the number. It was as familiar as the beat of my own heart. Once I hit that last mark, I pulled in a long, much needed breath as I slowly lifted my eyelids. For those four minutes, I'd forgotten all about Quinn being in the room with me, and seeing him watching me with an unreadable expression on his face gave me a start.

His eyes grew darker with every step he took in my direction, and I couldn't help but feel that, in that very moment, he was the predator and I was his prey. My heart began beating against my chest for an entirely different reason as he got closer, closer. Only inches stood between us when he finally stopped. I could smell the intoxicating spiciness of his cologne.

"S-so," I stuttered, out of breath from not only the exertion of dancing, but his heady presence. "What did you think?"

"That was..." The muscle in his jaw ticked, and his hands balled into tight fists at his side. "Fucking incredible," he finally finished, rendering me momentarily speechless.

"Yeah?" I asked on a sigh as the air around us went electric. Just like the night outside my apartment, my skin prickled with awareness as the moment stretched out between us.

"I've never seen anything like that in my life. The way you move… it's unbelievable."

I couldn't help but touch him right then. Reaching out, I placed my hand on his arm and whispered, "That's an amazing compliment. Thank you so much."

I meant for my touch to increase the connection I felt between us, but for some reason it seemed to snap him out of it. I could actually see the shutters falling down over his green eyes.

Taking a step back, he cleared his throat and lifted his arm, rubbing the back of his neck. His tone when he spoke next was completely void of any emotion. "You're very talented. I have no doubt Sophia will learn a lot from you."

Disappointment coursed through my blood, my shoulders drooped in defeat, but I did my best to paste a smile on my face. "Thanks. She's a fantastic student."

"Well…" Quinn glanced down at his watch, and I got the impression he was trying to look anywhere but at me. "It's getting late. I should probably go."

I kept my tone light as I said, "Okay. I'll walk you out."

"No need." He was already moving, reaching the door in a few quick strides. "Have a good night."

And just like that, he was gone, leaving me wondering what the hell just happened.

LILLY

J'D BEEN DRAGGING all morning long. Concerns over my father were weighing so heavily on my mind I had trouble finding sleep at night. And to make matters worse, it had been a week and a half since my private performance for Quinn, and he was *still* giving me the cold shoulder. If there was any chance of surviving the day, I needed one of Chloe's pastries and a cup of coffee STAT.

Taking the internal stairs, I headed down to the café below and made a beeline toward the bakery side.

"Morning," I announced, as I dramatically flopped down onto one of the barstools.

Chloe smirked at me. "Well good morning, sunshine," she teased, taking in my less-than-enthusiastic expression. "Coffee?"

"Intravenously, please. And two almond scones while you're at it."

She set about making my coffee and grabbed my scones from the pastry display. "Rough morning?"

I made a sarcastic face and stuffed half a scone in my mouth, talking around the delicious, crumbly goodness. "That's putting it lightly."

Chloe grimaced at my stellar display of table manners and opened her mouth, no doubt to lay into me for talking with my mouth full. Lucky for me, a handful of customers made their way to the counter and started placing their orders, giving me time to swallow my food.

By the time she made it back to me, I was one scone down and had already started sucking back my steaming cup of coffee. "So why the foul mood?" she asked, wiping the crumbs I'd left behind off the counter as she gave me that look. You know, the one that said she was in full on Mother Mode. "Does it have anything to do with whatever's causing those dark circles under your eyes?"

Grabbing a spoon from the counter, I held it up and tried to examine my warped image in the polished metal. Damn, I *did* have dark circles under my eyes. How had I not noticed that?

"You aren't sleeping, are you?" she continued in that motherly tone of voice. "Is there something going on?"

I should have known Chloe would be like a dog with a bone. During the months that Eliza was away in Denver, the woman nearly mothered me to death in an attempt to make up for missing her step-daughter.

"Just busy gearing up for the Winter Showcase," I lied, wanting to keep the truth about my father to myself for a little while longer. I spent my days and nights stuck in my own head, fretting over what I couldn't change. I couldn't bring myself to put words to it yet. It wasn't the most logical way of thinking, but part of me felt that by telling everyone in my life, by putting the truth out there into the universe, I could possibly lose him faster. And I wasn't ready for that.

Telling Quinn had been so much easier. He was, for all intents and purposes, a stranger. And it wasn't lost on me that we shared something thanks to our grief. Maybe that was why I felt that strange connection. But either way, I just couldn't bring it up yet.

Her face pinched in concern. "You push yourself too hard."

I heaved a sigh and took another bite. "I'll be fine."

I watched as she geared herself up to argue, but the door from the kitchen swung open, and one of her employees came out, carrying an overloaded basket stuffed full of every pastry imaginable. I stared longingly at the basket of goodies. "Please tell me that's for me, and I'll love you forever."

Chloe chuckled as she took the heaving basket from the poor girl who looked like she was about to collapse under the weight of it. "Sorry. This is for the guys at the fire station. I take a basket to them and the Sheriff's Department every month. Gotta keep our civil servants happy."

I cocked an eyebrow and smiled. "And it keeps you from getting traffic tickets."

She at least had the decency to blush a bit. "You'd have thought being the Sheriff's wife would come with those particular perks," she replied flatly, making me burst into laughter despite my exhaustion.

Another pack of customers hit the counter just then. Chloe looked from the quickly forming line, to the basket, to me, and I almost dreaded the question I *knew* was coming.

"Would you mind dropping this stuff off?" She pushed the basket in my direction and gave me a pitiful look. "Pretty please?"

I swallowed down the groan that wanted to come out. I'd been on the receiving end of Quinn's silent treatment the last several days. Traipsing onto his turf wasn't exactly something I wanted to do, but I couldn't say no to Chloe.

I wrapped my fingers around the handle of the basket and hefted it up, grunting at the unexpected weight of it. Who knew bread could weigh so much. "Fine. But if I strain a muscle, or throw my back out carrying this, I expect baked goods for life."

She laughed and waved me off. "Deal."

I moved slowly out of the restaurant toward my car, using the bulk of the basket as an excuse, when really I was just dreading a possible run-in with Quinn. If he was at the station, how would he act? Would he acknowledge me, or pretend I didn't exist? Would I be subjected to more of his coldness?

Trying to guess his mood was like trying to tell the time by the time of day by the sun. And considering I flunked out of Girl Scouts, it was safe to presume I could *not* do that.

I spent the entire—albeit short—drive to Pembrooke Fire Department worrying my bottom lip until I finally tasted blood. Why Quinn Mallick had such an intense reaction on me was anyone's guess.

When I pulled into the small parking lot in front of the brick building, I noticed the two big bay doors were open. I parked in the spot closest to one of the open bays in the hopes of getting in and out fast. Inhaling deeply, I shut the car off and opened my door, struggling to stand with the massive bundle of food in my hands. I couldn't even see over the top as I started walking in what I *hoped* was the direction of the door.

As I got closer, I started to hear voices, and breathed a sigh of relief when none of them sounded like Quinn. My relief, however, was short-lived when the toe of my shoe caught on a crack in the concrete. Thanks to the basket creating an off-balanced center of gravity I started going down... *fast*. I let out a loud, startled squeak as I squeezed my eyes closed and braced for impact. I was fully prepared for it to hurt like a bitch — Chloe was going to owe me *so huge* — but a pair of strong arms wrapped around my waist, catching me mid-fall, before I could face plant.

"Lilly?"

Well, shit. I squinted one eye open and chanced a brief glance over my shoulder. "Quinn... hey. How are you?" It would have been ideal if the ground beneath me had opened up and swallowed me whole. Unfortunately, no such luck.

He gave me a bewildered look as he studied my face, and I was acutely aware that he was still holding onto me tightly, my back pinned to his firm chest. "You okay?"

I took a step away, putting pressure on his arms so he'd let go. It took him a few seconds to break the connection, but once he did, I was finally able to take a full breath. "Yeah," I answered, as I worked to prop the heavy basket on my hip. "Just tripped carrying this damn thing."

He blinked, as if only just noticing the abundance of pastries. Reaching out, he tagged the handle and lifted it away from me like it weighed as much as a feather. "Thanks," I offered sheepishly, tucking a loose strand of hair behind my ear. "Those are from Chloe. She got busy and asked if I could drop them off."

"Yo, Mallick!" a man called out, his voice getting closer. "Move your ass before Carpenter peeks at your hand — Hell yeah! It's Delivery Day from the bakery? Score!"

The guy with a one-track mind for food rushed Quinn, pulling the cellophane wrapping from the basket then stuffing nearly an entire muffin in his mouth at once before realizing there was a woman present.

As soon as he did, he stopped chewing and gave me a very slow once-over. He was a handsome guy, in spite of the puffed out, chipmunk cheeks due to the muffin he had crammed in his mouth. He was about the same height and build as Quinn, but with darker features. He looked to be a few years older than Quinn, but the age didn't detract from his good looks one bit. And he had one of those faces that you just *knew* he could charm his way out of anything.

His gaze went from me to Quinn, back to me, back to Quinn. "Well, hello." He might have been going for a flirty smirk, but it was hard to tell with the mouthful of food. Either way, I couldn't help but laugh.

"Hello."

The guy swallowed hard, his throat bobbing in an attempt to get the muffin down. I silently waited and prayed it didn't get lodged in his throat. The last thing I needed was to be blamed for bearing the pastries that choked a firefighter to death.

Once he was finally able to speak clearly, he asked, "You the one that brought the basket of Heaven from Sinful Sweets?"

My grin widened. Yep, a total charmer. "I am. I'm on errand duty for Chloe."

"Delivery Day is like Christmas every month. Every shift hopes they're the ones working on that day. If I weren't a happily married man, I'd kiss you right on the mouth."

I giggled as Quinn glared. Extending my hand, I took a step toward Mr. Charmer. "I'm Lilly. It's nice to meet you."

"Tony." He brought my hand to his lips and kissed my knuckles as he gave side-eyes to Quinn. "And believe me, the pleasure's all mine."

I thought I might have heard Quinn growl low in his throat, but it was probably just my imagination. I pulled my hand free and gave them both an awkward wave.

"Well, it was good seeing you. I better go." I turned toward my car only to have Tony's voice stop me in my tracks.

"Oh, you can't go! We're in the middle of a poker game right now. You should stay and join us. After all, you did just guarantee we'd be well fed the rest of the shift."

Why was Quinn watching me like he was waiting for my reaction? And why was the fact that I could feel his eyes on me making my skin burn red?

"I couldn't." I started to back away, needing to get out of there, away from Quinn and my unpredictable reaction to him. "I don't even know how to play poker. I'd just be in the way." A lie. I knew how to play pretty damn well. On top of insisting I learn to change my own tire when I started driving, my dad also taught me how to hold my own at cards. But these guys didn't need to know that.

Tony snorted and waved me off. "We'll teach you. Don't even worry about that."

I opened my mouth to argue when Quinn finally spoke, and what he said floored me. "You should stay."

My mouth dropped open a bit as I stared. He wanted me to stay... after a week and a half of acting like I didn't exist. What was this guy's deal?

"Perfect!" Tony declared, throwing his arm over my shoulders and leading me into the station through the open bay door, and squashing any hope I had of escaping. "Just stick with me, gorgeous. I'll teach you everything you need to know."

Well... I guess I was playing poker whether I liked it or not.

And I was going to take them for everything they had.

10

QUINN

*S*HE WAS A goddamned card shark. Lilly had spent the past hour and a half scamming five men that were twice her size, and didn't even bat an eye.

And damn if that didn't make her all the more attractive. Even with my head as messed up as it was over this girl, even though I'd been doing my best to stay away from her *because* of how drawn to her I was, when Tony invited her to stay, my mouth opened before I could give it any thought.

Because I wanted her to stay. Because feeling her magnificent body against mine when I caught her was enough to blow my mind. Because she was the first person in three fucking years who could make me laugh.

I was fucked.

"Son of a bitch!" Carpenter shouted, slapping his cards down on the table as Lilly scooped up her winnings with an eager smile and did a little dance in her chair. It was safe to say she was cleaning all of us out.

"Beginner's luck?" She shrugged, giving us a look of fake innocence.

"Beginner's luck my ass." I chuckled. "You hustled us."

She stacked her chips in front of her, a pleased grin tugging at the corner of her mouth. "In my defense, I tried getting out of it, but your buddy over there," she pointed at Tony, "insisted. I didn't have much of a choice."

Tony glowered, his arms crossed over his chest. "Yeah? Well I take my invitation back. I don't wanna play with you anymore."

"Aw, poor baby." She pouted sarcastically. It was nice to see her revert back to the snarky, joking Lilly she normally was after how uncomfortable she seemed when she'd first arrived. I knew it was my fault she felt out of place. I knew it was because I ran hot and cold constantly. But she was tougher than most women I knew and she bounced back quickly. It was just another thing about her I respected and found dangerously attractive.

Yes, the discomfort I felt in her presence originally started because she reminded me of my wife, but now it was totally different. After getting to know her, the differences between Lilly and Addison stood out like a flashing red light. And even though the two women were like night and day, I still craved Lilly's company, her body, her spirited personality. *That* was why I had been trying so hard to keep my distance.

Lilly pulled her cellphone out of her pocket and gave it a quick glance. "I should probably be going anyway. I have to get ready for my next class."

My body had a mind of its own and stood from my seat. "I'll walk you out."

Now having officially become one of the guys by taking all their money, she was comfortable enough to pass out good-bye hugs to my crew without giving it a second thought. That was just the kind of woman she was. And as I walked her out of the station toward her car, I couldn't help but wonder if I'd be on the receiving end of one of those hugs… or if I'd be able to handle it if she did.

We walked the short distance to her car in silence, the awkward mood having returned now that we were alone. "So," I started once we stood at her driver side door. "Thanks for bringing the food."

She fidgeted with her purse, digging around for her keys as she said, "Yeah. Sure. You're welcome," and I got the distinct impression she was having trouble meeting my eyes. I opened my mouth, ready to apologize, when she suddenly spoke first. I shouldn't have been surprised. I was quickly learning that Lilly was the type of woman who spoke what was on her mind.

"Did I do something to piss you off?"

She was so direct I was taken off guard, and it took me a second to formulate a response. "What? No, of course not."

She gave me a speculative look, she didn't believe me. Finally she let out a shaky sigh. "Look, I know we don't really know each other well, but I thought... God, this sounds so stupid." She shook her head in embarrassment but pushed on anyway. "I thought, that night we had dinner at my place, that... well, we were kind of becoming friends. Maybe I was wrong?"

My mouth opened and closed while I tried my best to come up with something to say, something that would take the pained expression off her face. I *did* want to be friends with her. I just didn't have any idea how to do that. "Lilly—"

To my relief, she interrupted, because I really had no fucking clue what I was going to say. "If I misread the situation I can accept that. I'm not going to force you to be friends with me if you aren't comfortable. It's just..." She ran a shaky hand through her hair and swallowed. "...I could really use a friend right now. Things are really hard, and I don't have anyone to talk to. It was just so easy to talk to you that night, like a weight was lifted off my chest, you know? I haven't had anyone I could dump all this on. I didn't realize how much I needed that. But if you aren't comfortable I'd totally understa—"

Christ, she was killing me. She was so genuine about her grief that some protective instinct reared up from deep within me, having been buried in darkness since I lost Addy. It was right then that I wanted nothing more than to give her what she needed. And what she needed most was a friend. In the back of my mind I questioned why she didn't go to Eliza with everything that was hurting her, but the knowledge that I was the only one she felt comfortable turning to felt way too fucking good. I could push my own insecurities, my own demons, back in order to provide her with that.

"Lilly," I cut in, stopping her mid-rant, "I'd love to be your friend."

Her eyes went wide with shock. "Wait. What?"

I grinned down at her because she was too fucking cute. "I said I want to be your friend."

She bit into that plump bottom lip of hers and my blood started to roar. "Really?"

Friends, friends, friends, I chanted to myself. *She needs a friend, asshole, and you need to get your goddamned head straight.* I took a step closer, lowering my voice so the sincerity of my words would shine through. "Really."

I barely had a chance to get the word out before she launched herself at me and squeezed my neck tighter than I thought someone her size was capable of. "Thank you."

Those two heartfelt, whispered words made my stomach clench at the same time feeling her pressed against me made my skin tingle. Slowly, cautiously, I put my arms around her and returned the hug as she continued to whisper.

"I know I probably seem crazy right now, but that means a lot, Quinn. I really need a friend right now."

My arms clenched at that declaration. "You need me, I'm here. Any time."

Lilly sniffled and pulled away, rubbing the back of her hand across her cheek and alerting me to the relieved tears she'd just shed. "I should go," she said, only this time there was no awkwardness, no uncertainty. She was leaving with a smile on her face. A smile that *I* managed to somehow put there. That knowledge made me feel unbelievably fucking fantastic. "I'll see you at Sophia's next class."

"See you then." I lifted my hand and waved as she climbed in the car, started it up, and backed out of the space.

Friends. I could do that.

Or at least I hoped like hell that I could.

11

LILLY

I WAS STANDING in the café downstairs, having just ordered my first coffee of the morning, when I heard the terrifying sound.

"Ms. Lilly! Ms. Lilly! *Ms. Lilly!*"

I spun around from the counter at Sinful Sweets with my heart in my throat at the sound of Sophia's screams. The first thought that popped into my head was that she was hurt, the second one was that she was dying. There was no reason for a child to scream like that unless it was a life-or-death situation.

That was, until I heard Quinn's deep, familiar voice following right after. "Jesus Christ, Sophia. What have I told you about screaming like that?"

"Sorry. I got excited."

My wide-eyed gaze finally landed on the two of them, just coming through the door to the café. Sophia looked chastised, but not hurt, thank God, but that didn't mean she hadn't just taken years off my life.

"Good Lord," I breathed, putting my hand to my chest to prevent my heart from bursting through. "I thought she was really hurt. I almost had a heart attack."

Quinn rubbed a hand over his face, and my eyes instantly focused in on the sexy blond stubble that covered his square jaw. "I'm really sorry about that," he said, looking around the café in embarrassment. He put his hand on Sophia's head and ruffled her hair. "We're working on our inside voice... but it's slow going. Believe me, she's taken years off my life with that scream of hers."

I giggled as I looked down at an unapologetic Sophia. "I bet."

"Sorry for scarin' you, Ms. Lilly," she stated, not sounding apologetic in the slightest. "But I saw you through the window and wanted to invite you to my birthday party!"

I turned my smile on Quinn. It had been two weeks since we agreed to be friends, and in that time, things had been great. It really was nice to have someone around to help take my mind off things. With our work schedules we didn't see each other regularly, but we did text. And on the days he dropped off and picked up Sophia for dance class, he always hung around to chat for a while. It was nice. That connection I felt was still there, just as strong as before, but I had a friend in Quinn so I wasn't going to do anything to jeopardize that. We were slowly getting to know each other. He was giving me exactly what I needed during a difficult time in my life, and I was eternally grateful for that.

I wasn't going to ruin it by falling for someone who was so clearly unobtainable, no matter how much I was growing to like him.

I squatted down in front of Sophia and took the invitation from her extended hand. "A birthday party, huh? Will there be cake?"

I hadn't thought it was possible for her to look any more excited than she already had, but clearly I was wrong. "Yep! Ms. Chloe's makin' me a *humongous* princess cake! It's gonna be as big as our house!" She held her hands high in the air in an attempt to show how big it was going to be.

"Wow! That's really big."

"Uh huh. And I'll even let you have *two* pieces!"

I forced my eyes to go wide, mimicking her exuberance. "Two pieces? Well, then I *have* to come. I wouldn't miss your birthday for the world, Little Miss. Even if I was only getting one piece of cake."

She squealed loud enough to burst my ear drum before launching herself into me and wrapping her arms around my neck. "Yay! It's gonna be so fun! I can't wait!"

I looped my arms around her and stood up, keeping her tiny body propped on my hip for support. In the weeks Sophia had been in my class, I'd grown to adore the little girl. Her exuberance was infectious. She was so generous with her affection that it was impossible not to fall for her. "I can't wait either, sweetie."

She offered me up a smile that would have made her look exactly like her dad if his own smiles ever reached his eyes. I could almost picture Quinn's full-fledged grin in my head, and it caused a pain to shoot through my chest. I would kill to see a smile like that from him.

"Great," Quinn spoke up, pulling my and Sophia's attention in his direction. "Then we'll see you this weekend?"

"Absolutely."

He smiled... and it came *so close* to reaching his eyes that I was suddenly determined to make it happen one day soon. "All right, Angel. It's time for school." He reached his arms out and Sophia all but threw herself at him. Man, seeing him with her really was dangerous to the female population.

"Bye, Ms. Lilly!" Sophia shouted, as Quinn carried her toward the door.

"By, honey." I waved, as Quinn turned to look over his shoulder, shooting me a wink before disappearing outside and out of sight.

A wink. It was quick, there and gone in the blink of an eye. But damn if that one simple wink wasn't potent as hell.

Friends. You're just friends, my brain screamed.

If only my body would get on board.

As I MADE my way to Quinn's front door, my palms grew clammy. My fingers tightened around Sophia's present, the wrapping paper crinkling under my touch as I held tighter to not drop it. I wasn't sure why I was nervous, but there was no denying I was. I told myself that it was because of all the cars lining the street in front of his house; the loud sounds of the party coming from his back yard. I told myself it was because I wasn't a huge fan of crowds since I'd always been somewhat of a loner. But I knew that wasn't it.

For some reason the thought of seeing Quinn totally in his element, surrounded by family and friends, left me feeling off-balance. Normally our interactions took place in or around my dance school. That was *my* territory. Today, right now, I was firmly in *his*. And without Eliza, or even Ethan, here the only friend in attendance was Quinn.

Sure, I knew the people of this town pretty well, but, with the exception of *maybe* Kyle, one of my dance teachers at the school, most of them were acquaintances at best.

Pulling in a fortifying breath, I steeled my spine, shoved my nerves aside, and rang the doorbell. It took several seconds before I heard the familiar sound of the deadbolt twisting, and a moment later, the door swung open, revealing a very attractive, somewhat familiar-looking, blonde woman who appeared to be in her early-to-mid fifties.

"Hello," she said with a kind smile. "Are you here for the party?"

I shifted the present in my arms to free up a hand to shake the one she offered. "Yeah, hi. I'm—"

"Lilly," she finished for me. "Sophia's dance teacher. I know all about you. I'm Eve Mallick, her grandmother."

Well that explained the recognition. Not only did she look just like Quinn *and* Sophia, but I'd seen her in passing a time or two getting Sophia to and from class on the days Quinn was working at the station.

"Nice to officially meet you." I smiled and released her hand, allowing her to move to the side and let me in.

"Nice to meet you too. Sophia can't stop talking about how much she loves your class." She led me down a hallway that extended from the front of the house to the back. I caught glimpses of the other rooms off the hall; the living room, a study, what looked like a little girl's playroom. They were just cursory glances, but from what I could see, Quinn had done a fantastic job of making a comfortable home for himself and Sophia.

"I love having her in there," I continued as we came to a stop in the kitchen, the large wooden dining room table nearly groaning with brightly wrapped presents. I placed mine down and turned to face Quinn's mother. "She's a lively one."

Eve laughed. "That's a good way of putting it. The girl's wild. Definitely gives her father a run for his money. I didn't think it was possible for a kid to be more hyper than Quinn was when he was a boy, but Sophia managed to top him."

"Ah." I giggled. "Karma at work."

"Oh, absolutely! And well-deserved. I've been dying my hair since I was thirty-two because of him. It's only fair he has a taste of his own medicine."

"My mom says my time's coming."

"Smart woman."

The sound of kids yelling and laughing pulled my attention to the back door just as it opened and Quinn appeared, looking flustered and exhausted. "Mom, if we don't cut that cake soon, they're going to riot."

At that, I let out a full-blown laugh. His head jerked toward me and surprise registered across his handsome face. "Lilly. I didn't know you were in here."

"Just got here."

Eve moved around the kitchen, pulling the fridge door open

and unearthing a large cake box. "I had to let her in, that's why I haven't gotten the cake out yet. It'll just be a few minutes."

"Why don't…" He trailed off and pulled in a deep breath, like he was trying to calm himself. "I'll take care of the cake. Why don't you go help wrangle all the kids?"

Eve gave him a look I couldn't quite decipher but didn't say a word as she headed out into the back yard. As soon as the door closed behind her, Quinn propped his hands on the kitchen counter, dropped his head, and sighed.

"Hey," I said softly, coming up behind him. "You okay?"

He didn't bother to move. "Yeah, I'm good. You should get out there. Lilly's been asking for you."

Those familiar shutters started to come down. I opened my mouth to speak, to try and get him to confide in me, but the backdoor opened again, letting in screams of all the kids.

"Quinn?"

His head shot in the direction of the voice, and there was no missing the way his back went rigid. For the life of me, I couldn't understand his reaction to the pretty, middle-aged brunette woman standing in the doorway. And what was even more confusing was the fact that she looked just as uncomfortable as him. She wrung her hands in front of her as she continued speaking. "Sophia sent me to find you."

He moved to the cake box and lifted the cake out, setting it on the counter so he could put the candles on the top tier. It was as if he was doing everything in his power not to make eye contact. "Almost finished," he stated in a flat voice. "I'll be right out."

She looked like she wanted to say more, but forced herself to remain quiet. Moving her gaze to the floor, she whispered, "Okay." It was almost painful to watch. It was so obvious that, whoever she was, she wanted to reach out to him, but he was just as closed off with her as he was with anyone else.

Suddenly Sophia's loud, shouting voice came echoing into the kitchen. "*Grandma*! Where's Daddy?" Sophia barreled up next to the woman in the doorway and wrapped her arms around her legs, causing the air to freeze in my lungs.

Grandma. Oh, God. His wife's mother.

Quinn offered Sophia a tense, tight smile. "I'll be right out, Angel."

Sophia's eyes finally landed on me, and her smile nearly enveloped her entire face. "*Miss Lilly!*" She disengaged from her grandmother and came at me.

I returned her hug, loving how genuine it felt every single time. "Hey, Little Miss. Happy birthday."

"Thanks! You wanna come outside with me? I can show you my piñata!"

I looked from her to Quinn, and back again. "Give me just a second, sweetie. I'm going to help your daddy get everything ready."

Sophia headed back toward the door, back to her grand-mother. The woman smiled down at Sophia and reached for her hand. "Come on, sweet girl. Why don't we get everyone to sit down so we can serve up the cake?"

12

LILLY

"**I**'VE GOT THIS. You can just head outside."

I narrowed my eyes at Quinn. There was something weighing heavily on him, something he was determined to handle all by himself, even though I was standing right there, ready and more than willing to be a shoulder for him to lean on. We were friends. Friends helped each other.

And I was going to help him whether he wanted it or not, damn it!

I slid my purse off my shoulder and hooked it onto the back of one of the dining room chairs. The princess-designed paper plates and napkins were stacked on the end of the counter, so I grabbed everything and moved to hold the back door open for Quinn as he headed that way with the cake. As soon as he got close enough, just a handful of inches away from me, I lowered my voice and spoke adamantly.

"I'm helping you, so get over it. That's what friends do. There's clearly something wrong, and if you don't want to talk about it, that's fine, but I'm helping. Don't bother fighting me on it because I'll win. And I'm not above recruiting any damn person at this party to do so, you got me?"

His green eyes flickered, the dullness from seconds ago slowly creeping out of them as he gave me a tiny smirk. "You finished?"

I paused just long enough to consider his question. "Yeah. If you don't force my hand, I'm finished."

His smirk grew just a bit more. "No forcing necessary. You made your point and I accept it. But this cake's pretty fucking heavy, so if you don't mind…" He tipped his chin in the direction of the picnic table all the children were crowded around.

"Oh! Yeah, I got it." I stepped out of the way and let him through. Just as he cleared the doorway, he turned to look back over his shoulder.

"Hey, Lilly?"

"Yeah?"

"I'm glad you're here. Really glad."

My knees grew a little weak, but somehow I managed to get the plates and napkins to the table without completely melting into a puddle of goo.

Quinn just seemed to have that effect on me.

THE CAKE HAD BEEN SERVED before any of the kids went into shock from waiting. As soon as that was over, Sophia dove into the pile of presents Quinn and his father had moved outside. A few of the mothers from the dance school came up to say hello during that time, but mostly, I stood on the periphery, comfortable enough as an observer. I was having too much fun watching Sophia's face light up with every single present she opened. I didn't need to force myself into the very center of it all like some of the other mothers there.

If it hadn't sent a spike of jealousy through me, I probably would have laughed at the number of women who were unnecessarily helpful, overly touchy. It wasn't like I could blame them, really. Quinn was undeniably attractive. Any single, hot-blooded woman would want him, myself included. We were just friends, but that didn't make watching those women flirt any easier.

The only good thing about it was that Quinn didn't seem interested in the slightest. He smiled that smile that didn't come near his eyes, laughed when the situation warranted. But it was clear—to those watching closely—that he didn't return their attention.

Just as that thought occurred to me, I was hit with another, more unpleasant one. He wasn't interested in *any* woman. Myself included.

It wasn't like I didn't already know that, but the reminder didn't hurt any less.

Just friends. Just friends. Just friends.

The sound of Sophia's voice pulled me out of my head and back into reality. "Ms. Lilly! This one's from you!"

I smiled from a distance as she held up the wrapped present I brought. Then my heart gave a little jump when Quinn waved me over and added, "Come over here."

My cheeks heated as I picked my way through the crowd of unhappy-looking mothers to get to Quinn and Sophia's side. Quinn leaned in so close I could feel his breath across my neck as he whispered, "What are you doing all the way over there?"

I tried not to shiver as Sophia ripped into the wrapping paper. "Just watching. Didn't want to be in the way," I whispered back.

One corner of his mouth lifted in a smirk as he turned back to his daughter, muttering, "Impossible," under his breath.

I really was going to melt into a pile of goo if he didn't stop. Luckily, Sophia's high-pitched squeak distracted me from Quinn's potency and turned our attention back to her.

"Daddy, look!" She pulled the pale pink, satin ballet slippers from the box by the long ribbons that would wrap around her ankles. She held them up and stared at them, her face a blanket of wonder and awe. "Wow," she breathed after several seconds.

Turning from the slippers to me, her eyes were wide as she asked, "Can you put them on me? Please, Ms. Lilly?"

"Of course, sweetie." I sat down on the bench next to her and lifted her feet up. The ballet slippers didn't quite go with the princess dress she was wearing for the party, but she didn't seem to care. I showed her how to lace them up around her ankles and tie them in a little bow, and as soon as I stood up, she and her friends took off like they were on fire, screaming and running around the back yard. It always tripped me out how short kids' attention spans were. Present time was officially over and it was back to playing.

"Don't worry," I muttered from the side of my mouth to Quinn. "They're totally machine washable."

He let out a deep belly laugh, and I noticed the sound pulled the gaze of his mother, father, and the man and woman I now knew to be his wife's parents. The four of them seemed shocked to hear him laugh, and I was left wondering what that was all about.

Before I could think longer on it, Quinn's voice called my attention. "Well, thank Christ for that, because there's no way I'm getting those off her feet. Pretty sure she's going to sleep in them."

I beamed up at him and watched in amazement as his eyes traveled down to my lips. That telltale spark I felt every time he looked at me like that ignited beneath my skin, once again, making me feel like there was something deeper between us.

I knew it was more than likely all in my imagination, and that I needed to brush it off, so in an attempt to do that, I shook my head and began gathering up the plates and other trash scattered around the table from Sophia's cake and presents.

"Just leave that," he began to argue. "I'll get to it later."

"I don't mind helping. Besides, two hands are better than one, and if we get this cleaned up now, you won't be stuck with the mess later."

That smile of his grew just a tad closer to his eyes as he reached down and started gathering up more trash. "Thanks."

———

THE PARTYGOERS HAD STARTED to clear out a while later. I hung around, wanting to help clean up as much as I could before taking off. I was standing at the kitchen sink washing the last of the dirty dishes when a voice spoke up behind me.

"You're Sophia's dance teacher, aren't you?"

I looked over my shoulder at the pretty brunette, Sophia's grandmother. "Yes ma'am."

She closed the distance between us as I dried my hands and offered hers up for a shake. "I'm Janice Benson. It's lovely to meet you."

I shook her soft hand as I studied her sincere expression. "It's nice to meet you too."

"She talks about your class every time we have a call." She must have read my confusion as she went on to explain, "My husband and I live in Seattle. We don't get to see Sophia as much as we want to anymore, so we have regularly scheduled phone calls three times a week."

That was incredibly sad, and judging by what I saw behind her eyes, she felt the same way. I didn't know what I was supposed to say, what she *expected* me to say. There didn't seem like any right words, so all I could offer was a heartfelt, "It's really nice you take the time to keep in contact."

Her face only grew sadder, even with her attempt at a smile. "We miss her... them. We miss both of them."

I was about two seconds away from crying if I didn't get my shit together. She sniffed, clearly trying to hold back her own tears and gave me another wobbly smile. "Is he..." She stopped suddenly and cleared her throat against the rush of emotion that caused her words to break. "Quinn, is he… okay? I mean, does he seem happy?"

My mouth opened and closed several times before I was finally able to stutter, "I-I don't… I'm not… I…" I had no clue how to answer that question. The truth was, some days he seemed content, but as far as *happy*, I just wasn't sure about that. And I didn't think she wanted to hear the truth. She wanted hope.

"He laughed with you, earlier today. He actually laughed. I haven't heard that in… well, I don't know how long. That has to mean something, right?"

I couldn't let her continue with the worry she was carrying around, not if I was able to do something to help. "Yes," I whispered. "He seems happy."

The weight dropping off her shoulders was almost palpable. "Thank you," she spoke in a ragged whisper. "Thank you. That means—"

"Everything okay in here?" We were both startled by the unexpected voice and turned to find Quinn standing in the doorway leading to the back yard.

"Yeah," I answered brightly, trying to cover up the intensity of the moment that had just occurred. "All good. We were just finishing up the last of the dishes."

He hesitated before stepping fully into the kitchen. "You didn't have to do that."

"Oh… I didn't mind. I—" I was suddenly cut off by the man I'd come to know as Janice's husband. Quinn's deceased wife's father.

"Janice… you about ready, darling?"

Quinn's body went on alert, his posture stiffening as the man stopped just feet from him. Not once did he look over at the man he'd known as his father-in-law. I couldn't for the life of me understand the dynamic between all these people, but there was one thing I knew for sure. It wasn't healthy. For any of them.

"Sure," Janice smiled and moved toward her husband. "Let me just say goodnight to Sophia."

The man looked from his wife to Quinn before saying, "I'll go with you." Then, just like that, they were both gone, but the tension still hung heavy in the air.

"You okay?" Quinn asked, giving me a start.

"Uh…" A nervous laugh bubbled from deep within. "I'm pretty sure I should be asking you that question. You get any more rigid and you just might crack."

He came closer, his face suspicious. "Did she say something that upset you?"

"What? No, not at all. She was really nice, actually. Why would you think that?"

I could tell he didn't believe me. "You looked upset when I walked in, that's all. Things with them can be…"

"Can be what?" I asked when he didn't finish his sentence.

"It's a difficult situation, that's all. They do what they can to maintain a relationship with Sophia, but we don't really talk."

I was shocked to hear him admit something so personal. He was normally so closed-off that his openness about his in-laws was surprising. I had expected those shutters of his to come down. Seeing as they hadn't, I decided to take my chances and asked, "Why?"

What he said next broke my heart. The words, coupled with the emptiness in his beautiful eyes killed me. "They blame me," he admitted raggedly.

I closed the gap between us in two steps, grabbing hold of his hands in an attempt to offer some sort of comfort, no matter how small. "What? No, Quinn, that's not—"

"It's all right. I blame myself, too. It's just…" He looked so ravaged, so pained. I would have given anything in that moment to take it all away from him. "I wish things were different between all of us. For Sophia's sake."

"I think you're wrong," I told him softly, reaching up to hold his face in my hands. "She's worried. She told me herself that they miss you. She didn't sound like a woman who placed blame, Quinn."

His eyes grew dark as those shutters began to lower. "You wouldn't understand."

I was just about to argue, to tell him that maybe I could understand if he'd just *talk to me*, but Sophia called out from the backyard, interrupting the moment.

"I need to get out there. Thank you for everything today." He turned and walked out, effectively closing the door on our conversation and leaving me hurting for him.

1 3

LILLY

*S*INCE MY FATHER'S diagnosis it had been hard to keep from stopping by my parents' house unexpectedly every chance I had. The only thing that kept me from going over constantly was the fact that we'd changed our monthly dinners to weekly, so I was able to keep a closer eye on my father. Other than being tired and losing weight, he'd been in pretty good spirits recently. It wasn't until I walked into their kitchen the day after Sophia's party and got a look at my mother's face that I knew something wasn't right.

Her eyes were bloodshot, dark circles made them appear sunken in. Her skin was pale and her normally put together appearance was disheveled. She looked like she hadn't been sleeping.

"Mom? What's wrong?"

She gave me a sad, tired smile as she slowly chopped a stalk of celery. "Oh, hi, sweetie. I didn't hear you come in."

I walked to her and took the knife from her hand. "Maybe that's because you're half-asleep? What's going on?"

She let out a weary sigh and all but collapsed onto the

barstool at the island. "Sorry. It's just been a little rough. You're father hasn't had a very good week."

It felt like someone reached into my chest and squeezed. "Is he okay?"

Hearing the worry in my voice, Mom reached over and placed her hand on top of mine. "Oh, honey, I'm sorry. I didn't mean to scare you. He's okay. He's just been a little under the weather. You know how it gets when a person's sick. The nights are always the worst. I've been staying up to take care of him."

"Why didn't you call me?"

"Lilly," she said softly. "You're already juggling enough with the studio and your big show coming up. Fall and Winter are a stressful time for you as it is. I didn't want to burden you."

That tightness in my chest returned and my eyes began to burn. "Mom, how could you think that? You're my parents. You and Dad could never be a burden. When Dad is sick, or you're not getting any sleep, I want to help. Please, let me help."

She looked so tired, so sad. This was the woman who kissed away every ache and pain, who held me when the kids at school teased me, who'd been my rock my entire life. I was twenty-four years old and she was *still* looking out for me. It was time for me to pitch in. I owed it to her to carry some of *her* burden for a change.

"You know what? There's really no reason for you to go all out on dinner every night. Why don't I handle it for a change while you go take a nap?" She gave me a look that spoke volumes about her faith in me when it came to cooking, so I amended by saying, "I'll order a pizza. You and I can eat that, and I'll make Dad a sandwich. I can't possibly screw up a sandwich, right?"

Her smile was one of relief as she gave my hand a gentle pat. "Okay, sweetheart. You do that. I'm just going to rest in the living room for a bit. Your father's sleeping in the bedroom and I don't want to disturb him."

Mom went to lay down while I prepared a grilled cheese sandwich and some tomato soup for Dad and put in a call for a mushroom and pepperoni pizza.

The ache in my heart only grew worse when I pushed the bedroom door open and saw my father, so small and frail, lying asleep in the bed. He'd always been such a force of nature when I was growing up. I even remembered back when I thought my father was invincible. He was a strong, proud man. Seeing how cancer was slowly ravaging his body was tearing me apart.

"I smell tomato soup and grilled cheese," he spoke, pulling me from my dreary thoughts. I smiled as he cracked his eyes open. "I knew it. That smell could only mean one thing — Lilly's on dinner duty."

"Ha ha," I deadpanned, as I made my way into the room and set the tray down over his lap. "Very funny, Daddy. Not everyone can have Mom's skills in the kitchen." I helped him prop up on a few pillows and took a seat next to him.

"That's okay, Lilly Flower. You make up for it with the way you dance. Always felt like I was watching magic every time I saw you."

"Stop it, or you're going to make me cry," I teased, even though I felt dangerously close to bursting into tears.

Dad might have looked worse than he had the week before, but I could still see the love and humor in his eyes. He slowly lifted the spoon to his mouth and sipped the soup. "So, I take it your mom's finally resting?"

I could hear his concern for her in his voice. "She is," I sighed. "Dad, when things get like this, you need to call me so I can help. Mom doesn't need to exhaust herself and you don't need to worry when I'm just a phone call away."

"Lilly Flower, that's just what parents do. You'll understand one day. No matter what's happening, it's our job to take care of our children. We didn't want you to get upset."

I sniffed, trying my hardest to fight back the wave of emotion. "Daddy, you have to let me help." I took his hand in mine, noticing how frail it was. The man I once thought could save me from every bad thing that existed was slowly withering away before my very eyes. "I *need* you to let me help," I managed past the lump in my throat.

"Oh, baby girl." He wrapped his arm around me and pulled me into him for a tight hug. It was then that I lost my fight and let the tears fall silently. "I'm sorry. I'm so sorry for all of this."

"It's not your fault," I whispered. "None of this is. It just…" I hiccupped through another wave of tears. "It sucks. I hate this."

"I know, honey." We were both silent for several minutes, just holding each other as sorrow filled the room. "Hey," Dad finally spoke up. "Remember that winter the blizzard came through and dumped so much snow the whole town shut down for a week?"

"Yeah."

"Everyone was stuck in their houses. You were going stir-crazy, driving your mom up the wall."

I giggled at the memory. "I remember. You finally had enough of listening to us argue, so you came up with the brilliant idea to take me sledding."

"Only we didn't have sleds."

At that, I let out a full belly laugh. "Yep. So, in your infinite wisdom, you decided I was small enough to use the massive silver serving platter that Grandma Rose had passed down to Mom on your wedding day. Remember her reaction when she found out what I'd been sliding down the hill on? I don't think I've ever seen her turn so red in my life."

Dad chuckled, his chest vibrating against my ear. "Hey, how was I supposed to know it was a family heirloom?"

We both burst into laughter. Silence filled the room once the humor had petered out. "Lilly Flower, look at me."

I tipped my head up and looked into my father's loving eyes.

"Those are the memories I want you to hold onto when I'm

gone. I know this will be hard, baby girl. I know it's going to hurt. But we've managed to make a lifetime of memories just like that one. Remember those times when it starts to get hard. Can you do that for me?"

A lone tear spilled over onto my cheek as I smiled up at my dad. "I can do that, Daddy."

"That's my girl." He returned my smile and I knew that this moment was going to be yet another among years worth of happy memories that I held on to once he was finally gone.

THAT NIGHT, I decided it was best for me to stay the night with my folks. I wasn't teaching until later the following day and Mom really needed a break. She was so exhausted that when I tried to wake her for pizza, she mumbled a few unintelligible words, rolled over, and passed back out. I pulled a blanket over her and let her be, hoping that she'd catch up on the sleep she so desperately needed.

I closed down the house for the night and had just crawled into my old bed when my cellphone began to ring from the bedside table, the light from the screen creating a soft glow in the otherwise dark bedroom.

I was surprised to see Quinn's name, and quickly slid my thumb across the glass face to answer the call. "Quinn? Is everything all right? Is Sophia okay?"

His deep, rough voice came through the line, sending a tingle across my skin. "Yeah, everything's fine. Why do you ask?"

A quick glance at the clock on my nightstand showed it was a few minutes past ten. "It's just kind of late. I didn't know if something was wrong."

He was silent for a second before whispering, "Shit. I didn't realize what time it was. I'm sorry. Did I wake you up?"

I found myself smiling in spite of the weight still resting on my chest from the stress with my father. "No. I wasn't asleep. So, what's up?"

"I was just…" When he trailed off, I got the weird sense that he wasn't sure of himself, like he was nervous to be calling me in the middle of the night. "I knew you had dinner with your folks tonight and I wanted to check on you. See how you're doing."

Warmth spread threw my limbs and my heart gave a little jump in my chest. He was checking up on me. He knew how hard all of this was, and just wanted to make sure I was okay. At that realization, the weight seemed to lessen just a bit.

I was suddenly choked up at the show of support. "Thank you," I managed to say on a whisper. "That… that means a lot."

"So how's your dad doing?"

I let out a sigh and stacked the pillows behind my back in an effort to get comfortable. "He's had a tough few days. I'm staying the night to try and give my mom a break. She was exhausted by the time I showed up."

"I'm so sorry, Lilly."

"It's okay," I spoke. "It sucks, but it is what it is."

"Is there anything I can do to help?"

God, this man. The more time I spent getting to know him, the blurrier the line between friends and something more became. He made it damn near impossible to *not* fall for him.

"Just talking to you helps," I answered truthfully. "It might sound crazy, but knowing I can vent to you if I need to really helps."

His voice was soft as he said, "I get it. Believe me. And I'm always here. You need me, you call. Day or night. Got it?"

I giggled into the phone at his bossy demeanor. "Yes sir."

His voice sounded thicker, gravelly when he spoke again. "I should let you get some sleep. See you tomorrow?"

"Yeah," I breathed. "And Quinn?"

"I'm here." And he really was. That meant more to me than he could ever know.

"Thank you for calling."

"Always. Night, Lilly."

"Night, Quinn." I ended the call and snuggled down into the bed, closing my eyes on a heavy exhale.

Thanks to Quinn being my friend when I needed one the most, sleep came easily that night.

14

LILLY

I HATED HAVING to leave my parents the next day to make the drive back to Pembrooke, but the two of them had teamed up against me and practically forced me out the door. They said I had classes to teach and responsibilities of my own. I wanted to stay and help take care of them both, but they insisted they'd be just fine without me. I knew it was their way of looking out for me, but that didn't help to lessen the tension I was carrying around in the pit of my stomach.

I tried throwing myself into work, tried pouring all my stress and anxiety out in dance, but it just wasn't working. I was on edge, and it showed. By the time my last class of the day came to an end, I felt ready to snap.

Pasting a fake smile on my face, I began winding my way through the crowd of parents picking up their kids, looking for an escape, when a hand on my elbow caused me to stop. I spun around to find Quinn looking down at me, his pale green eyes full of concern.

"Hey," I greeted.

"Hey. You okay?"

With a sigh, I tucked a few strands of hair behind my ear. "Yeah, I'm good. Just ready for this day to be over, I guess."

"I know the feeling." It was then that I noticed the tension around his eyes and mouth. Something was on his mind.

"I get the feeling I should be asking you the same question. What's up?"

"What? Nothing. I'm good." It was clearly a lie. He'd been a good enough friend to ask how I was doing, but I could tell he was holding something back. It was written all over his face.

One of my brows quirked up in skepticism, and I crossed my arms over my chest. "Yeah? Well, for someone who's *good,* you're looking rather constipated."

By the way his eyes bugged out and a rumble of bewildered laughter broke from his throat, I knew my comment had shocked him. "Constipated?" His eyes sparkled with humor that made my heart leap just a little bit. "Wow. Colorful analogy, Lil."

Lil. It was the first time he'd ever used any type of nickname with me, and I was suddenly ridiculously giddy at the thought that our friendship had evolved to that level of comfort. "You're welcome." I smiled. "Now tell me what's up, because I know you're not as fine as you're claiming to be. We have a truce, remember? We're supposed to be trying this whole friendship thing out. Grumpy Quinn is only allowed to come out once a month."

His eyes brightened just a bit more, but despite all my effort, I still couldn't pull a genuine smile from the man. It was almost infuriating. "I'm not grumpy," he stated softly, "I'm just..."

"Just what?" I pushed.

He let out a sigh and ran his long fingers through his sandy blond hair. "Stressed, I guess. Tony asked if I could work half his shift for him so he could take his wife out for his anniversary. I said yes before checking with my parents. They're going to Yellowstone for the weekend. Now I'm committed to working tonight and don't have anyone to watch Soph."

Sympathy washed over me as I took in his concerned expression. I couldn't imagine how hard it was for him, trying to be a single father to a little girl, especially to one as rambunctious and lively as Sophia. Without thinking, my mouth opened and the words came out. "I'll watch her for you."

His surprise registered for a brief second before he replied, "I can't ask you to do that."

"You didn't." I shrugged. "I offered. I don't mind. Really. I like Sophia, and we're friends, right? Let me help you."

Just then, the girl in question came scurrying over. "Daddy! Did you see me? Did you see?" She jumped up and down excitedly and, at her enthusiasm, coupled with the genuine, happy smile on Quinn's face, my belly swooped.

"I did, Angel. You were terrific."

"Miss Lilly said Imma fast learner," she rambled.

Quinn's eyes quickly met mine and he gave me a wink that made my knees tremble just a bit. "I can see that. You'll be spinning around in circles in no time."

She rolled her eyes dramatically, like only a little girl can do. "I can already do that, Daddy." She proceeded to spin around over and over, wobbling around until she finally lost balance and fell on her behind. Without batting an eye, she jumped back to her feet and grinned triumphantly. "See?"

"I stand corrected." Quinn chuckled. "You sure you can handle all this energy over night?" he asked, looking back at me.

I scoffed. "*Pfft*. Totally."

Sophia's gasp drew both our attention to her. "Is Miss Lilly coming for a sleepover?" She clasped her hands together in front of her chest. "Oh please, please, please, please!"

Quinn eyed me questioningly, leaving the ball in my court. I leaned down, running my hand over Sophia's soft ponytail. "If you want me to, yeah. Your daddy has to work so I told him I'd come over and keep you company for the night. You can cook, right? Because I'm horrible in the kitchen. If we don't want to starve, it's up to you to feed us."

"Yeah!" she shouted, throwing her hands in the air. "I can make you Daddy's pancakes! They're the best in the *whole world*!"

I couldn't help but laugh at the fear written across Quinn's face. "I don't think your dad's too fond of that idea, Little Miss."

"I think I might be more comfortable if the two of you stay out of the kitchen. How about I leave some cash for pizza?"

I took no offense to that. Besides, it wasn't too long ago the fire department was at my apartment. But still, I couldn't help but tease. "It was only a teeny-tiny kitchen fire. No big deal."

He looked like he was two seconds from having an aneurism, so I took pity on him. "I'm kidding! Me and Soph will order a pizza so we can Netflix and chill. Don't worry."

His lips quirked just a fraction, and I would have given anything to get a real smile from him. That quirk did nothing but make me more determined to wear him down. I was going to get a smile from him that actually reached his eyes if it killed me.

"I must be losing my mind," he muttered under his breath. "Okay, fine. Lilly's watching you tonight, Angel. That means you have to do exactly what she tells you. And no tricks."

I hadn't thought it was possible for a kid her age, but Sophia actually looked affronted as she declared, "I don't trick!"

Quinn gave her what could only be described as *The Father Face*. I knew it well. I'd gotten it from my own dad quite a bit growing up. The reminder of my dad sent a pang of sadness through me that I had to work to swallow down.

"Yeah?" he asked, unconvinced. "What's your bedtime?"

"Nine."

"Nice try," he grunted, turning from his daughter to me. "Her bedtime's eight. Don't let her play you. Trust me, she'll try."

I winked down at a bereft Sophia, earning myself a grin. "I think I can handle it."

"Famous last words," Quinn replied before taking his daughter's hand. "All right then. Does six work for you?"

"Yep. I'll be there."

Maybe it was the little girl in me, maybe it was because I was happy to have something to fill my time with so I could keep my mind off my dad, maybe it was just because I really liked Sophia and her father. But whatever the reason, I was excited for my sleepover tonight.

IT WAS JUST a little after eight-thirty when my cellphone rang. Picking up the remote, I clicked pause on the episode of *Vikings* I'd found in Quinn's DVR. I had to admit, the show was addicting. I was only on the first episode, and if Sophia hadn't run me ragged in the two hours she'd been awake, I would have probably stayed up all night binge watching.

Hitting the green button on my phone I lifted it to my ear. "Hello?"

"Oh good," Quinn's voice came through the line. "You're still alive. I was afraid one or both of you would have burned the house down by now."

Despite the twitch in my lips, I fought a smile and deadpanned, "Your faith in me as a babysitter is touching, really. I'm swooning as we speak."

His deep, rough chuckle sent a shiver up my spine. I loved it when he laughed. He didn't do nearly enough of it. He was a good man, he deserved to laugh more. "She asleep?"

"Out like a light," I confirmed. "That shot of whiskey I gave her right before we watched *The Walking Dead* knocked her right out. Can't promise it'll help with the nightmares though. That show's gory as hell, Quinn. I couldn't believe it when she told me you let her watch it. What were you thinking?"

"*What?!*"

I burst into laughter. "I'm kidding! Would you relax? We watched some cartoon movie that now makes me wish I had a snowman of my own, and I read her *Cinderella* three times before she finally passed out."

He remained silent long enough for me to question my decision to joke around. When he finally spoke again, it wasn't what I'd been expecting to hear.

"I never thanked you for watching Sophia for me. I know you acted like it wasn't big deal for you, but it means a lot to me that you'd put your plans on hold for the night to babysit her at the drop of a hat."

For a man of few words, he sure was good at talking when he wanted to be. And seeing as our relationship started off with him pretending I didn't exist, hearing him say something like that felt really, really nice.

"She's a great kid," I said softly, pulling my knees up and hugging them to my chest. "You're doing well with her, Quinn. It might not feel like it sometimes, but you're a great dad. She adores you."

He spoke just as quietly as I just had when he said, "I can't tell you how much it means to hear that. Sometimes I worry that I'm screwing everything up."

Unable to sit still as Quinn opened himself up to me, showing me a new side of him I'd never seen before, I stood from the couch and began walking aimlessly. "I wouldn't have said it if it wasn't true. I work with children enough to know when they've got it good at home and when they don't. You'd be shocked how many parents are checked out of their own kid's life. You're doing the best you can, Quinn. It shows."

My words ended just as I my feet stopped moving. Right in front of his bedroom door. The door was opened just a crack and, for some reason, my curiosity was peaked.

"Thanks." His voice was gruff, but I knew he was being sincere.

"You're welcome," I replied, just as my fingers reached out of their own accord and pushed the door open a bit more.

"Well, I should probably let you get some sleep. I know Soph's probably worn you out."

I was hit with a wave of regret, not wanting the conversation to end, and the intensity of it was startling. "Yeah. Good night."

"Night, Lilly."

"Be safe."

He hung up without another word, and my curiosity finally got the best of me. Pushing the door the rest of the way open, I stepped quietly into Quinn's room.

The masculinity of the room didn't surprise me. Quinn was the very definition of masculine so the dark espresso finish of the wooden headboard and matching bedside tables and dresser fit. It was the cleanliness that was shocking. The bed was made perfectly. The navy and gray chevron-patterned comforter was tucked in around the sides and covered the pillows with almost military precision. I bet I could bounce a quarter off it if I weren't concerned with leaving wrinkles.

The only thing on the dark hardwood floors was a pale gray throw rug, no clothing strewn about, no miscellaneous socks or shoes, nothing. With the exception of some pocket change and a couple folded receipts on the dresser, there wasn't even any clutter. I was sure that if I scoped out his closet, it would have been organized to precision. Not that I was going to do that. I was already invading his privacy enough as it was, I refused to cross the line further by going through his closet or rummaging through his medicine cabinet.

The only personal effect in the entire room was one single picture frame that sat on the far nightstand. My feet carried me around the foot of the bed, and when I saw the picture of the blonde woman smiling over her shoulder at a laughing Quinn, my heart stopped. Addison. Quinn's wife. She was remarkably beautiful, and the smile stretching across her face made it clear she loved her life. But it was Quinn's expression that made my chest ache. I picked up the frame and brought it closer to my face. I don't think I'd ever seen him looking so happy and carefree. It was like looking at a totally different person. The Quinn I knew now was just a shadow of the Quinn captured in the snapshot I was holding in my hands. And that realization gutted me.

Setting the picture back where I found it, I couldn't help but think how sad it was that he'd lost so much at such a young age, so much that it changed him into someone else. I hated that for him. I wanted to fix it.

But before I could let my worry over his wellbeing take over, the sound of Sophia's screams from down the hall had me running out of the room as fast as I possibly could.

"Daddy!" Sophia screamed at the same time I grabbed hold of the doorframe, sliding around on my sock-clad feet and almost falling before I finally made it into her room.

Her face was pale, her blue eyes wide and shining like crazy as she sat in her bed, panting heavily.

"Hey, hey," I cooed, rushing to her and dropping to my knees at the side of her bed. "It's okay, sweetie. I'm here. I've got you."

My heart was pounding so hard I thought it might come through my breastbone as she grabbed the sleeves of my sweater and pulled until I was sitting on the mattress next to her.

"I had a bad dream." Her voice shook as she laid her head on my lap. My fingers found her hair and I slowly started sliding them down in the hopes of soothing her.

"Do you want to talk about it?" I asked, as I lifted my legs and rested back against the headboard, stretching out along the length of her little girl bed. She shook her head against my legs and burrowed closer.

"No. It scared me. I don't wanna be scared again."

A memory from my childhood pushed its way to the forefront of my mind; one of those memories my father wanted me to hold on to. "You know, when I was a little girl, my dad used to lay with me and sing me a song any time I had a bad dream. He said it was a special song that would keep all the scary thoughts away. Would you like me to sing it to you?"

"Uh huh."

I settled further into the bed and started to sing Fleetwood Mac's "Landslide," just like my father did countless times. I didn't hold a candle to Stevie Nicks' sultry voice, but that didn't stop me from giving it my all. I remembered how that song would chase away the monsters every time Dad sang it to me, and I wanted to give Sophia that very same comfort.

By the time I finished singing, she was asleep, breathing deep and steady as I ran my fingers through her soft hair. I continued to hum the tune, taking the very same comfort I'd just offered her from the memory of my father. I must have eventually dozed, because the next thing I knew, I was startled awake by Quinn's low, gravelly voice.

"What are you doing?"

My eyes flicked open and it took a second for me to get my bearings and remember where I was. Sunlight was streaming through the slats of the blinds on Sophia's bedroom window, lighting everything in a pretty combination of pink and orange. Quinn was standing in the doorway, his face completely blank and unreadable, thick arms crossed over his broad chest. If I wasn't still half asleep, I probably would have drooled at the sight of him in his navy work uniform.

"Hey," I spoke, my voice raspy from sleep as I lifted my right arm that was resting around Sophia's and carefully pulled my left from beneath her body, mindful not to wake her. "You're home. What time is it?"

"7:15." It was the short, choppy way he answered that put me on alert. As I stood from the bed and made my way to the door, I noticed the air was almost static. I'd been wrong. Quinn's face wasn't blank. The closer I got, I realized something had seriously pissed him off. I just had no idea what.

"You okay?"

"You haven't answered my question. What the hell are you doing?"

With a quick glance behind me to confirm Quinn hadn't woken Sophia, I grabbed his arm and pulled him into the hallway, closing the door behind us so as not to disturb her.

"What are you talking about?" I asked, my voice still a whisper as we moved a few feet from the door. It was when I finally registered my hand on Quinn's arm that I realized his entire body was strung tight.

"Why were you in her bed?"

My forehead wrinkled as my eyebrows dipped in a V. "She had a pretty bad nightmare last night, and didn't want me to leave. I held her until she fell back asleep, and I must have dozed off."

"She has a nightmare, you stay with her until she's asleep, then you get the hell up and leave. You don't sleep in there with her."

My jaw dropped as I tried to figure out what was going on. "Quinn, I—"

"You're not her fucking mother, so don't pretend to be. First, it was cleaning up after the party like it was your job, now this? You couldn't replace Addy if you tried, so don't. Fucking. Try," he barked out angrily. His words forced me to jerk back like he'd just hit me, and in a way, I guess he had, because I certainly felt what he'd said like a physical blow.

"I wasn't..." I started, but the lump forming in my throat blocked what I was trying to say. Swallowing painfully, I tried once more. "I'd never try to do that..."

He let out a sarcastic laugh as he dropped his arms and rested his hands on his hips. The new stance didn't make him any less threatening, and as I stared at him, my nose burned and my eyes began to sting. "Could have fooled me. Looked like you were trying pretty fucking hard to cozy up to my daughter in there. You're her dance teacher, that's it. Don't try and be something more, you'll just be disappointed when you can't live up to the real thing."

I had to take a step back with each word as they hit me, over and over, each hurting worse than the last.

"Wow," I breathed, it was the only word I was able to say for several seconds as I fought to keep from crying. Quinn had just flayed me open without missing a beat. I wouldn't give him the satisfaction of letting him see me cry. For every step forward I think we've taken, he did something so callous, so mean, we take at least thirty steps back. And standing in front of him just then, having just taken the brunt of yet *another* mood swing, I wondered why I even wanted to be friends with this man. There hadn't been someone in my life who made me feel so low since I was a kid, picked on for being a little different.

"Glad to know that's how little you think of me. I'll be sure not to forget that." I stomped into the living room, picking up my shoes, lifting the overnight bag I had onto my shoulder, and grabbing my purse from the coffee table. I wasn't going to wait the extra seconds it would take to slide my feet in and lace them up. Fuck that, I was getting out of there.

I stopped just long enough to look at him over my shoulder and say, "You know, I get that you're hurting, I do. And I'm sorry for everything you lost. But that pain doesn't give you the right to be an asshole to every person in your life. You don't hold the fucking monopoly on suffering, Quinn, but if you want to spend the rest of your life miserable and alone, have at it. I'm done trying to help someone who'd rather hurt the people who care about him than try and feel better."

I wanted to slam the door, take my anger and pain out physically, but I wasn't willing to risk Sophia overhearing and possibly getting upset. No matter how much of an asshole her father was, I still cared deeply for her. So I shut the door quietly and walked as fast as I could to my car, tossing my stuff over to the passenger side. From the corner of my eye, I saw the front door open as

Quinn's large frame filled the doorway, but I wouldn't let myself look.

Putting the car in reverse, I pulled out of the driveway and took myself back to my apartment. It wasn't until I made it to my bathroom and got the shower running that I finally allowed what he said to fully register. As I stood beneath the hot spray, I let myself feel each wound he inflicted with his words. Then I cried. I gave myself until the water ran cold to let it all out. Because he wasn't worth more than fifteen minutes of my time.

15

QUINN

*I*T TOOK WAY too goddamned long for my feet to become unstuck from the floor, but once they did, and I rushed to the front door, it was too late. Her car was gone, and I was left with a sense I'd just screwed up something amazing.

God, I was such a fucking asshole.

As soon as the words left I mouth I regretted them. I wish I could have taken them back, erased the pain I caused to fill her beautiful eyes. But I couldn't.

Falling to the couch, I dropped my head in my hands and worked on breathing deep. I hadn't had a panic attack in over a year. Yes, the nightmares from that night still plagued me, but I'd been stupid enough to think I was making some sort of progress. If that had been true, I wouldn't be sitting in my living room, a cold sweat coating every inch of my body as my heart threatened to pound right out of my chest.

I inhaled through my nose and slowly exhaled through my lips while I counted silently in my head. That was the only goddamned thing that joke of a shrink taught me. A year of talking about my feelings from that night, and all I came out of it with was knowing how to stave off a panic attack once I felt it coming on.

I knew it wasn't going to do me any good, but the department in Seattle wouldn't let me return unless a doctor signed off. My body might have healed, but they wanted to make sure my head was screwed back on straight before letting me fight fire. That was just one of the many reasons I left, came back to Pembrooke after the accident.

Without Addison, there was nothing for me in Seattle, so I figured why stick around? Her parents hated me for killing their daughter. The department was watching me like a hawk. Addy was gone. Pembrooke was the only option. At least here I had my folks to help out with Sophia. And with my dad's reputation, I knew I wouldn't have any problem getting on with the fire department. I expected to start feeling better.

But that never happened. The guilt of what had happened followed me from Washington to Wyoming. There was no escape for me. My carelessness had killed my wife, the love of my life. There was no chance of me being happy *anywhere*.

Or at least that's what I thought. But then I met Lilly.

She made me remember how to laugh, how to find the little pleasures in day-to-day life. The guilt was still there, always would be, but when I was in her presence, I actually felt like I could breathe. Something about her soothed me, calmed the tumultuous swell of emotion that raged inside of me for the past three and a half years.

And how did I repay her? I hurt her... *again*.

I hated myself for how I'd acted, but stepping through that doorway and seeing her and Sophia curled up together? Well, it was like being transplanted back in time. It actually took me several seconds to realize it wasn't Addison lying in that bed with our daughter, that I hadn't gotten my family back. And when that realization hit, all rationale thought flew out the window.

I just... reacted.

Badly.

Because what I felt when I realized it was Lilly, not Addison, was something so disconcerting I couldn't handle it. I *liked* seeing Lilly curled up with my daughter. No, that's not right: I fucking loved it. For just a split second, I'd let myself enjoy having a woman in my house, taking care of not only Sophia, but in her own way, me as well. And I wanted that. I wanted *her*. And I realized then that I could never truly be *just friends* with Lilly.

So I did the only thing I could think of to push her away. Her parting shot was still resonating in my head several minutes later, making me feel like complete shit.

My heart rate was finally starting to return to normal by the time Sophia woke up. "Where's Ms. Lilly?" she asked drowsily, as she rounded the couch, rubbing the sleep from her eyes.

"She had to get home." I scooped my daughter up and rested her in my lap. It was something I did with her every morning I was home. Even when she crawled out of bed, she was still only halfway awake. She'd sit with me until she woke up all the way, resting her tiny head on my chest. It was the only time during my days that I was able to push the past from my mind and live in the moment. "I heard you had a bad dream last night," I said a few minutes later.

"Uh huh. But Ms. Lilly sang me a special song that her daddy sang to her to keep the scary thoughts away."

That knot of guilt in my stomach grew even tighter. "Yeah?" I croaked. "Did it work?"

"Yeah. It was a pretty song."

Just when I thought I couldn't possibly feel any worse about myself, I was proven wrong. Shifting topic, I asked. "You want some breakfast?"

She nodded against my shoulder and mumbled, "Pancakes."

I gave a little chuckle at her standard answer. One day I was going to have to write Bisquick a thank-you letter for their ready-made mix. Those damn bottles made me look like a culinary genius as far as Sophia was concerned.

"KNOCK, KNOCK."

I had to restrain myself from rolling my eyes as my mom and dad came traipsing through my front door. Stopping by unexpectedly at least twice a week was turning into a nasty habit. When Soph and I first moved back, it was only once or twice a month. Now it was like they thought they had free rein over my private space. It wasn't unusual for me to come home after a shift and find that Mom let herself in to clean and do laundry. Hell, the woman had even gone as far as stripping my bed and washing the sheets once a week.

And Dad was no better. Keeping beer stocked in my fridge was impossible. Apparently my house was his sanctuary when it came to watching any sporting event. The man used my cable like it was his own. I could have sworn I hadn't signed myself up for the NFL package. Normally their spontaneous visit wouldn't annoy me too badly, but my foul mood from my early morning fight with Lilly hadn't gotten any better. I'd been wracking my brain all day, trying to think of what I could say to get her to forgive me for my behavior, but the best I'd come up with was *I'm sorry*. And something told me that wasn't going to cut it.

"Hi sweetie," Mom chirped, as she walked into the living room and leaned down to give me a kiss on the cheek. Several seconds later, Dad walked in behind her and, sure enough, there was a freshly opened beer in his hand.

He took a big swig and collapsed in my recliner with a loud *ahhhh*. "Oh good, you've got the game on."

"*Meemaw! Papaw!*" Sophia came barreling out of her room at the speed of a freight train, like she hadn't seen her grandparents in years as opposed to just a day or two.

Mom scooped her up and peppered her cheeks and neck with kisses that made her squeal happily before putting her back on the ground so my dad could do the same.

My gaze bounced back and forth between my folks. I picked up the remote and muted the commercial currently playing on the TV and I finally asked in a deadpan voice, "To what do I owe the pleasure?"

"I thought I'd take Sophia to spend the gift cards she got for her birthday." Sophia shouted excitedly, throwing her fist in the air. "We can have a girls' day," Mom told her. "Shopping and lunch, no boys allowed."

"Yeah! I'll go put my shoes on! No boys allowed! No boys allowed!" she chanted as she headed back for her bedroom. I was just about to get up and get my own beer when the sound of Sophia singing from her bedroom froze every single cell in my body. I couldn't breathe as those familiar words came echoing down the hallway. Hell, even my parents were still with shock.

Two minutes later she came back out wearing those ballet slippers that didn't go with the outfit at all, not that she'd care.

"Hey, Angel?" I squatted down in front of Sophia and tucked her hair behind her ear. "Where'd you hear that song, baby?"

"That's the song Ms. Lilly sang to me to chase my bad dream away," she answered innocently. "Her daddy sang it to her when she was little and had bad dreams too."

Christ, what were the odds that the special song Lilly sang for my daughter the night before just so happened to be my wife's favorite, the very song she walked around singing all the time. Did coincidences like that really happen?

Mom gave me a look that told me no, coincidences like that certainly *didn't* happen. She'd always been a firm believer that everything happened for a reason, and I knew she'd take this and run with it. I ignored her look and helped Soph put her jacket on.

Kisses were exchanged and the two of them left for their girls' day, leaving me and my old man to relax in front of the TV without interruption for the rest of the day. At least I could count on some peace and quiet.

Or so I thought…

It was halftime in the game, Dad had just come back from the kitchen with his second beer, and my eyes were growing heavy as I leaned back on the couch, my feet propped on the coffee table. I had started contemplating a nap when Dad spoke up, effectively killing any hopes I had of catching some much-needed sleep.

"What's going on with you and that pretty dance teacher?"

I'd just taken a swallow of my beer when he blurted that out, and I proceeded to choke on it. At least he wasn't bringing up the song. Once I stopped sputtering and was able to breathe again, I managed to croak, "What?"

Dad gave me a knowing look. "Please, son. I'm old, not stupid. I'm also not blind."

"Dad…" I shook my head, dropped my feet to the carpet and sat up. "It's not like that."

His face grew serious as he turned to face me fully, completely forgetting all about the game. "Not like what, exactly?"

I started to feel defensive for some insane reason. It was hard enough trying to battle my feelings. Having someone else reaffirm them only set me further on edge. I stood from the couch and began pacing. "There's nothing between us," I insisted, even though the lie left a sour taste on my tongue. There *was* something between us, something intense and frightening. I could deny it to myself all damn day, but putting a voice to that denial just felt… wrong. Almost as wrong as having those feelings in the first goddamned place.

Dad stood tall as well and stepped in front of me, forcing me to stop. "Quinn, do you even realize that Sophia's birthday party was the first time any of us have heard you laugh in over three years?"

"That's ridiculous," I sneered, turning on my heels in the direction of the kitchen.

"It's true!" Dad grabbed hold of my shoulder, thwarting my pathetic attempt to escape.

"Jesus, Dad. I laugh all the fucking time."

"Not like that. Not genuinely. That laugh came from deep in your gut. So fucking unexpected it scared your mom and me."

Tension coiled inside me so tightly I thought I might snap. "Stop," I snarled, jerking from my father's hold. But he wasn't done.

"And all it took was a few words from that girl to get you to let go and laugh. That means something, son."

"Stop!"

"You deserve happiness. You've been walking around, half a man since Addy died. Watching you with Lilly, I saw flashes of the man my son used to be. I miss that man."

"*I said stop!*" I roared, so loud Dad took a step back.

His voice lowered, his expression grew pained. "What are you so scared of?"

With that one simple question, asked by the man I respected most in the entire world, that coil inside me broke. "It's wrong!" I shouted, unable to hold it in anymore. "It's fucking wrong! I don't deserve that, no matter what you or Mom think. It's my fault Addy died. *Mine.* If it wasn't for me, she'd still be alive. I had happiness once, and I fucking killed it, okay? So just drop it! It doesn't matter what you think you saw between me and Lilly, because nothing's ever going to come of it. The man I was, the man you miss, died with Addy in that car. Just let it go, Dad. Let it fucking go."

In all my life, I'd only seen my father cry two times. The first time was when I woke up in the hospital room after the accident. The second time was during my wife's funeral. He'd never really been the type to cry. He was the strongest man I'd ever met. But as he stood there, watching me unravel *again*, his eyes grew glassy.

"Oh, son," he whispered, his voice ravaged with heartache that only made my own that much worse. "That's not true."

"It is!" I demanded, raking my hands threw my hair in agony. "It is. I killed her, Dad. It was my fault."

His expression grew fierce as he charged me, grabbing hold of my shoulders and giving them a rough shake. "It was an accident. You hear me? An accident. You aren't to blame for Addy's death."

"If I'd been paying attention—"

He cut me off. "The events of that night were a tragedy, but it was *not your fault*. You can spend the rest of your life analyzing every single second, wondering how you could have reacted differently, but there is no way you could guarantee the outcome would have been any different. You can't walk around blaming yourself for something that was beyond your control, Quinn. That's no way to live."

"Dad…" my voice was like gravel. It physically hurt to force the words from my throat. "You don't understand…"

"You're right," he whispered. "I don't. And it kills me a little more every single day to see you suffering this way. I wish I could undo it all. I wish I could take this pain for you, but I can't, and I pray to God you never have to experience what it's like to feel so goddamned helpless when it comes to your own child. If I could carry this burden for you, I would, in a heartbeat." He gave me another shake as he repeated, "That accident was not your fault. You can't spend the rest of your life punishing yourself."

"That's not what I'm doing," I insisted, even though each day felt like a test to see how miserable I could make myself feel. I kept myself mired in the past for that very reason. Even my memories were part of my penance for what I'd done.

"For a brief moment that day, I got a glimpse of my son while he wasn't crippled with grief. You looked at that girl and for just a second, you forgot to blame yourself for everything. Hold on to that, son. I'm begging you, for your sake *and* Sophia's, hold on to that. If that girl can give you an ounce of peace, you hold on to that. No matter what you believe, you deserve some peace."

He was so adamant with everything he said that I knew in my heart that he truly believed them.

The problem was... I wasn't sure that I did.

16

LILLY

I'D BEEN SITTING at my desk, staring at my calendar for so long my eyes were starting to cross. After my fight with Quinn I'd left his house with an uncomfortable knot in my stomach that refused to go away. I thought that maybe a trip to Denver might have been a good idea, a change of scenery for a weekend to clear my head. But the brightly-colored boxes on my computer screen were mocking me, telling me a mini-vacation was out of the question.

A knock at my office door startled me and made me jump. My head jerked up to see Kyle standing in the doorway, smirking at me. "Jeez. You scared the shit out of me."

"Well, if you weren't so focused on trying to blow your computer up with your mind, maybe you'd have noticed me sooner."

I scowled. "Funny. I wasn't trying to blow it up. I was just…" I banged the computer mouse a few times to let off some steam. "Trying to get my calendar to do what I want, but the asshole refuses to cooperate."

Kyle plopped down in the chair across from me and propped his feet on my desk. "What are you trying to get it to do?"

I let out a frustrated huff and collapsed back into my chair, spinning it around in circles as I spoke. "I was hoping to get away for a few days, maybe go to Denver, but I've got too much on my plate right now. It's not possible." Kyle gave me a look that I couldn't quite decipher. "What? What's that look about?"

"It's about the fact that you have me and Samantha to handle your classes for you for two or three days so you can get out of here and take a load off for a while."

It was an argument I'd heard several times over the few years he and Samantha had worked for me. Any time Kyle thought I was over-extending myself, he'd say he and Sam could carry more of the weight. It was his way of looking out for me. Being his boss made it a little hard to consider Kyle a true friend since the fact I paid him sometimes blurred the lines, but I had to give him credit, he never stopped trying. His insistence made me wonder if it was just my own insecurities that were the real issue.

"I don't know," I hesitated. "You each have your classes, plus we're gearing up for the Winter Showcase. I just don't think it's the right time."

He rolled his eyes dramatically. "It's never the right time, as far as you're concerned. What's the worst that could happen, huh? We burn the place down?"

That certainly didn't make me feel any better. "Yes. That. Exactly that."

"Please," he scoffed. "Just admit it. You're a total control freak. That's why you have so much trouble letting go."

"Am not!" I objected, even though it was the truth. I was a *complete* control freak.

He gave me a serious look and sat forward in the chair. "Come on, Lil. It's just a few days. Trust me, Sam and I can handle that. Besides, whether you want to talk about what you've been dealing with the past several weeks or not, we aren't blind. We know it's heavy. You need a break, admit it."

I suddenly felt bad for keeping such a tight hold on everything. I hired both Kyle and Samantha because they were talented and capable. And he was right. I definitely needed a break. "Is it that obvious?"

"That you've got some serious heavy in your life right now? Uh, yeah, babe. It's pretty damn obvious. Look, I'm not telling you to sit here and pour your heart out if that's not what you want to do, but if taking a little vacation will help you deal with whatever it is that's going on in your world, then let us help."

For the first time since this morning, I was actually able to take a deep breath. Kyle couldn't possibly know it, but his concern for my wellbeing eased some of the weight that had been sitting on my chest for weeks.

I smiled my first real smile since Quinn's blowup earlier that morning. "Thank you."

"Anything, honeybun." Kyle stood and headed for the door, but stopped long enough to look over his shoulder and offer, "I know you're a private person and all that, but if you ever need to talk… about anything, I'm here. I just want you to know that."

Maybe I needed to start reevaluating my relationship with Kyle.

"YOU'RE HERE!" ELIZA squeaked as soon as she opened the door to her and Ethan's loft.

"Oh my God!" I screeched at the sight of her little baby bump. She moved in for a hug just as I ducked down and reached for her belly. It wasn't until I laid eyes on her belly that I realized how real it was. "You're going to be a mommy!"

We both let out a tiny scream and jumped in place, embracing each other tightly in celebration.

"Dear Lord," Ethan's deep voice echoed around us. "I forgot you two reach ear-bleeding decibels when you're around each other."

I laughed and disengaged from Eliza in order to hug Ethan. "And you're going to be a daddy!"

He squeezed tightly and lifted my feet off the ground for a few seconds. "We're so glad you're here," he told me once he put me back down. "Eliza's been going crazy up here without her partner in crime."

"Aw," I pinched his cheek playfully. "I've missed you too."

He swatted at my hands playfully and stepped back so Eliza could come up beside me and loop her arm across my shoulders. "It's true. We *have* missed you. And I can't wait to take you to the game tomorrow, you're gong to have so much fun!"

That was exactly what I was counting on. Fun. The perfect thing to keep my mind off the fact my world seemed to be spiraling out of control.

THE GAME WAS INSANE... in a very good way. I'd never seen Eliza as out of control as she was watching her husband on the field. Maybe it was all the extra hormones from the pregnancy, but I don't think I've ever seen her scream at Ethan to *'Kill him!'; 'Stomp him into the ground!'* before. Watching the other players' wives and girlfriends shy away from my bestie had been the icing on the cake. They seriously thought she was demented. It was great.

After the game, we headed over to a dive bar a few minutes from the stadium where the guys liked to go and decompress. Luckily they'd won, so no one would be drinking their sorrows away. I was on my third IPA, Eliza on her second Shirley Temple, when she dropped the bomb.

"Don't be mad at me."

I swallowed my beer and gave her a curious look. "Why would I be mad?" I looked around the bar. Sure, it was weathered and had probably hit its heyday back in the seventies, but it was clean and bug free. "This place isn't that bad."

"No. Not about the bar." I followed her gaze through the dingy window and spotted Ethan on the sidewalk just outside. And he wasn't alone. That was when it dawned on me.

"What did you do?"

Just then, Ethan's loud, boisterous laughter rang out, resonating through the semi-empty bar.

Eliza's voice lowered to a whisper and she began talking at a fast clip. "I know you said you weren't up for any blind dates, but he's a really nice guy, I swear. His name is Alex Sanders, he's twenty-seven, single, never been married, no arrest record, and a Defensive End for the team. And I never would have done this, but he saw a picture of you and found out you were here for the weekend. He asked Ethan about setting him up."

"Shit," I hissed out, picking up my draft glass and downing the rest of the contents, then waving at the bartender for another. "I should be pissed, but I can't when you're carrying my niece or nephew." I gave her a fake glare as she burst out into laughter. "I came here to relax," I admitted quietly. "I needed to get away and de-stress for a few days, Eliza. *This* doesn't really help me with that."

Her eyes grew concerned and she tipped her head to the side to study me, however, Ethan and his friend reached us before she could say a word.

"Ladies." I turned around and pasted a smile on my face as Ethan introduced me to his teammate.

Alex took the barstool on my left, putting me between him and Eliza. "Can I order you another drink?" he asked just as the bartender set my fourth beer in front of me.

"Sorry." I gave him an apologetic smile. "But I'll let you get the next one?

He laughed and I noticed then that he was actually pretty cute. Tall, really flipping tall, built, light brown hair and eyes, but that spark I probably would have felt from looking at him a few months ago just wasn't there.

"I'll take you up on that." He ordered a Bud Light from the bartender and turned back to me, holding out his hand for me to shake. His entire hand engulfed mine and I almost giggled thinking of all the women who probably compared the size of his hands to the size of his penis. Okay, so maybe I was a little buzzed. "It's nice to meet you. Eliza and Ethan talk about you all the time."

"It's nice to meet you too."

Alex was a pretty laid back guy, and the longer we all hung out at the bar, the more I enjoyed his company... in a strictly platonic way. After beer number five, my cellphone vibrated in my purse. I knew I needed to switch to water when I pulled my phone out and had to close one eye in order to read the text.

They were two simple words that came two days too late. But they still hit me right in the chest.

Quinn: I'm sorry.

So much for leaving my stress back in Pembrooke. With a large sigh, I hit the button to make the screen go black and shoved the phone back into my purse.

"Everything okay?" Alex asked, his expression one of curiosity.

I tried to smile but knew it felt short. "Yeah. It's all good." My phone vibrated again, and like the masochist I was, I pulled it out and read it.

Quinn: And I'm sorry it's taken me so long to apologize. Can I come over so we can talk?

Well shit.

"Boyfriend?"

Alex's voice startled me back into reality. "What? Oh, no. No boyfriend." I exited out of my texts and sat the phone down on the bar top.

"So, if there's no boyfriend..." I really didn't like the way he trailed off and smiled. "Maybe you'd be willing to go to dinner with me tomorrow night?"

Well shit.

I pulled in a deep breath and prepared to give my first ever rejection. Thank God I was a little drunk. "Look, Alex. You seem like a great guy—"

"Oh wow. The kiss of death."

"I'm sorry," I said sympathetically. "I really am. I've just got a lot going on in my life right now. I'm kind of a mess."

"Well, how about this?" Alex picked up my phone and started typing something out. "I've enjoyed hanging out with you tonight. If there comes a time when you're feeling like less of a mess, why don't you give me a call, yeah?"

He handed my phone to me and I saw he'd saved his number in my contacts. I smiled and answered, "I'll be sure to do that," even though I knew I wouldn't be calling him.

———

ELIZA HANDED ME a mug of hot tea and plopped down on the couch next to me later that night. We'd stayed at the bar long enough for me to sober up. By the time we got home, Ethan and I were both ready to crash, but Eliza had some sort of crazy hormonal surge which made her as alert as ever. Since Ethan had played earlier, he had an excuse to go to bed. I decided to stay up with her so we could catch up, just the two of us. "So…" she started with a sly grin. "You and Alex seemed to really hit it off."

I rolled my eyes. Of course she'd think that. She and her husband had spent seventy percent of the evening with their tongues stuck down each other's throats, clueless to everything going on around them.

At least she wasn't *totally* wrong. We had hit it off enough to keep each other company while our friends went at it like horny teenagers.

"Not going to happen, Eliza. Drop it," I warned.

Her head cocked to the side as she regarded me, her face

suddenly awash with concern. "What's going on with you, babe?"

I brought the mug to my lips and blew before taking a sip, all the while, keeping my eyes diverted. "What do you mean?"

"Something's off. You haven't been yourself lately. And I'm not just talking about this weekend. Every time I call you're... I don't know, distracted or something."

I tried to look placating as I shrugged. I came to escape, not rehash all the bad shit going on in my life. "I don't know. I guess I'm just busy with the school and stuff."

She shook her head and leaned forward, sitting her own mug on the coffee table so she could turn her entire body to face me. "That's not it. I've seen you busy around this time of year. I know what that's like. This is different." She paused and studied my face, like she could read me. "Talk to me, honey. You've always been there for me whenever I needed you. Let me do the same."

I let out a deep sigh and placed my mug down next to hers as my nose began to sting. There was no point in trying to keep it to myself any longer. I knew Eliza well enough to know she wasn't going to let this go. I also knew I needed her more than anything at this very moment. For those reasons, I found myself opening my mouth and admitting, "Dad's dying." It physically hurt to say those two words out loud.

"What?"

"Cancer," I said in a raspy, pained voice. "It was too far gone by the time they found it. There's nothing they can do." My chin quivered as the first of many tears broke free. "He's dying."

"Oh my God." And just like that, she was across the couch, wrapping me in her arms and holding on tight. "I'm so sorry. So, so sorry, Lilly. I can't believe this."

I pulled back with a sniffle and wiped at my cheeks. "Yeah. Me too."

"So that's why you wanted to come this weekend? To de-stress?"

Part of the reason, I thought. Instead of saying that out loud, I simply nodded. "Yeah."

"Shit. And here I am, trying to set you up on a date. God, I suck so bad!"

I managed a laugh and took her hand in mine. "You don't suck. You didn't know."

Her shoulders squared and she lifted her chin in determination. "Well, if you need to de-stress, then that's *exactly* what we're going to do for the rest of the weekend. I'm talking manicures, pedicures, facials, massages… the full spa treatment."

My head fell back against the couch. I could just imagine how amazing it would feel to be pampered. "That sounds amazing."

"Totally. And to make you feel even better, we're going to put the whole thing on Ethan's credit card." She winked and we both burst into laughter.

"You know me so well," I teased.

"Damn right I do." She picked up her mug and settled back into the couch, her entire demeanor shifting from humorous to serious. "I'm here, Lilly. I might not physically be in Pembrooke, but I'm always here for you. Don't ever doubt that."

"I know, sweetie," I whispered. "But you're pregnant and I didn't—"

She shot me a cutting glare. "Pregnant or not, that doesn't change the fact that you've been my best friend since elementary school. I practically grew up in your house. I love your folks like they're my second family. You've always had my back whenever I needed it. Now it's my turn to return the favor. Let me do that for you."

Somehow I managed to speak past the mass of emotions building up in my throat. "Okay." There was no point in arguing with her.

"So what can I do for you, huh? How can I help?"

I looked from the mug back to her and answered, "You can get me drunk. Very, *very* drunk."

She smiled brightly at me. "I can totally do that."

17

QUINN

I WASN'T EVEN sure how it happened, but I'd somehow managed to sink to a whole new low.

I was stalking Lilly's Facebook and Instagram pages like a creep. But when I stopped by the dance school and found out from that Kyle guy that she'd gone to Denver for the weekend, I kind of lost my mind. I hadn't seen her in three days. I was like a junky in need of a fix. If Eliza's last comment on her Facebook page was anything to go by, Lilly should be on her way back home today. Unfortunately, I was in the middle of a shift at the department and had another twelve hours to go.

I needed to talk to her. I had to apologize face to face and try to make things right. But mostly, I needed to find out why the fuck there were so many pictures of her on Alex Sanders' Instagram page and what happened over the weekend to make them look so goddamned cozy together.

I'd texted her countless times over the weekend, even called twice, trying to get her to talk to me, but each one went unanswered. That was, until earlier this morning. She finally replied back saying: *In Denver. Will be home tonight. See you at Sophia's class Wednesday.*

I had no fucking clue how to interpret that, but it left me feeling uneasy. I'd asked her if we could talk, and instead of saying yes or giving me a time to meet, I had to wait two goddamned days after she got home to see her, and even then, it would only be in passing when I dropped my daughter off and picked her up.

I was going out of my mind.

"Hey man." I jumped at the sound of Tony's voice coming from behind me. Before I had a chance to shut my laptop down, he and Carpenter moved in. "Hey, isn't that Lilly? And is that..."

"Holy shit!" Carpenter exclaimed. "Is that Alex Sanders?"

"Yes," I hissed through clenched teeth.

"Dude, his hand's really close to her tits. I thought she was your girl."

I gave Carpenter a bewildered look even as the image of that particular picture of Lilly and Alex seared itself to the backs of my eyelids. "What? She's not my girl. Where the hell'd you come up with that idea?"

Tony and Carpenter glanced at each other, both with a cocked eyebrow, before turning back to me. "Uh... maybe because you watched her like you wanted to take a bite out of her that time she stopped by?" Carpenter said.

"Or because you talk about her all the damn time like a pussy-whipped teenager?" Tony added.

"Or that you're constantly texting her?"

"Or stalking her social media accounts in the middle of work?"

"All right!" I shouted, cutting them both off. "You've made your point." I slammed the laptop closed and scrubbed my face with both hands. "Fuck," I hissed. "This whole thing's a goddamned mess."

Carpenter grabbed an apple from the bowl on the counter and leaned back, crossing his ankles as he took a bite. "So, she's *not* your girl?" he asked through a full mouth.

"No," I grunted.

"Then… you wouldn't mind if I made a move?"

All I saw was red as I glared at him. "Touch her, and I'll break every bone in your fucking body."

He shot a smirk in Tony's direction and muttered, "Not his girl my ass," before taking another bite.

I was just about to rip into him when my cellphone rang from my back pocket. I stood and pulled it out, and as soon as I saw the name on the screen, moved out of the kitchen into the empty bay for some privacy.

"Ethan, man. What's up?"

"Hey, you got a second?"

The tone of his voice instantly set me on edge. "Sure. What's going on? Everything okay?"

"Yeah, everything's good. I just need to ask a favor. You know Eliza's friend, Lilly?"

My shoulders went stiff at the mention of her name. "What about her?"

He let out a sigh. "She came to Denver for the weekend, and she confided in Eliza that things are pretty tough for her right now. Apparently her dad's really sick. It's not looking too good, and even though she tried to hide it, Eliza said she's taking it pretty hard."

I'd spent the past few days in misery as jealousy gnawed at my insides over the photos of Lilly with another man, and now, knowing that she'd confided in Eliza about her father—something that she'd only shared with me up to this point—only compounded that ache.

Yep, it was official. I really *had* lost my mind. I had no right to be jealous over her relationship with her best friend. But logical or not, I was.

"So what's that got to do with me?" I snapped. I hadn't intended for my words to come across as harsh as they did. I guess it was all par for the course of going insane.

"Uh…" he trailed off, obviously reading my sudden mood change and not knowing how to react. "Well, it's just that we're worried about her. She's heading back to Pembrooke and we're both in Denver for another couple of months, so we can't really keep an eye on her. I know you two don't know each other that well…" *Oh, if you only knew.* I guess Lilly hadn't confided in Eliza about our so-called friendship while she was there. And for some crazy reason, that pissed me off even more than goddamned Alex Sanders. "But I wanted to see if maybe you'd watch out for her? Just for a little while. You know, make sure she's doing okay until we can get there. I just want to make sure she's all right."

My mouth opened and the words began pouring out before I could consider pulling them back. "And why is it suddenly *your* job to look after her?"

There was no mistaking the bite my tone carried. Ethan remained silent for several seconds, then finally he asked, "What's with the fucking hostility, dude? If you can't take some time out of your goddamned day, then never mind. I'll ask someone else."

"You know she's not your responsibility, right?" I sneered. "You already have a wife."

"Whoa! What the hell? Seriously, man. What's your problem?"

It was like I'd detached from my body, like I was hovering over myself yelling to shut the hell up, but the word vomit just wouldn't stop. "My problem is that you've got a pregnant wife you need to be looking after, but instead of doing that, you're thinking about another woman."

"Wait…" I could hear his breathing coming through the line, and it finally dawned on me what I'd just let slip. "I haven't told you Eliza's pregnant."

He hadn't. I'd gotten that bit of news from Lilly. She'd even gone as far as to ask me not to let on I knew so Ethan could tell me himself. "Sure you did," I lied… *badly.*

"No. I haven't. I'm pretty sure I'd remember telling you. The only ones that know so far are our families and… *fuck me.*"

I dropped my head and closed my eyes, rubbing at my temple with my fingers. "Look, man. I'm sorry. I—"

"Do you have something going on with Lilly?"

I sighed through the phone. "It's not like that."

"Holy shit," he cut me off. "This makes so much sense now! I couldn't figure out why she wouldn't go for Alex when she was here. I mean, he's a cool guy, can get tail pretty much whenever the hell he wants. But she wasn't having any of it. I just thought it was because of everything with her dad."

My jaw ticked uncontrollably as I tried not to picture that fucker putting the moves on Lilly. "Or maybe she just wasn't interested."

He scoffed and I wanted to reach through the phone and punch the shit out of him. "Not interested in the pro-football player that has more money in the bank than he knows what to do with, and was just voted one of *People's* most eligible bachelors? I'm straight as an arrow, brother, and I love my wife, but even I'm not *that* blind. What's going on with you two?"

My hand moved from my temple to rake through my hair as I began to pace around the bay. "Nothing. We're just friends."

"I'm not stupid either, man. You just ripped me a new asshole for voicing concern about my *wife's* best *friend*, so don't try and sell me that 'just friends' bullshit. I'm not buying."

"I fucked up," I finally admitted after a long, tense silence. "Several times. I acted like a dick. We really are just friends, but I need to make it right somehow, and I don't have the first fucking clue how to do that."

I expected advice, or maybe even some ribbing at my own expense. What I didn't expect was what came out of his mouth next. "Don't go there with her, Quinn. Not right now."

I stopped mid pace and asked defensively, "What's that supposed to mean?"

There wasn't an ounce of humor in Ethan's voice as he explained, "What it means is, you aren't capable of something long term. I get it, man. I do. I can't imagine what you've gone through, but Lilly's in a bad place right now. She doesn't need you jerking her chain at the same time. If you can't be there for her... like *really* be there, then you need to back off."

The fuck? "I'm not jerking her chain," I snarled.

"Yeah. You are. I saw that girl when she was here. I didn't get it then, but I do now. She barely even looked at another guy. And believe me, it wasn't for lack of trying on the dudes' parts. Whether or not something's going on *now*, or just leading in that direction, she's already invested. I'm not trying to be a dick—"

"Really?" I snapped sarcastically. "Could have fucking fooled me."

"I'm looking out for both of you, all right? Unless you're ready to move on, this is going to end badly. For everyone involved."

"Ethan, you don't know what you're talking about."

"I don't? Really? So that means you aren't still wearing your wedding ring, right?"

I looked down at my hand, the gold band still prominent against my tanned skin. At my lack of response, he continued. "She needs peace right now, Quinn. Her dad's dying and you're still mourning a ghost. Just move on."

I was still staring at my hand as my fingers curled into a fist so tight my knuckles turned white. It took everything I had to keep from exploding as I warned, "You're coming dangerously close to crossing a line with me you do *not* want to cross. You don't talk about my wife, understand? And my relationship with Lilly is none of your goddamned business."

He sighed heavily. "Look, I'm not going to keep pushing. I've said my piece, but know this. You hurt her and I'll be on the first goddamn plane to Pembrooke to kick your ass."

With that, he hung up.

Leaving me reeling.

18

QUINN

ALKING THROUGH THE glass doors of the dance studio, I scanned the front desk area and the window behind that housed Lilly's office, desperate for a glimpse of her. When I dropped Sophia off earlier, she hadn't been anywhere in sight, and I was forced to leave, disappointment resting heavy on my shoulders. It had become an addiction of mine, seeing her. That dimpled smile, the way her amber eyes glimmered every time she laughed, it frightened the shit out of me, how desperate I was for just those little tastes, but every time I tried pulling back from her, something was there to jerk me right back. Usually it was the pain on her beautiful face every time I did or said something to hurt her in an attempt to keep her at arm's length.

I just couldn't help myself. I knew Ethan was right to warn me off, but staying away was impossible. What I felt for her was more than just a physical attraction. That was definitely there, believe me. But I found I craved her infectious sense of humor just as much, if not more. I fought her friendship, knowing that if there was one person who'd be able to breach the impenetrable walls I'd surrounded myself with it'd be her, but I was a glutton for punishment and couldn't stay away.

Even though I knew hurting her was inevitable. I could never be the man she needed. I didn't have it in me to give her a life. There would never be a white picket fence with babies and pets running around. I'd had that dream once and I still burned from the memories.

When I didn't find her anywhere in the lobby area, I gave up my search and headed for the studio where Sophia's class was being held. Usually the kids were running around like they'd just executed a successful prison break at the end of class, but pushing through the door and stepping into the studio, I was taken aback to find that not only were they all sitting completely still, facing the wall of mirrors, but even the parents weren't moving, with smiles on their faces as they faced forward.

"Come on. Miss Lilly!" One of the girls cried. *"Pleeeeeeeease?"*

I watched in fascination as Lilly's face blushed an enticing shade of pink as her gaze darted to the ground and that dimple popped out with her shy smile. "Okay, okay," she started, holding her hands up as the kids started shouting. When they finally quieted down, she continued. "But only if Mr. Kyle is okay with it."

Something unpleasant twisted in my gut as the guy who taught some of the classes at Lilly's school walked over all cocky-like, a confident smirk on his face as he threw his arm around Lilly's shoulder. I was officially losing it, because I had a sudden urge to lunge and rip that goddamned arm off and beat him to death with it.

"I don't mind if you don't, sweetheart." He smiled brightly down at her. The fucker. The kids went crazy and the adults all chuckled quietly as Lilly moved from under Dick Head's arm and walked to the dock that held her iPhone.

Seconds later a song began to play and she and the douche moved to the very center of the room facing everyone. They began to move in sync to some punk who sounded like he hadn't even hit puberty yet as he sang about begging some chick to have mercy on him.

The longer the song played, the tighter my fists clenched at my side, until my knuckles turned white. And it only got worse when they moved, pressing their bodies flush against each other as she wrapped her lean arms around his neck and he grabbed hold of her hips and pulled him even closer.

Was everyone else blind? They were in front of a bunch of first and second graders, for Christ's sake! How did they not find this shit inappropriate?

Lilly finally moved away from him, and I started to breathe easier, until she executed some sort of jump through the air and he caught her, tossing her high before letting her slide down his body. I thought my head might explode. Just as my vision started growing red, the song ended and everyone in the room—except for me—burst into cheers.

Everybody acted like it was the most magnificent thing they'd ever seen. And although I couldn't deny that both of them were clearly talented, while everyone else celebrated them, I wanted to commit homicide. I told myself it was because they had no business dancing like that in front of impressionable children, but the truth was, I couldn't stand the sight of another man's hands on Lilly.

"Daddy!" Sophia came charging through the crowd of kids and parents. "Weren't they *awesome*?" she screeched, as she threw herself into my arms.

Before I had a chance to respond one of the soccer moms close by turned and spoke up. "They truly are amazing, aren't they? I'd kill to learn how to do the Argentine Tango."

Was that what they were doing? I thought they were just dry humping around the floor. "Amazing," I gritted out through a fake smile. "You ready to go, Angel?" I asked, turning back to my daughter and disregarding the woman next to me. She was obviously an idiot.

"I wanna say bye to Miss Lilly," she pouted. I was just about to tell her we didn't have time if she wanted to make it to her classmate's slumber party when Lilly's voice spoke up from beside us, causing every muscle in my body to tense up.

"Hey guys."

It had been a week, a fucking *week* since I'd last seen her. I'd been going out of my head picturing this very moment, but right then the best I could do was a quick glance over my shoulder. I couldn't look for too long or there was no telling what I'd do. I gave her my attention just long enough to notice that her chest was rising and falling, still somewhat out of breath from her dirty dance with the needle dick.

"You were so good, Miss Lilly! I can't wait until I can dance like you."

Yeah. Over my dead fucking body.

"Thanks, sweetie." She smiled sweetly and some of that anger knotting my gut untangled a bit, but not enough for it to matter. When her eyes hit mine, the sparkle dimmed slightly, and Christ, that hurt. She asked, "How are you, Quinn?" but I needed to get out of there before my head exploded. Nothing was going right. Anxiety mixed with an unhealthy dose of jealousy raged in my blood, and if I didn't leave, I was going to cause a scene.

"Come on, Soph," I stated in a flat tone. "We have to go."

"Okay," she answered sullenly. I caught a glance of Lilly's face, just enough to notice that I'd hurt her feelings again, but there was nothing to be done. If I stayed any longer the chances of me making the situation worse continued to grow. As I grabbed my daughter's hand and led her from the building without a backward glance, I hated myself just a little more.

LILLY

QUINN'S PROPENSITY TO run hot and cold was beginning to become too much. There was something about him, something I saw in him that drew me to him, kind of like a kindred spirit. I could see the pain, still fresh behind his eyes, and knew we shared that in common, but I was getting whiplash from his mood swings. He'd been texting all weekend, asking to talk, but the first time I saw him after arriving home from Denver, he acted like a jackass.

Fuck him.

As I puttered around my apartment with a glass of wine in hand, trying to keep myself from calling Eliza and laying all my problems on her shoulders, that sense of loneliness began to creep back in. I wanted my best friend. I wanted to bitch and whine to her about all the bad shit going on in my life, but I knew that wasn't fair. She was happy, pregnant with her and her husband's first baby. She was finally in a good place after so many years of sitting stagnant, she didn't deserve for me to heap all my problems on her.

Maybe I just needed to cut my losses with Quinn, accept that we couldn't be friends and just move on. But every time I considered doing that, my heart physically ached. It wasn't the attraction to him that kept me holding on. Sure, that was definitely there, but it was more. After the night I danced for him, I couldn't help but feel a connection. I'd opened up to him, sharing pieces of myself that I hadn't shared with anyone but Eliza.

He'd been so easy to talk to, and with him listening, there had been brief snatches of time where the loneliness was beaten back. The question was, were those brief snatches worth the other times he made me feel undeserving? Less than important? He had the uncanny ability to make me feel on top of the world one second and lower than pond scum the next.

I knew he regretted every time he hurt me, it was written all over his face. But wasn't the definition of insanity doing the same thing over and over and expecting a different outcome? I kept expecting for Quinn to shed the rough exterior, stop letting me close only to shove me away again, but every time I thought I'd made progress, he reverted back to his usual asshole ways.

Was that insanity?

None of the answers I was seeking came to me as I paced my apartment, so I eventually caved and turned on the TV after refilling my glass, flipping from channel to channel in the hopes of landing on some mind-numbing show that would help to turn my brain off for just a little bit. I stopped when I landed on an episode of *Vikings*, a wave of nostalgia washing over me. I wanted to watch, see what my girl Lagertha was getting up to, but the damn show reminded me too much of Quinn.

"Damn it!" I shouted, turning the TV off and throwing the remote across the room. "What's wrong with me?" I shouted at the ceiling. Before I got an answer, there was a knock on my door.

I stared at the door for several seconds, long enough for a second, more insistent knock to follow. "I'm coming," I called out, as I stood from the couch and headed for the door. The wine had affected my senses just enough that I forgot to check the peephole, and once I opened the door, I instantly regretted my decision to imbibe.

"Quinn?" Yep, it was Quinn, all right. And he looked like he could breathe fire at any moment. Looked like Angry Quinn was in full force tonight. "What are you doing here?"

"What the fuck was that, today?"

My head shot back and I had to hold onto the door to keep my balance. "Excuse me?"

"You heard me."

"Yeah, I did," I snapped. "And the last fucking thing I need right now is your attitude. I haven't done anything to warrant you being a jackass… just like I didn't deserve it *every other time*. So do me a favor and take it somewhere else."

I moved to slam the door in his face, but his booted foot shot out, stopping my progress. I frowned and demanded, "Move your foot."

"We need to talk."

"Like hell we do! I'm sick and fucking tired of the way you bounce from happy to asshole in the blink of an eye. I'm not doing this. You need to leave."

I gave the door another shove, but his hand came up at the same time, and since he was *much* stronger than I was, the door flew all the way open and he waltzed into my apartment like he owned the place.

"Oh, please. Do come in," I said dryly, as I slammed the door closed and stomped in after him. So he'd invaded my personal space. Whatever. Didn't mean I had to talk to him. I'd had just enough wine that acting like a bratty child sounded like the perfect idea, so that's just what I did. Snatching my wineglass from the coffee table, I clicked the TV back on and began flipping channels again as I took a huge gulp. He wanted to talk? Well he could talk to his own damn self. I had no interest in listening.

19

QUINN

THE GODDAMNED WOMAN was infuriating.

I came over to get some answers, and instead of even looking at me, she was hitting buttons on her fucking remote like I wasn't even there. Like I hadn't just spent the past two and a half hours pacing my house after dropping Sophia off at her slumber party, trying to calm myself down without any success.

"You mind?" My voice came out more of a growl, but it was taking everything I had not to go all caveman on her ass and toss her over my shoulder, tying her to the bed until she finally listened.

"Not at all," she replied casually, waving her wine glass through the air. "Carry on like you intended. I'll just pretend you're not even here."

"How much wine have you had?"

"Not enough to put up with you. That's for goddamned sure."

With that, I'd had enough. "For Christ's sake, Lilly!" I barked. "Will you fucking look at me?"

"No thanks."

And I snapped. Snatching the remote from her hand, I

powered the TV off and shoved it into the pocket of my jeans. If she wanted it, she could come get it. And I couldn't lie, the idea of her digging around in my jeans held a hell of a lot of appeal.

"Hey! I was watching that!"

"And now you're not. Start talking."

She shoved up from the couch and got in my face. "Start talking? *Have you lost your mind?!*" Christ, she was something else. How I ever thought, for even a second, that she was anything like Addy was beyond me. She was harsh where Addy was soft, argumentative where my wife was compliant, loud when my Addison was quiet. She pushed back. That was something Addison had only ever done once… right before she died. They couldn't have possibly been more different. But in spite of that — maybe even *because* of that — I was unbelievably attracted to the woman. It was that attraction that scared the living shit out of me. It was unlike anything I'd felt before, even for my wife, who'd been the love of my life. It was why I pushed Lilly away, causing her pain that I felt down to my very bones. But something in me had snapped tonight, and despite the fear, I couldn't make myself stay away.

"You show up at *my house*, force your way in after being a *complete dick* earlier today, and you have the nerve to bark orders at me? You've got to be kidding!"

"And you let some fucking guy put his hands all over you right in front of me!" I shouted back.

"Oh my God," she laughed in bewilderment, as she raked her hands through her long, silky hair and took a step back. "You have. You've totally lost your mind."

I couldn't have stopped myself from moving toward her if I tried. The more I got to know Lilly, the more that tether, that unseen force I felt between us grew stronger. I couldn't *not* touch her.

"Wait," she paused, holding her hand up to stop me. "Where's Sophia?"

That one simple question hit me in a place inside I'd long thought dead. The fact we were in the middle of an argument, the fire inside her raging as strong as always, and she stopped everything out of concern for my daughter? I felt that in a way I had never wanted to feel again. And it made me lose all control.

My voice came out in a growl as I stalked toward her. "At a sleepover."

LILLY

OH GOD.

There was no denying it. In that very moment, Quinn was the predator and I was his prey. And how I wanted him to devour me.

But self-preservation kicked in before I could do what I wanted and lose myself in him completely, because no matter how badly I craved this man, in the back of my mind I knew it was only a matter of time before he did something else to hurt me, to push me away and keep me at arms length.

And I was tired of being hurt.

"Quinn, stop," I demanded, but judging by the feral look in his eyes, he was beyond reason as he continued to move. My hands hit his chest at the same time the fire in my blood ignited. "Who the hell do you think you are, huh?" I shouted, slamming my palms against his chest. "Who the *hell* do you think you are?! You treat me like shit over and over *and over*, drive me crazy with your fucking mood swings, and you think you have the right to come in here and make demands? Screw you, Quinn! I'm tired of letting you make me feel bad about myself." I laughed without humor again, because the longer he stood there, so close, the more hysterical I began to feel. "And you know what? It's all my fault! Because I actually *want* to be your friend." I punctuated the statement with another smack to his chest. "How stupid is that? Because on the rare occasion you aren't a jerk, I actually like being around you. I'm not so damn lonely all the time."

"Lilly—"

But I wasn't even close to finished. It was like the dam had broken, and I couldn't hold it back any longer. I was now ranting, and even though I was pretty sure I wasn't making any sense, I couldn't stop. "I'm just so damn tired of not having someone to talk to, you know? I thought I could talk to you, but every time I think I'm getting close, you push me away again. I just..." My voice dropped to a whisper as the fight began to drain out of me. "I'm so *tired* of feeling alone."

I dropped my head, unable to meet his eyes as I fought back the tears. I wished he would just leave. No matter how much I was drawn to him, no matter the connection I thought I felt between us, I was mentally and physically exhausted. I just needed space.

But apparently he wasn't having that. With his thumb, he put pressure under my chin and forced my face up. "I'm sorry," he whispered reverently. "I'm sorry." I could hear the sincerity laced around those two words. My breath stalled when his eyes traveled down to my lips and the green grew dark.

I licked my lips as my body started to shake, responding to that one simple look. "Q-Quinn..." I stuttered as I moved back. "What are you—?"

He cut me off with a curt, "What I've been dying to do for way too fucking long." Then, before I could pull in a full breath, his mouth was on mine in a fierce, hungry kiss that made every bone in my body go weak on impact.

My lips parted on a startled gasp and he took that as an opportunity to dive in. His tongue wrapped around mine as his hands grabbed hold of my hips and molded my body to his. I was so consumed by him, his smell, his taste, the way he touched me, that I hadn't even noticed we were moving until the backs of my knees hit the couch and I was going down.

Quinn was like a man possessed, touching wherever he could, and I couldn't get enough. My brain was on sensory overload, unable to process anything other than his hands on my body or his lips against mine. My legs spread, almost of their own accord, cradling his narrow hips between them as I tangled my fingers into that mass of sandy blond hair, pulling him impossibly closer. I could feel his hard length through the denim of his jeans, and when he rolled his hips, hitting that sensitive spot that ached for him, I had to tear my mouth away on a wanton moan.

One hand skated up my side, over the material of my thin sweater until he cupped one heavy breast in his large hand, causing a whole new flood of arousal to rush through me.

"God *damn*," he groaned, trailing his teeth along the cord in my neck. "You feel even better than I imagined."

Hearing his gruff, lust-filled voice helped to clear some of the fog from my brain. Untangling my hands from his hair, I set them on his shoulders and gave a soft push. "Wait, wait, wait. Quinn, wait."

This time his groan was pained as he dropped his forehead to my shoulder and hissed, "*Fuck.*"

"What..." My body shook with want as he remained on top of me, but what I was thinking had to be said. "What are we doing?"

There were several tense seconds of silence. Only our labored breathing filled my living room before he finally sighed heavily against my neck. I could have sworn I heard regret in his tone as he whispered, "I don't know."

My heart sank just a bit, even though my body protested against stopping what we'd just started. My feelings for Quinn had been growing out of control the past few weeks, and to have him kiss me like he did, have him touch me like he couldn't keep his hands off me, it had given a glimmer of hope that the words he'd just spoken extinguished.

I opened my mouth, to say what, I didn't know, but before I could form any words, his head lifted and those green eyes, so full of lust, landed on me. "But whatever it is, I'm tired of fighting it. So fucking tired, Lilly. I don't want to think." He punctuated the sentence with another sinful roll of his hips that stole a whimper from deep in my throat. "I don't want to stop. I've been out of my mind, wanting you. Staying away is too hard. I can't do it anymore."

I knew I should have said more, should have forced him out of my apartment for my own peace of mind. I knew I was just asking for my heart to be broken. But rational thinking had flown out the window. I wanted him just as badly as he wanted me, maybe more because all I wanted to do was hold him close while he used every opportunity to push me away.

The smart thing to do would have been to tell him to leave, close the door in his face, and spare myself the pain that was inevitable. But damn it, I just couldn't bring myself to do the smart thing. Ever since I found out my father was dying I'd felt more alone than ever. The only times in the past month the loneliness had been bearable was when I was with Quinn. I wanted to feel more of that. And for that reason, instead of kicking him out, I found myself whispering, "Take me to bed."

20

LILLY

*H*E DIDN'T HAVE to be told twice. Once again, his lips fused with mine and I was lost. My arms and legs wrapped around Quinn's muscular body as he stood from the couch and made his way down the hall toward my bedroom. We didn't break contact until he dropped me onto the mattress. Reaching for the waistband, he pulled my leggings and panties down in one quick swoop. Sitting up, not wanting to delay feeling him inside me, I pulled my sweater over my head and unclasped my bra, letting the straps fall down my arms and exposing myself to him completely. Before there was a chance for self-consciousness to kick in, he reached behind his neck and yanked his shirt over his head, giving me my first glimpse of all that toned, well-defined muscle.

"Oh my god," I sighed, reaching out with both hands to trace the lines of his abs, counting eight in total before leading to that delicious V that dipped into his jeans.

Quinn toed off his boots and socks while I worked the fly of his jeans, desperate to get to where that V ended. Never in my life had I been so consumed with the need to touch and be touched. I wanted him in a way I'd never wanted another man in my life.

As soon as I had his zipper down, I grabbed hold of the waist-band and jerked his pants down. His hard cock sprang free, thick and straining. I wasn't a virgin, not by a long shot, but the sight of Quinn in all his glory took my breath away. I'd never seen anything so perfect, so beautiful, in my life. The desire to taste him had me licking my lips just before I bent my head and ran my tongue along the very tip of his erection.

"Oh, Christ," he grunted. His hips jerked and I opened my mouth to suck more of him inside, wrapping my fingers around the base as I began to move my head. "Fuck, baby, stop. You have to stop." He pulled back and I was hit with a sudden wave of self-consciousness. I'd never been a fan of giving blowjobs before, but I wanted to please Quinn in a way I'd never experienced. And having him pull back left me feeling bereft and embarrassed.

I moved to cover my naked breasts. "Did I…" I swallowed thickly. "Did I do it wrong?"

"What? No. Fuck, no." He leaned over me until I was forced to lay back, then he grabbed my wrists and pinned them above my head. "It was amazing. *Too* amazing. If I let you continue, I was going to come in your mouth, and that's not what I want."

A shiver worked through my body as the throb between my legs deepened. "Wh-what do you want, then?"

His mouth hovered over mine as his knees pushed my legs further apart. His cock nudged against my opening and I lifted my hips in an attempt to pull him closer. "Tell me you're protected."

It took me a few seconds to understand what he was saying, but when it finally registered, I nodded. "The pill."

"I want to feel you. Nothing between us. You okay with that?"

Oh damn, I was more than okay with that. But I didn't want this to be something he'd eventually regret. "Are you sure?" I asked. "I have condoms—"

My words were cut off, and I cried out in ecstasy as he sank himself inside me as deep as he could go. "So goddamned perfect," he gritted, as he pulled out and thrust back in, filling me so completely. I felt him *everywhere* as he moved over me, inside me. I whimpered and struggled, trying to free my hands from his unrelenting grasp as every powerful drive of his hips brought me closer to my release.

"Quinn," I moaned, as his cock hit the perfect spot inside of me. "Let me touch you. Please."

His fingers tightened around my wrists as he shoved my hands deeper into the mattress. "You feel me, baby?"

"Yes," I gasped. "Please, let me touch you."

"You're all I've been able to think about," he grunted, picking up his pace, moving so hard and fast my body shifted across the bed every time he pushed back in. "Tell me you've been thinking about me."

"All the time," I admitted.

His forehead dropped to my shoulder. "Thank God." He finally released my hands at the same time every cell in my body exploded. My legs clamped around his waist and my nails dug into his shoulders as I lost all control. Everything inside me tightened until it snapped, and my head shot back as I cried out with the most intense orgasm of my life. I was still riding the high when Quinn buried himself to the hilt and groaned my name against my neck.

Tiny shockwaves of pleasure sparked through me as I felt his cock twitch with the last of his release. Minutes later, we were both breathing heavy and unable to move. I kept my hold on him, afraid that if I let go he'd somehow disappear.

My bones felt like rubber as exhaustion began to envelop me, and the last thing I remembered before sleep took over, was Quinn shifting his weight and turning us both so that his back was to my chest. And then everything went black.

Wʜᴇɴ I ᴡᴏᴋᴇ up the early morning sun was just beginning to filter through the slats in my blinds, painting my room in pale shades of gray and pink. It took several seconds for the disorientation of sleep to wear off, and once it did I realized I wasn't alone in my bed and images of the night before came flooding back. Quinn had shown up at my apartment. We fought. He kissed me. *We had sex.*

Shame began to seep from every pore, not because it wasn't good. It had been nothing less than *amazing*. But because that one act could have possibly ruined the already rocky friendship we were working so hard to maintain. I knew him well enough to know that he'd more than likely wake up with regrets... regrets that would cause him to push me away indefinitely.

Squeezing my eyes closed as pain lanced through my chest, I bent my head on the pillow and did my best to talk myself out of the inevitable freak-out I felt stirring in the pit of my stomach. Just the thought of losing him completely killed.

When I opened my eyes once more, the glint of the sun hitting something caught my attention, and my chest seized. Quinn's arm was wrapped firmly around my stomach, holding my back to his chest. Normally, waking up like that would have filled me with a riot of butterflies, but the sight of his ever-present wedding ring still on his left ring finger made my blood run cold.

Oh yeah, he was going to wake up with regrets. I was certain of it.

Needing to escape and collect my bearings for the blow I was about to face, I slowly lifted his hand and slid from the bed, keeping as quiet as possible so as not to wake him.

I crept from the room into the bathroom, refusing to allow myself to turn and look at the gorgeous man asleep in my bed. That would have just made it harder. I brushed my teeth, splashed water on my face, and slid my robe on to conceal my naked body. Then I moved to the kitchen to start a pot of coffee. I was going to need it if I had any hope of getting through this morning.

QUINN

THE STRONG AROMA of coffee invaded my senses and stirred me from the deepest sleep I'd had in years. I woke in an unfamiliar bed in an unfamiliar room, but as soon as the subtle scent of Lilly's perfume on the sheets hit me, my cock started to get hard.

Christ, last night had been... *phenomenal*. I kept my eyes closed, taking in the lingering smell of flowers as I slid my hand across the sheets in search of the woman who'd made me come so hard the night before, I'd seen stars. My eyelids snapped open when my hand hit nothing but air. A glance around showed that Lilly wasn't even in the room.

Slipping from the bed, I snatched my jeans from the floor and slid them on, sans underwear. I didn't even bother to button them as I started from the bedroom toward the kitchen. Reaching the end of the hall, I stopped at the sight of Lilly sitting quietly at her little dinette table. I had the perfect view of her profile, elbows on the table, a cup of coffee held between her hands. She wasn't moving, just sitting perfectly still, a distant expression on her face, like she was deep in thought. There wasn't even the slightest flinch in her frame that led me to believe she'd heard me moving around.

"Hey," I spoke softly, coming up behind her and resting my hands on her shoulders. At my touch and the sound of my voice, she did a startled jump and let out a yelp as she spun in her chair, nearly dropping the coffee cup in the process. "Sorry, didn't mean to scare you."

Setting the mug on the table, she brought one hand up and

held it against her chest as if trying to hold her heart in place. "Jeez, Quinn. Are you a ninja or something? I didn't even hear you enter the room."

I chuckled as I pulled the chair next to her out and took a seat. "Well, I wasn't really all that quiet."

She smiled, but it wasn't even enough to bring that dimple out I loved seeing so much. One long look at her face and I knew something wasn't right. I pulled the chair beside her out, and turned it so that, when I sat, I was facing her directly and my thighs were bracketing her legs. "Hey, you okay?"

I got the side of her face again when she looked away and lifted her coffee to her lips. "I'm fine," she said quietly against the rim of her cup.

My stomach dropped, because she was anything but fine. When it came to women I'd learned early on, 'fine' never meant *fine*. "Lilly."

She hummed, keeping her gaze diverted.

That sinking feeling grew more intense as I demanded, "Look at me." I finally got her eyes, but what I saw in them didn't do a damn thing to ease the knot in my gut. She looked skittish... almost scared.

"What's going on? And don't lie to me this time."

She set the cup down, once again, but this time turned to give me her full attention. Her voice was low as she said, "I'm just waiting for the other shoe to drop."

My brow furrowed in confusion. "Huh?"

"We had sex last night," she added on a whisper.

"I know. I was there. Thank fucking God."

It was her turn to look confused. "Y-you... you don't regret it?"

That was when it hit me. And the feeling wasn't a good one. Thanks to my shitty actions over the past several weeks, I'd trained Lilly to expect the absolute worst when it came to me. I

158

couldn't fault her for being leery. I'd basically taught her to expect the worst. And just knowing that cut so deep I wasn't sure the wound would ever heal right.

"No," I stated firmly before growling, "Fuck no. I don't regret it."

Her eyes started to shine as they darted down to my hands, more specifically, to the finger my wedding ring rested on. Shit, I'd made such a mess of everything. "How can you say that?" Her voice grew thick as she continued. "How can you even expect me to *believe* it? Every time we get close, you shove me away. Well, last night was the closest two people could get, wasn't it?"

I leaned forward and cupped her cheeks in my hands. To my relief, she nuzzled into my hold instead of pulling away. "I'm so goddamned sorry for everything I've put you through. I'm a mess, Lil. My head's all twisted up, and I can't promise I won't fuck up again, but I swear, I don't regret last night."

"Maybe not now—"

"Not ever," I interrupted. "I know I've given you no reason to believe me, but I'm telling the truth."

She studied my expression, searching for anything that would prove my words were less than genuine. Again, I couldn't blame her, but fuck me, did that ever sting. "What are we doing here, Quinn?"

It was a question I dreaded, mainly because I didn't have an answer. I wasn't lying when I said I had no regrets about what happened last night, but that didn't mean I wasn't confused as hell about where it was leading. "I don't know," I answered as honestly as possible. And from the way her face dropped and her expression became guarded, I knew it wasn't a good one.

I tightened my hold on her and scrambled to give her an explanation that wouldn't have her running in the other direction. "Look, I don't have all the answers you're looking for, but I want to try this. I haven't been able to stop thinking about you, and trying to keep my distance is only making us both miserable. Can we just… can we take this one day at a time?"

It wasn't a very reasonable request on my part, but it was the best I could do. I knew I wanted her, but the guilt at the thought of betraying my wife hadn't lessened. I felt like I was being ripped in half, pulled in two different directions, and neither of them felt totally right. I didn't know what else to do.

"One day at a time," she repeated softly.

"Yeah."

"Like… dating?"

The idea of labeling what we were doing was uncomfortable, but at least *dating* was a label I could live with. Anything more concrete would have sent me over the edge, and I couldn't stand the idea of hurting her again. Dating was the best I could do. At least for now. I just prayed to God she could accept that.

"Yeah, I guess you could call it that." I ran the pad of my thumb along her cheekbone. "I know I've given you no reason to trust me, and I have no idea what tomorrow is going to bring, but I want to try this… with you."

"One day at a time."

"Yes," I said softly, my eyes pleading with her. "It's all I've got right now, Lilly. Please, tell me you understand."

"I do," she whispered on a nod. "I understand that this has to be hard for you."

I couldn't keep the hopefulness in my voice in check as I asked, "So you'll try?"

And when she gave me another nod, I breathed a sigh of relief as the knot in my stomach unfurled. "Thank you," I breathed, leaning in to close the distance between us and repeated, "Thank you," against her lips.

She pulled back just enough to draw my attention to her eyes. "Just… promise you won't hurt me again, okay?"

I didn't answer. Instead, I devoured her lips — tasting, licking, and nipping until her entire body went pliant and fell against me, her question long forgotten. I couldn't promise her that, because somewhere deep inside I knew that promise would be the hardest one to keep.

21

LILLY

"*A*LL RIGHT, GUYS. You did great today! I'll see you next week."

Choruses of "Bye, Ms. Lilly" rang out around the room as the little girls scattered to their parents. I lifted my gaze just as Quinn pushed through the studio room door.

My heartbeat kicked up several notches at the sight of him. He stood at least a head taller than the rest of the parents in the room, so I didn't miss the tiny smirk that played on his lips as he crossed his arms over his chest and leaned back against the wall like he didn't have a care in the world. God, he was *fine*.

I felt like a teenage girl with a silly crush. My stomach swooped and my skin got tingly as I diverted my attention, staring at anything and everything except him. I could feel the heat in my cheeks as I passed out hugs and good byes to my students.

I finally started in his direction, working to push my nerves back, telling myself I was being ridiculous. But everything about our relationship had changed. Two nights ago I'd seen him naked, felt him move inside me. I had intimate knowledge of his body, and just thinking about it made me want to blush and giggle. We hadn't really had a chance to see each other since he stayed the night at my apartment, but he'd called and texted several times, and each time my phone lit up with his name I got all giddy.

"Hi." *Damn it.* My voice came out a lot breathier and low than I'd intended.

That smirk of his grew, coming dangerously close to his eyes. "Hi back."

"Daddy!" Sophia came rushing over. "Look what I learned today!" She went down in plié just like I'd taught them before doing a pretty damn good pirouette.

"That's amazing, Angel. You're doing so good."

Sophia's entire face brightened at her father's praise, causing my heart to jump. Quinn was attractive all on his own, but watching him interact with his daughter only made him that much hotter. And judging by the looks on some of the other moms' faces, I wasn't the only one who thought so.

"Go get your stuff, baby girl. I'm going to have a word with Ms. Lilly then we'll go home and I'll get dinner started."

She rushed off to go grab her backpack and Quinn turned back to me, whispering, "How are you?"

My face got hot all over again, and I knew he saw it because his green eyes began to shoot sparks. "Why do I suddenly feel like a fourteen-year-old with a crush when you're around?" It was meant to be a rhetorical question, but that didn't stop him from answering... and making my face flush even worse.

His voice dropped so low only I could hear it as he said, "Maybe because I've been up close and personal with every inch of your body and now know exactly what you look like when you come. Or maybe it's because you know I plan on seeing that look on your face again... *very* soon."

Sophia came running back just as my mouth dropped open and my eyes bugged out. "Daddy! Can we have tacos for dinner? *Pleeeease?*"

I was still stunned speechless, a tremor building between my thighs from Quinn's statement as he turned to look at his daughter.

"Yes, we can have tacos."

"Yes!" She pumped her little fist then asked, "Oh! Can Ms. Lilly come?" She gave me her attention and stated enthusiastically, "Daddy's like the best cook *ever*. His tacos are *awesome!*"

"Oh, I—uh… I don't think—"

"Great idea," Quinn interrupted, stunning me for the second time in as many minutes. "You should definitely come. We eat around seven. That work for you?"

"Um…" I wasn't quite sure how to react. I knew he said he wanted to *try*… whatever that entailed, but I couldn't help but compare dating Quinn with trying to successfully navigate a minefield. I never knew when I'd take one wrong step. And even though it had only been two days, I still felt that everything could turn on a dime, that I was just waiting for *something* to happen to make him push me away again. I'd be lying if I said I wasn't surprised he was so cool with the idea of a cozy dinner at his house with his daughter. I was sure that would cross one of the million invisible lines he had laid out between us. So knowing he not only liked the idea, but insisted upon it, made that floaty feeling in my belly that much stronger. "Sure. Seven works great."

"*Yay!*" Sophia screamed.

"Perfect." He did that little wink thing that sent a quiver of pleasure through my core. "See you then."

SOPHIA HADN'T BEEN LYING. Quinn's tacos were delicious. And the entire evening had been surprisingly comfortable, even with the potent sexual tension that filtered between the two of us.

"So, what did you think?" Quinn asked after I polished off the last of my fourth taco. If he hadn't been sitting right in front of me, I might have gone so far as to lick my plate clean.

"So good," I groaned through a full mouth, giving two thumbs up.

"Told ya!" Sophia giggled. "My daddy's the best cook in the world. You should try his pancakes."

"She's exaggerating," Quinn added. "Pancakes and tacos are about the extent of my culinary prowess."

I swallowed and smiled brightly. "Then I guess we're all lucky Sinful Sweets expanded, huh?"

He lifted his bottle of beer and tipped it in my direction. "I thank God every day." Then he took a pull, and I was mesmerized by the way his Adam's apple bobbed up and down. Damn, even his *throat* was sexy.

"It's almost bedtime, Angel," he spoke, pulling me from my lusty haze. "Go brush your teeth, and I'll pick a book to read to you."

"Can Ms. Lilly read me a story tonight?"

I glanced sideways at Quinn. After his blowup the one and only time I babysat Sophia, I didn't want to risk pushing my luck by overstepping my boundaries, so I said, "Why doesn't your dad read you a story while I clean up."

I stood and began gathering the dishes when I felt Quinn's hand land softly on my forearm. "You don't have to do that."

That simple touch sent a spark of electricity through my bloodstream. "I don't mind. Besides, you cooked, it's only fair, right?"

His eyes held mine for several seconds, and I swear, I could feel something intense coming from the pale green depths, but before I could place it, he stood and broke the connection. "Okay." He looked to his daughter and gently commanded, "Get a move on, sweetheart."

Sophia pushed from her chair and came at me, wrapping her arms around my waist. "'Night, Ms. Lilly. I'm glad you had dinner with us."

"Me too, honey." I returned her hug as best as I could with my hands full of dirty plates.

She bolted from the room and Quinn started to follow, but stopped before passing me, leaning in close to whisper in my ear, "Don't leave yet. I'll be back in a few."

Another tremor worked through my core. "Okay," I whispered back.

He disappeared down the hall and I headed for the kitchen and dove into scrubbing dishes like my life depended on it in an effort to temper my raging hormones.

I was so busy scouring the skillet Quinn had used for chicken that I hadn't heard him enter the kitchen. My body gave a startled jolt as he reached up and brushed my hair over one shoulder before placing his lips on the sensitive skin. This time I jolted for an entirely different reason.

"You scrub that any harder and you're going to take the Teflon right off."

I dropped the scrubber and moved the skillet under the water, giving it a good rinse. I'd just picked up a plate to wash when Quinn's tongue darted out and ran along the cord in my neck. It felt so good, no… it felt *amazing*. I didn't want him to stop, but in the back of my mind, I knew it probably wasn't a good idea. "Should you be doing that right now with Sophia only a few rooms away?"

"She's dead asleep. Won't hear a thing."

I cocked my head to the side to give him better access as my eyes fluttered closed. "Jeez. That was fast."

He stood and placed his hands on my hips, spinning me around to face him. "Babe. I've been with her for twenty minutes." My eyes got big, making Quinn smirk. "Just how long were you scrubbing at skillet?" he asked, humor laced through his words.

"Uh…"

He chuckled and bent close. "Fuck, you're cute."

I grinned widely, watching as his gaze trailed down my face to my mouth. "That dimple kills me," he muttered, closing the rest of the distance and placing a kiss on my cheek, right where it depressed every time I smiled. I melted into his big, strong body as he moved from my dimple to my lips and began kissing me. It started soft and slow, feather-light pressure of his mouth against mine. Then his tongue ran along the seam of my lips. I opened for him and the tone of the kiss changed completely.

He kissed me so thoroughly, with such deliberateness, that I got completely lost in the feel of him. My hands snaked around his back and yanked up his sweater in order to get to the warm skin of his back. My nails dug in and I moaned into his mouth as pleasure coursed through me.

Something about that noise spurred him on. A deep, low growl worked its way up his chest and down my throat. His fingers on my hips clenched then moved. Before I could process what was about to happen, he grabbed my ass in both hands and hauled me up his body. My legs wrapped around his waist, locking at the ankles, and I twined my arms around his neck as he set me down on the counter beside the sink.

His cock was hard, the pressure of it pressing again me oh-so perfectly that another — more wanton — groan escaped. "Quinn," I breathed as his head lowered and he kissed a scorching trail down my jaw and neck.

"Christ," he grunted, pushing himself harder against me. "Want you so fucking bad." Tiny bombs detonated between my thighs. I was so wet. So ready.

I'd just started contemplating ways to get us both naked and in his bed when a tiny voice called out, "Daddy? Can I have a glass of water?"

Everything stopped. The heat instantly disappeared like a tub full of ice water had just been dumped on us. "Shit," he hissed, dropping his forehead to my shoulder. "Shit, shit, *fucking shit.*"

I gave his shoulders a little push and tried not to giggle at the murderous look on his face as he called out, "Yeah, Angel. Be right there."

At that, I lost hold of my giggle. Quinn's eyes lowered once more to my dimple and his eyes grew hooded. "I'm really sorry about that," he said quietly.

I reached up and did what I'd been wanting to do since the first time he walked into my dance school, I ran my fingers through that mass of sandy blond hair, letting them trail down over the stubble on his square jaw. "Don't be sorry. It's hot watching you be a good dad."

One of his brows quirked up as he mumbled, "I'll have to keep that in mind."

"You do that," I grinned, unlocking my ankles so he could step back and I could hop down. "I should probably go."

"Yeah," he nodded, then leaned in and gave me a soft kiss. "But we're picking this up again as soon as possible."

"Oh, I'm counting on that. Go get Little Miss her glass of water. I'll talk to you later?"

"I'll call you." I stood on my tip-toes and landed one last kiss on his lush lips. Then I turned and headed for the door, smiling the whole way.

Sure, it had only been two days, but this whole *dating* thing was going pretty damn good so far.

2 2

QUINN

$\mathcal{L}$ILLY AND I had been seeing each other for close to a month. We kept it casual, no expectations; we just enjoyed spending time together. We didn't flaunt the fact we were sleeping together in public. As far as our families, the townspeople, and my daughter were concerned, we were good friends.

It worked for us. Or at least that's what I was constantly telling myself. Lilly hadn't given me any reason to think she wasn't happy with our arrangement, and I didn't want to consider that she might want more.

I was giving her all I had, all that was left of me. I hoped it was enough.

It had to be.

For the first time in years, I woke up without the suffocating weight of knowing it was just another emotionless, bleak day where I simply walked through life instead of leaving it resting on my chest. I could breathe knowing what was waiting for me. I could smile and almost feel it to my soul. *Almost*.

So yeah, it *had* to be enough. Because with Lilly in my life now, I felt better. I was content; which was more than I could have hoped for. Happiness for a guy like me—a guy who was the blame for tearing his family apart—wasn't in the cards. I could settle for contentment. That was the most I deserved, after all.

I should have known that something would dredge up from the dreary, bottomless pits of my despair to try and cast darkness on the goodness that was settling over me. But somehow, a month with that constant acute ache suddenly dulled, I'd let my guard down, so when the call came, I hadn't been properly prepared. Stupidly, I'd let my guard down.

I'd just dropped Sophia off at a sleepover with some of her friends from dance class. It seemed the older she got, the more she spent nights at other people's houses instead of ours. I wasn't sure if I was ready for my baby girl to grow up yet, but she was intent on doing it whether I liked it or not.

Taking advantage of the free time, I'd called Lilly and made plans to meet at The Moose, Pembrooke's local watering hole, for dinner and a few drinks before going back to her place for the night.

My cellphone rang from the cup holder in the center console and, not taking my eyes off the road, I picked it up, engaged the call, and brought it to my ear.

"Yeah."

"Quinn?"

The sound of Garrett Benson's voice coming through my phone set my entire body on edge. We never talked. If Addy's parents needed to talk to me about something specific, or even when it was just one of their regularly scheduled calls to Sophia, it had always been Janice. In the past three and a half years, we probably hadn't said more than five sentences to each other. And most of those weren't all that pleasant since they consisted of a pissed-off Garrett cussing me out when he found out I was taking Sophia and moving back to Pembrooke.

To say that my late wife's parents weren't my biggest fans was putting it mildly. We'd been so close when Addy was alive. They were as much a family to me as my own folks were. But then I took their daughter from them. I couldn't fault them for hating me. Luckily they were good people and, over the years, they'd learned to deal with me for their granddaughter's sake. Janice was pleasant enough, but Garrett was tolerant at best.

"Garrett. What can I do for you?"

He breathed through the line, and I got the sense that I was the last person he wanted to be talking to. "Look, I know it's difficult with your work schedule, but Jan and I would really love to see Sophia for Thanksgiving." Then he lowered the boom the rest of the way by adding, "In Seattle."

I sighed heavily through the line as I turned into the parking lot of The Moose. "Listen, Garrett. I know you want to see your granddaughter, but—"

I found a spot, pulled in, and put my truck in park just as he barked, "It's not an unreasonable request. We get to see her once, maybe twice a year since you took her away."

"I didn't take her *away*," I snarled, feeling my temper start to boil. "The move was the best thing for the both of us." But even as I said it, I began to question if that was really the truth. I blamed the department in Seattle for giving me the runaround when it came to going back to work. I used the excuse of needing my parents' help with Soph. But the truth was, I ran. Shit got too hard, and I tucked tail and fucking ran.

And I knew he knew it, too, when he muttered, "If that's what you need to tell yourself to sleep better at night."

My grip on the steering wheel tightened until the leather creaked and the skin of my palm began to burn. But I refused to engage. I knew he wanted to argue, to possibly hurl insults my way, but Garrett sucked in several breaths before speaking again.

"If you can't get time off work, then Jan and I are more than happy to fly there to pick her up. But we want to spend the holiday with Sophia in *our* home. The home we raised her mother in."

I closed my eyes and reached up to rub one of them with the ball of my free hand. I didn't want to give up a holiday with my daughter, but he wasn't all wrong, it wasn't an unreasonable request. However, the way he went about *making* that request was bullshit. Still, I couldn't bring myself to refuse. Whether or not he and I ever got along again, he was a terrific grandfather, and Sophia loved him and Janice like crazy. It wouldn't be fair to her to say no.

"I'll check my schedule with the department, all right?" I finally relented, guilt tearing at my insides. "I'll call you back to let you know whether or not you need to come get her."

By his silence, I knew I'd surprised him with the ease in which I'd agreed. He'd been expecting a fight on his hands. I just didn't have the strength — or the right — to give him one.

"Thank you," he finally said, gruffly.

"I'll be in touch." Before I even finished the sentence, the line went dead. I stared out the windshield of my truck at the entrance to The Moose, wishing I could just throw the gearshift in reverse and get the hell out of there. The thought of having to make pleasant conversation in a crowded bar while I was pissed off sat like a lead ball in my stomach. But just as I considered shooting her a text, cancelling our dinner, a flash of blonde hair caught my attention.

Through the large windows that made up the front of the bar, I saw Lilly. The hostess had placed her at a booth right up front, so I had the perfect view of her as she looked up and offered the woman a full-fledged smile. One that brought forth that dimple that drove me crazy. Just the sight of her calmed the turmoil inside of me.

It was then that I realized I was sinking deeper and deeper every day when it came to Lilly Mathewson. That scared the absolute shit out of me, but I was helpless to stop it. Every day my feelings for her grew stronger. Every goddamned day. If I was smart, I'd end things right then and there, hurt her *now* in order to prevent even worse pain down the line, because I saw the way she looked at me. What she felt was written in those amber eyes of hers, clear as day. She was falling just as fast—maybe faster.

I knew it, but I was too selfish to stop it. I needed her to quiet the voices, to lessen the burden of guilt. I needed her light.

I'd have given anything to be strong enough, to be the man she truly deserved for the long haul. I wanted nothing more than to lower my walls and allow her to heal my broken soul.

But I didn't deserve that.

I didn't deserve her.

However, as long as she was willing to take me as I was, there was no way in hell I was letting her go.

"QUINN."

Oh yeah. *Fuck* yeah. The breathy way she moaned my name as I fucked her drove me wild. The way her silky, wet heat squeezed my cock as I pumped in and out of her nearly killed me.

Nothing existed when we were like this. The world outside of the two of us disappeared every time I was buried deep inside her. It was yet another thing she gave me, another piece of goodness I'd never be able to return.

"So goddamn beautiful," I grunted, as I watched her beautiful face twist with pleasure *I* was giving her. Her eyes opened and those amber depths flashed darker as she lifted her hips in time with my thrusts, reaching for her release.

My greedy girl.

I fucking loved it.

She gave so much of herself to everyone she cared about. The fact that she *took* when we were together gave me a high unlike anything I'd ever felt. If this was all I had to give her, then I was determined to make it count.

"Please," she whimpered when I slowed down, dragging it out

as long as possible. "I'm so close."

My jaw clenched as I bit out, "Not yet."

"Oh God." Her neck bowed and I could feel her getting closer. Her pussy clenched around me every time I pulled out. I was seconds away from blowing, but I wouldn't let her come. Not until I was ready.

"Not. Yet. Hold on, baby. Come with me."

"I can't." Her head began to thrash, sending waves of blonde hair cascading over her pillow. "Oh shit, hurry. *Please*."

I drove into her... hard. Once... twice... three times then buried my cock deep and held, a growl bursting from my throat as I poured myself into her.

"*Now*, Lilly!"

The second I started coming, her mouth opened on a silent scream that turned into a long, drawn out moan as every muscle in her body locked up.

"Quinn!" she shouted at the very peak of her release as she drained every drop from me. Each orgasm with Lilly got better and better, to the point I worried that one of them might actually kill me. But shit, I'd die a happy man.

I dropped my head into the crook of her neck as we both worked to get our breathing under control. I stayed that way for what felt like an eternity, simply enjoying the feel of her silky hair on my face, her soft skin against mine. In the rare moments like this one, I was able to let everything go and just *be* as Lilly's fingers trailed gentle paths up and down my back. She was greedy while we fucked, but once it was finished she went back to giving, with no hesitation. And I readily accepted the comfort she offered.

Once feeling came back in my limbs, I lifted my head and looked down at her. Lilly's eyes were smiling, her dimple prominent, and I couldn't help but think that, even though she was always beautiful, nothing topped what she looked like in the afterglow of amazing sex. She was take-your-breath-away stunning. Several seconds passed in complete silence as I committed every inch of her face to memory.

"Hi," she finally whispered up at me, breaking through the quiet of the room.

I felt one corner of my mouth curl up in a half grin as I replied. "Hi back."

Her smile dimmed, the dimple disappeared, and the happiness on her face faded enough to let concern seep in and take it's place. Lilly's fingers moved to my hair and she brushed it back off my forehead. Her voice remained quiet as she asked, "You want to talk about whatever was bothering you over dinner?"

I jerked back just a bit, bewildered that she'd been able to read me so well. I thought I'd covered up the fact that my conversation with Garrett was still heavy on my mind. But she saw right through my façade. Warmth spread through my chest at the same time my gut constricted with anxiousness. I did my best to push the fear and guilt back, wanting to stay wrapped in Lilly's goodness for a little while longer.

"I don't want to think about the bad shit," I answered.

Her expression didn't grow any less uneasy, but she nodded anyway.

Wanting to erase her apprehension, I continued. "All I want is to be here with you, right now. Can we do that? Just stay with me in this room for tonight. We can let the real world back in tomorrow."

Lilly's eyes drifted shut as she inhaled deeply. They opened once again on an exhale, and the worry was gone. "If that's what you need."

It was. "It is."

She nodded her head and wrapped her arms around my neck, pulling me down for a hug. Once again, giving me a beautiful gift.

No. I didn't deserve her.

But as long as she could make me feel like this, I was going to keep her.

LILLY

*H*E WAS STILL holding himself back from me.

It had been just a little over a month since we started this relationship, and it didn't take a genius to see that he still had that invisible line between us firmly in place. I thought he'd warm up, *open* up. But — with the exception of sex — he was as closed off as ever.

He didn't talk to me about Addison. He kept us a secret from everyone he knew. He still wore his wedding ring. And any time I asked what was weighing on his mind, he'd divert, either with conversation or sex. He was a master at changing the subject.

But I loved what we had so much I couldn't bring myself to push him. Hell, if I were being honest with myself, it wasn't what he *had* that I loved. It was just *him*. I was falling. Steadily and surely. More and more every single day.

I couldn't remember a time when I'd ever laughed so hard or so much than when I was with him. He showed concern for my wellbeing, always asking about my father when he knew I went to see him. He made the pain in my heart easier to deal with. We spent every available minute together, and when our schedules didn't sync up, we talked and texted all the time. But he refused to put a label on what we were.

I told myself I was okay with that when really, I'd begun to worry. Even though I was falling in love with Quinn — and his actions showed me daily that he could possibly be feeling the same way — I couldn't ignore the nagging sense that something unpleasant was just around the corner.

But instead of heeding the warning in my head, I chose to ignore it and move forward. I'd never felt for someone like I felt for Quinn, and the thought of giving that up ate away at me. I just couldn't bring myself to do it, even though I knew, with each passing day, the pain of potentially losing him would be that much worse.

He was worth it to me. He was worth the pain. Problem was, I couldn't be sure I was worth it to him.

"What are you thinking so hard about?" he asked, and the sudden sound of his voice caused me to jump and spin around, nearly dropping the dish I'd been holding.

It had been a week since our dinner at The Moose, and I was back at his house, having had a homemade dinner of macaroni and hotdogs with him and Sophia. He'd gone to get her ready for bed and I'd started on the dishes. Once again, I hadn't heard him enter the kitchen, and when my gaze finally landed on him, he was leaning against the doorframe, his arms crossed over his powerful chest, that sexy smirk on his face.

I was beginning to hate that smirk. Not because it wasn't gorgeous. It so was. But because it still didn't reach his eyes. And every time his lips curled up, I wanted to do everything in my power to give him reason to smile with his beautiful green eyes as well.

"I didn't hear you."

Quinn pushed off the door and made his way to me, taking the soap covered plate from my hand. "I got that when you nearly jumped out of your skin, Lil." He chuckled, as he placed the dish back into the sink. Once he finished with that, his arms banded around my waist, holding me firmly against him. "What's got you so preoccupied you couldn't hear a garbage truck if it drove through the room?"

I twisted my lips and gave him a glare. "I wasn't *that* preoccupied."

"Baby, I said your name like, five times."

I started at his declaration even as my skin tingled as his calling me *baby*. "Okay. So maybe I was that preoccupied."

His arms gave me a squeeze and I lifted my hands and placed them on his chest. He didn't seem to mind I was getting his sweater wet. "So tell me what's on your mind."

I couldn't. I couldn't tell him that I was worried he was still keeping me at such a distance. He'd feel pressured, cornered into either giving me more or cutting and running, and I knew exactly which of those he'd pick if it came down to that. Maybe it made me a coward, but I just couldn't lose him... not yet. Hopefully not at all.

So, instead, I brought up *another* topic I'd been hesitant to bring up, but less so than the state of our relationship. It was the lesser of two evils.

"I was just wondering..." I trailed off and lowered my eyes to where my hands rested on his chest. I played with the cotton there as I forced the words out. "We haven't talked about it, and it's only two days away, but... I was wondering if you and Sophia would like to come to my parents' house for Thanksgiving?"

The shutters slammed down over his face. His entire body froze, freezing mine right along with it. Oh God, I shouldn't have asked. I really, *really* shouldn't have asked.

"I can't."

My heart sank, but I did my best to mask that by smiling, wide and fake. "Oh... yeah! Totally. I mean, I get it," I began to ramble, pushing back and putting pressure on his arms around me. He didn't let go. "It's last minute and you're probably going to be with your folks, and we're still, like. New. Whatever. It's whatever. Just forget I even asked. I shouldn't have asked."

Damn it, I was *not* going to cry. But he wouldn't *let me go*.

"Lilly—"

"I mean, it was presumptuous, right?"

"Lil—"

"Seriously. It is. We're only dating. It's not like I'm your girlfriend."

"Can I talk, please?"

But I was on a roll. "Who does that? Who asks the guy she's just *dating* to meet her *parents* on *Thanksgiving?*" I let out a slightly hysterical laugh, and kept trying to get him to release me. "It's ridiculous! I'm ridiculous."

"Damn it, Lilly. Just—"

"I should probably finish these dishes and get home. If you'll just…"

I trailed off and pointed at his arms. He loosened one, but held firm with the other. And the arm that released me came up so his hand could cover my mouth.

"Baby. Stop." I'd been mumbling against his palm, but the moment his clipped command left his lips, I shut up. I couldn't read his expression, and at that very moment I really needed to know what he was thinking. Had I screwed up epically? Had I pushed too far? Was he going to end us?

I was expecting the absolute worst, so what he said next shocked me. "Sophia's going to Seattle for Thanksgiving, and I'm on shift at the department." He held my eyes for a beat before finally lowering his hand from my mouth. "*That's* what I was trying to say. But you went on your rant and wouldn't let me get a word in edgewise."

"Sorry," I mumbled before pulling my lips between my teeth and biting down to keep my word-vomit at bay.

Quinn's grin returned as he tucked some of my hair behind

my ear. "Christ, you're cute always, but even cuter when you're rambling."

My face went hot, but I ignored my blush in order to ask, "So, you're not going to have Sophia for Thanksgiving?"

The humor dissipated from his face. "No."

I was suddenly terribly sad for him. "Is this something that happens every year?"

His thunderous expression told me all I needed to know, but he still vocalized his response. "No, it's not. Her grandparents on her mom's side called and requested they have her for the holiday. I didn't feel like I could say no."

I rested my hands on either side of his neck, hating how upset he seemed at the thought of not being with his daughter on such an important day. "Of course you could say no! Or maybe they could come here instead. You're her father, Quinn. All the decisions are yours."

He then let me go and took a step back, rubbing at the back of his neck anxiously. "You wouldn't understand."

That did not sit well... *at all*. And despite my fear of overstepping, I found anger spiking and myself saying, "Maybe I would understand, if you talked to me about it."

He sighed and kept his gaze diverted down. "It's not something I want to discuss, okay? When I'm with you, I want to be *with you*. I don't want to have to think about all the shit swirling around in my life."

"But you know I'm here, right? If you ever need to talk?" I stepped close and took his hands in mine. "That's what you're supposed to do with people you care about. You talk to them and they listen. You can't push the real world out all the time, Quinn."

"I can goddamned well try," he grumbled, shaking my hands loose and moving to the fridge. He yanked it open, pulled a beer out, popped the cap off, and chugged. Once he was done, his eyes came back to me, and his voice sounded devoid of all emotion when he said, "It's late. You should probably get home."

Yep, I'd definitely pushed too hard. But was it really too much to ask that he *talk* to me? I wanted to argue. I wanted to get in his face and tell him that this wasn't how relationships worked, that it wasn't healthy. But I didn't. Not because I was scared of losing him, but because I knew then just how pointless it would be. And I was tired of beating my head against a brick wall.

Instead of arguing, I nodded and went for my purse where it rested hooked on the back of one of the kitchen chairs. "Yeah. You're right. I should go."

I moved to step past him, concentrating on the floor at my feet as I walked, when his hand shot out and caught me around my arm. "Lilly, I'm sorry."

I lifted my head just enough to look at him through my lashes and offered up a tiny smile. "It's fine, Quinn. I get it, really. Don't worry about it."

Uncertainty flickered through his eyes as he asked, "Can I call you tomorrow?"

"Of course."

The uncertainty remained, and I understood why with his next question. "Will you answer?"

God, he was breaking my heart. "Yes, Quinn," I whispered. "I'll answer. Because in spite of everything, I really do care about you. Nothing's going to change that."

I stood on my tiptoes and lifted, placing a chaste kiss against his lips. Then I walked out of the kitchen, through the house, and out the front door. I wasn't sure who I was madder at… me for pushing too hard when I knew better.

Or Quinn for keeping that cold, miserable distance between us.

LILLY

I STOOD IN my mother's kitchen chopping onions and celery for the cornbread dressing — that was the extent of what my mother would allow me to do — while Mom and her sister, Aunt Jenny, worked on different side dishes. The house was full of family, many of them having traveled the distance to Jackson Hole to spend the holiday with my father, knowing it would more than likely be his last.

It was great to have everyone under the same roof again, but the underlying reason as to why sat in the back of everyone's minds, not really allowing for a totally festive Thanksgiving.

The football game was on in the living room, and every few minutes, masculine shouts could be heard, either from triumph or disappointment. From the sounds of the yells that just reverberated through the kitchen, they weren't too happy with whatever just happened on the screen.

I turned in the direction of the door and smiled, loving how normal everything seemed.

"Well, I'll tell you one thing," Aunt Jenny started, "Hank and Keith better be prepared to scrub these dishes spotless when we're done eating," she said about her husband and grown son.

"I'm not slaving away, making this meal for them so they can just sit on their butts and watch football all day."

My mother laughed softly from her place at the stove. "Jenn, in the twenty years Keith's been born, and the thirty you've been married to Hank, when have you ever known those two to leave you a dirty kitchen when you've spent the day cooking?"

Aunt Jenny paused and looked up, pondering Mom's question. "You're right, Lizzy. I've trained them well."

We all laughed just as my cellphone rang from my back pocket. I wiped my hands on a dishtowel and pulled it out. Quinn's name shone up at me from the screen. True to his word, he'd called yesterday after the little drama we'd had the night before. I could tell he was still concerned about my mindset, but I was doing everything I could to put him at ease.

Yes, I was still unsettled by how stagnant our relationship seemed to be, however, I couldn't help but to hope Quinn would finally let go of the past enough to let me in.

"Be back in a sec," I told my mom and Aunt. I headed out the back door for some privacy, too eager to take the call to worry about bundling up against the cold temperature outside. I engaged the call and brought the phone to my ear. "Hey," I said softly, a smile splitting my face.

His deep, rumbly voice carried through the line. "Happy Thanksgiving, baby."

"Happy Thanksgiving. How are you? Did Sophia get to Seattle safely?"

He sighed into my ear, and I knew he still wasn't happy about sending his daughter to a different state for the holiday. "Yeah, got a call from her earlier this morning. She's excited to be with her grandparents."

"Well that's good," I said, trying to give him a bit of comfort. "And it's just two more days. She'll be back before you know it."

"I know. You're right. And she's having a great time. I just hate being away from her."

My heart gave a small tug. "You're a good dad."

I could hear the grin in his voice when he said, "Thanks sweetheart. So, what are you up to today?"

I looked through the window into the kitchen to see Mom and Aunt Jenny chatting and laughing. My feet carried me along the back deck until I got a perfect view into the living room. Dad looked good… better than he had in weeks. It was like having a house full of people breathed life into him. He was happy.

"I'm helping my mom and aunt cook. The men are camped out in front of the TV watching the game."

"Oh Lord, you're in the kitchen?"

I rolled my eyes toward the blue sky. "Ha ha, smart ass. You'll be happy to know I've been relegated to chopping duty. What about you? Are you guys planning on making a turkey or anything?"

"Nah. We tried that a couple years ago and got called out in the middle of cooking. By the time we got back the food was ruined."

I frowned, thinking about him and the rest of the guys not having anything to commemorate the day. "Well that kind of sucks."

"Part of the job," he replied nonchalantly. "We've all gotten used to it. At least with us working Thanksgiving we won't be on shift Christmas Day."

My mouth dropped open and a gasp trickled out. "You've had to work on *Christmas*?"

He laughed through the phone at my outrage. "Fires and accidents happen every day, baby. Someone has to take care of them. Besides, Thanksgiving and Christmas are two of our biggest days. You get overeager husbands who want to fry a turkey but don't have the first fucking clue how. Might be a disaster, but it leads to some pretty entertaining stories. And at least we don't have time to think about not being with our families if we're constantly busy."

"I guess you have a point," I pouted, hating that he was alone and working on the holidays and didn't even get to enjoy all the delicious food.

"Aw," he said teasingly. "You're worried about me. That's sweet."

I let out an inelegant snort. "Please. I'm not worried. Just don't want you to be jealous that I'll be in a hardcore tryptophan coma in a few hours and feel like you missed out."

His gravelly chuckle did crazy things to my insides. "Believe me, I'd much rather be curled up next to you with a turkey hangover than here. But then I remember that I get you to myself tomorrow, no interruptions, makes it all worth it."

A quiver worked its way through my belly at the sinful tone of his voice, and I suddenly couldn't wait for tomorrow. "Don't turn me on when I have to spend the next few hours stuck in a kitchen with my mom and my aunt."

That got me another chuckle. "Well, don't say something like that and turn *me* on when I have to go back into a room full of guys who'll give me shit for sporting a hard-on."

I wouldn't have giggled at the picture he painted if the thought of Quinn hard didn't send a flood of arousal through my core.

I must have let out a tiny moan, because he suddenly growled into the receiver. "Okay, I see I'm going to have to cut this conversation off here if you're going to keep making sounds like that."

I giggled and shifted from foot to foot, the cold finally starting to seep into my bones. "I should get back inside anyway. Be safe, okay?"

"Promise, baby. I'll talk to you later."

We hung up, and I took a few more seconds to get my raging hormones back under control. I was just about to turn and head into the house when the back door opened and Dad walked through with my coat in his hands.

"You're going to catch your death out here, Lilly Flower."

I turned and slipped my arms into the coat he held open for me. "It's not so bad." I looked out at the expanse of snow-topped trees and mountains that provided a stunning view as far as the eye could see. "It's so beautiful out here."

Dad threw his arm around me and pulled me into his side as we both stared out at the horizon. "Why do you think me and your mom refuse to live anywhere outside of Wyoming? Nothing but God's country out here, baby girl. Beauty as far as the eye can see."

"I get it." I nuzzled into him, taking in his familiar scent mixed with the fresh snow. "I'd never want to live anywhere else either."

"So…" he dragged out. "I'm taking it from that smile you had on your face when I came out here that you and your young man have found equal footing?"

My head shot to the side, my eyes shooting up at him. He wore a grin on his face that told me he hadn't forgotten our conversation from over a month ago. I hadn't talked to my parents about Quinn since we started seeing each other. I felt like if I admitted it out loud, I'd somehow jinx it. I shouldn't have been surprised that he remembered. I was his baby girl, and even sick he was still as protective as he'd always been.

"We're… working on it," I answered slowly.

He looked back out at the landscape. "Well, that's better than nothing. What's he up to today?"

"He's working. He's a firefighter with the Pembrooke Fire Department so he's on shift today."

"Honorable line of work," Dad said.

"Yeah, but it's sad they have to miss out on days like today with their families."

Dad turned to me and grinned before guiding us back toward the door. "Then I guess you should pack up whatever leftovers we have so you can take them a bit of the holiday, huh?"

I could have smacked myself for not thinking of that sooner.

We stepped back into the house, and I lifted up on my tiptoes to place a kiss on my father's cheek. "You're a smart man, Dad. Anyone ever tell you that?"

He chuckled and hugged me tight. "Don't let your mother find out or she'll start expecting more from me. All these years later I've still got the woman convinced I don't have the first clue how to use a washing machine."

We laughed and made our way back to the family, and I was comforted by the fact that, even if this was my dad's last Thanksgiving, at least it was a great one.

THE SUN HAD LONG since set by the time I pulled up to the fire station. I breathed a sigh of relief at the sight of the engine in an open bay, meaning they weren't out on a call. By the time I pulled into my spot and cut the engine, Quinn and the guy I remembered as Carpenter—I couldn't think of his first name—were coming out to see who'd just driven up.

"Lilly?" Quinn's voice carried with a threat of surprise. "What are you doing here?"

I opened the back door to give him a good look. When I'd told Mom about the guys at the station not getting to have a proper Thanksgiving meal, she and my aunt had been all over helping me pack up the leftovers. And there had been *a lot*. There was enough food to feed twenty lining my parents' table, and the six of us hadn't even come close to making a dent in it. Needless to say, the guys at the station were going to be eating very well.

"I figured since you guys were missing out on Thanksgiving, I'd bring a bit of it to you."

"Oh, hell yeah!" Carpenter hooted and threw his fist in the air. "Please tell me you've got sweet potato pie."

I giggled at the excitement on the grown man's face. "Two, actually. We made three and couldn't finish the rest off."

Carpenter scooped me up in a bear hug, lifting my feet off the ground and spinning me in a circle. "If I wasn't afraid of getting my teeth knocked in, I'd kiss you," he declared once he put me back down.

"Smart man," Quinn stated with a scowl on his face. "Now do you mind removing your hands from her before I have to break your fingers?"

Carpenter threw his hands up and took a big step back, causing me to burst into laughter. "I'll just… take some of this inside."

He grabbed as many containers as he could carry — which wasn't even half — and booked it back into the station. I was still laughing when I suddenly felt Quinn's fingers brush across my cheek. I opened my eyes to find him standing *right there*, less than two inches separating us. "Thank you, baby," he said in a low, melodic voice.

I beamed up at him and his gaze traveled down my face to my dimple. "No problem. There was no way we were eating this all. Seemed wasteful to toss all this perfectly good food."

He wrapped his arms around me and pulled me flush against him. "As long as you didn't have a hand in cooking any of it, I'm sure it's delicious."

I managed to get one swift punch to his gut in before he leaned in and planted a kiss on my lips while we both laughed. "Let's get the rest of this stuff inside and get you boys fed," I breathed once he pulled back, his kiss leaving my legs wobbly.

The smile he gave me then came so close to meeting his eyes that I considered it a win.

As we loaded our arms with containers and headed into the station I couldn't help but think: One day I was going to get a real smile from this beautiful man.

LILLY

"OKAY, GUYS," I called out, as my heels clicked along the wooden floor back stage. "We've been preparing for this for months. You know your steps forward and back. You're going to do great. So let's knock 'em dead, yeah?"

My students all let out cheers of excitement. Some looked more anxious than others, but I had complete faith that each and every one of them was going to do amazing.

The Winter Showcase was a big deal in Pembrooke. It was a community event, not just the parents of the students enrolled at the school. Almost the whole town came out to watch the kids put on a show, and as I peeked through the curtain that led to the front of the auditorium, my belly fluttered with nervous butter-flies. We had a full house.

I lived for moments like this; moments when my kids were front and center, the spotlight shining on them. For me, dancing wasn't about showing off my talent; it was about teaching an art to others so they could pass along that gift.

"Seven minutes," Kyle announced, as he and Samantha scur-ried around, helping kids fix costumes, hair, makeup, or the like.

He planted a quick kiss on my cheek as he passed by, and Samantha reached for my hand and gave it a squeeze.

"Miss Lilly! Miss Lilly!" I looked down just as Sophia rushed me, wrapping her arms around my legs. I bent with a laugh and scooped her up. "Hey there, Little Miss. You ready for your number?"

She nodded enthusiastically. "Yep! Does my bun look okay?"

I set her down and examined her hair. Over the past few months, Quinn's skill at putting his daughter's hair in a bun had really grown.

"It's perfect, sweetheart. And you're beautiful. Is your daddy in the audience?"

"Uh huh," she nodded. "With Meemaw and Papaw too. They can't wait to see me." I was about to agree with them when one of the other little girls called Sophia's name. She offered me a distracted wave and bolted off in that direction. I grinned after her, then turned toward the gathered crowd.

"All right," I spoke loud enough for everyone to hear. "First number's about to start. I need the intermediate ballet class to take their places."

The students scattered to all corners of the area backstage, some taking their places, some waiting in the wings to watch the performances they weren't in. The air was a full of excitement and quiet chatter.

"Five minutes," called Samantha.

I peeked back around the curtain, scanning the sea of faces for one in particular. I wasn't sure why, but I knew seeing his face would help ease some of my nerves.

"Lilly," Kyle spoke, calling my attention from the audience. "You've got visitors."

I spun around and my face broke out into a bright smile at the sight of my mom and dad making their way up the stairs. "Hey! I thought you guys weren't going to make it."

"Miss your biggest show of the year? Are you crazy?" Mom

scoffed. She held onto my father's arm, and I could tell she was offering him her support. He looked more tired today than usual.

"Hey," I said quietly, stepping up to kiss his cheek. "You okay?"

"Right as rain." He smiled, but I could see pain flicker in his eyes. This wasn't a great day for him, but he was determined to be there for me.

"And don't you look so pretty," Mom cooed, eyeing the pale pink, long-sleeved wrap dress I'd bought for tonight. I hardly ever dressed up, more comfortable in leggings and sweaters, or dance clothes than anything else, but I always tried to look nice for the showcase. I matched the dress with a pair of tan heels that were murder on my feet, but made my legs look *fantastic*. I was hoping Quinn would get a chance to see me in it before the night was through.

I hugged her and took a step back. "Thanks, Mom. You two better find your seats. We're about to start."

"Okay, honey," she spoke. "We'll be watching."

Dad leaned in for one last kiss. "Your kiddos will be amazing, Lilly Flower."

"Thanks, guys. Love you."

They waved and gave their love back before disappearing toward the front of the auditorium.

The auditorium lights lowered and the ones on the stage brightened just seconds before the music for the first number began.

As the program progressed, I ran around the backstage area like a mad woman, getting my students ready. It was a mix of modern numbers combined with classics to keep with the holiday spirit.

I'd just finished getting Sophia's class in place for their dance. The lights lowered and they filtered out onto the stage. The Dance of the Sugarplum Fairies began to play and I found myself stuck in place, watching Sophia move around with the biggest smile on her face. There were a million things I needed to be doing, but I couldn't have made myself move from that spot if I'd wanted to. I was enthralled.

She was so happy, so excited to be performing, and that radiated from her as she danced. Sophia was absolutely adorable in her dark plum-colored leotard and pale pink tutu, and whether or not she landed each step correctly didn't matter. She owned that stage with personality alone, causing my chest to swell with pride and love, because I really and truly loved that little girl like crazy. It was impossible not to. I was so damn proud of her.

I looked away from her and scanned the audience again, and when my eyes finally landed on Quinn my heart picked up the pace, beating frantically against my ribs. The look of his face was sheer awe as he watched his little girl. I hadn't been lying when I said it was a turn on watching him with his daughter, but seeing that expression? Well, I fell deeper in love with him.

I was crazy about Quinn and Sophia Mallick. I just hoped the feeling was mutual.

ALL THE STUDENTS — right along with myself, Kyle, and Samantha — were riding the high of another amazing Winter Showcase. I was so proud of each and every one of them. They'd finished the final number, where we included every class at every age level, and before the curtain dropped, the kids dragged Kyle, Samantha, and me onto the stage, giving each of us a massive bouquet of flowers. We all took a bow as the crowd cheered and whistled.

The lights finally came up, and the crowd in the auditorium was slowly beginning to thin out as everyone rushed backstage to grab their stuff and come back out to meet up with their families. I'd shaken hands with several of the parents, reminded them of the lock-in we were doing at the school the next day to celebrate, when my folks came up to stand next to me.

"Such a good show, honey," Mom exclaimed happily.

Dad looped his arm around her shoulder in a show of support, but I understood it was more his needing to rest on her than a show of affection. "Your kids are all so talented, Lilly Flower. You should be proud."

"I am," I answered just as Sophia's voice rang through the auditorium yelling my name in the way only Sophia could. I turned and instantly sucked in a deep breath at the way Quinn's eyes were eating me up, the green depths turning dark with want. I could say with certainty that the feeling was totally mutual. I'd never seen him in a suit before, but *damn* did he wear it well.

"Miss Lilly! Did I do good!?" Sophia came to a halt only after her arms wrapped around my legs. Quinn stopped two feet away, and I noticed he wasn't alone. His parents were standing right behind him, both looking happy to have seen their grand-daughter up on that stage.

"You did amazing, Little Miss." I smiled affectionately and leaned down to give her a hug. "And look," I poked her bun with the tip of my finger. "Your hair stayed in place perfectly."

She beamed proudly. "That's 'cause Daddy used a whole canna hairspray!"

I let a giggle loose as I looked at Quinn, but his eyes were darting back and forth between my parents, and he suddenly seemed to tense.

"I wanna be a sugarplum fairy again next year, Mrs. Lilly? Can I, please?"

From the corner of my eye I saw my mom and dad smile down at the adorable little girl. Yep, everyone who ever came into contact with Sophia was instantly smitten.

Sophia looked from me to my folks and asked, "Who's that?"

"These are my parents. Mom, Dad, this is Sophia, she's one of my best students." Sophia sucked in a breath, the compliment I'd just paid her making her glow. She loved hearing that just as much as I loved watching her reaction.

"You were a wonderful sugarplum fairy, sweetheart," my mom told her, making that glow so much brighter.

"Best I've ever seen," Dad added.

"Thank you," she whispered.

"Wonderful show, dear," Mrs. Mallick spoke up.

"Thanks." I smiled and offered up introductions between the adults. "Mr. and Mrs. Mallick, this is Will and Elizabeth Mathewson."

The foursome shook hands then broke apart, allowing me to continue. "Mom, Dad. This is Quinn, my—"

"Hi," Quinn interrupted, his hand shooting toward my dad. "I'm a friend of Lilly's."

Every muscle in my body grew tight. I did my best to school my features to hide the utter disappointment that was suddenly flowing through me, but judging by the quick glance my father gave me, I hadn't masked it in time. *A friend of Lilly's.* I wasn't sure what I wanted to do more, scream or cry. However, I couldn't do either in front of an audience.

The fact he'd cut me off hurt like hell, because not only did he not want anyone to know what was going on with us, but also he didn't trust me not to throw a label on whatever we were the first chance I got. It was as if he'd expected me to just spit out that he was my boyfriend right there in front of his daughter. It was just another reminder, slapping me in the face that he was nowhere near letting me close. It was like he'd allowed me to include myself in every part of his life *except* his heart. Some days I felt like an integral part of his world, then something like this would happen and put everything into painful perspective.

"Nice to meet you, Quinn," my mother replied politely. Dad followed suit, holding out his hand to shake Quinn's, but I could see the questions dancing in his eyes. Unfortunately, I couldn't give him those answers, especially when I didn't even have them myself.

"We were just talking about going to grab a bite to eat at that fancy new steak place that opened up just outside of town," Mr. Mallick stated. "Why don't the three of you join us?"

I was trying to form a quick excuse in my head to get us out of a big, cozy family dinner, when my father spoke up to say, "That's very kind of you to offer, but I'm afraid I'm not feeling my best. I think I should probably be getting home."

I spun around, concern for my dad overshadowing the fact that Quinn had managed to hurt my feelings yet again. I stepped close to his side, opposite my mom and whispered, "Are you okay?"

He smiled, but I could see the pain he was trying so hard to hide. "I'm fine, Lilly Flower, just tired."

I chanced a quick glance at my mother and saw she was just as worried as I was. It appeared my father was no longer on the upswing and had taken another turn downhill. I hated that he was suffering so much.

Mom linked her elbow through Dad's and gave his hand a gentle pat. "It's been a long day. I think we're both pretty worn out."

Compassion flittered across Quinn's face as he gave me a look, but I wasn't in the mood. He could take his pity and shove it, as far as I was concerned. I turned back to his parents and smiled as politely as I could. "It was so nice seeing you again. I'm going to walk them out. Thank you for coming out tonight."

Mr. Mallick's face was soft and kind as he reached out and gave my forearm a squeeze. "Of course, darling. Have a good night."

"You too." I leaned down, placing a quick kiss on Sophia's forehead before linking my arm with Dad's other one.

As we passed, I offered Quinn a glance and a nod before leading my parents from the auditorium. Once we reached the sidewalk Mom went ahead to pull the car around, not wanting my father to have to navigate the parking lot. I stayed with him, keeping a firm hold on his arm the whole time. I felt like I was getting slammed with heartbreak from both sides. One side was Quinn, the other was my father. And I felt ill-equipped to handle either. I wasn't sure how much pain one person could take before it all finally just became too much.

"Don't be too hard on him, baby girl," Dad muttered while we waited for the car.

I gave my father my eyes. "What are you talking about?"

"Your young man. He's struggling. It's written all over his face."

I let out a sigh of defeat and looked back out into the night. "I know, Daddy. But what's the point if he's content to just hold on to that struggle for the rest of his life?"

His arm tugged mine, calling my attention back to him. "You love him."

I nodded, feeling the tears well in my eyes. "I do."

"Then show him there's a light at the end of the tunnel."

My dad. God, I loved him so much. "I don't know if I have the power to make him see it."

He reached up and brushed my cheek with his thumb. Until he did that I hadn't realized a tear and broken free. "Don't sell yourself short, baby girl. Whether this works out between you two or not, never forget, there's someone out there worthy of everything you are. It may be him, or it may be someone else. But either way, the heartache will eventually dull and you'll meet someone who will show you just how special you are."

I grinned and gave a little laugh, resting my head on his shoulder. "My dad, the smartest man I know."

His lips brushed the top of my head as he said softly, "No, just a man lucky enough to have a woman show him how wonderful life could be. Then she graced me with a daughter who drove that point home."

Oh yeah. I loved my dad.

26

QUINN

THE MORE TIME I spent with Lilly, the more I grew to care about her. And the more I hated myself, because I just couldn't seem to stop hurting her. She was quickly starting to become a person who meant the absolute world to me. I was falling for her hard and fast, no matter how much I told myself I didn't want to. But I was such a goddamned coward that I was scared shitless when I woke up a few days ago and instantly wished she was next to me. That was the day I started slowly pulling away from her, despite my heart protesting.

I knew she sensed it. And when I called her a friend in front of our parents, I saw the devastation on her face. The smart move would have been to stay away, keep my distance to lessen the impact when my anxieties finally became too much for me to handle and I shut myself off permanently.

But I couldn't stay away.

I was a selfish bastard, but the idea of going to sleep that night after seeing her face was just something I couldn't take. That was why, after I dropped Sophia off at her sleepover, I found myself standing on the stoop of Lilly's apartment. I knocked and waited for what felt like an eternity for her to answer. The knot of tension in my gut coiled tighter with each passing second.

It wasn't until I heard the sound of the lock disengaging that I was finally able to take my first real breath.

Her eyes gave nothing away as she stood in the doorway, looking just as beautiful as ever. "What are you doing here?" she asked on a sigh. I hated that my behavior over the past few months had trained her to be skeptical. Deep down, I really did want to make her happy, I just couldn't seem get past all my hang ups to allow that to happen.

"I'm sorry," I blurted out.

Lilly's eyelids fell closed as she dropped her head and gave it a shake. When she finally looked back up at me, the hesitance that stared back at me from those warm amber eyes was almost too much to bear.

"You're always sorry, Quinn, and I'm really getting sick and tired of hearing your apologies."

I knew that one of these days I'd push her too far, but the thought that this could actually be that day sent a spike of desperation straight through my chest. I couldn't let her go. Not yet. Not now.

"Can I come in? Please, Lilly."

She didn't move from the doorway. Instead, she landed a well-placed blow by saying, "You know, I wasn't going to call you my boyfriend. I wouldn't do something like that in front of your family, and especially not in front of Sophia. I'd never intentionally confuse her like that."

I was such an asshole. "I know."

She crossed her arms over her chest, the picture of animosity as she continued to stare me down. "Then why'd you feel the need to cut me off like that? Like you were scared I was going to slip up and *actually* admit out loud that we're carrying on like more than friends when no one's watching."

Shame so strong it nearly choked me twisted inside me throat. "I-I don't know."

She let out a sardonic laugh that cut me right down to the bone. "Well, you don't need to worry, Quinn. Your dirty little secret is safe."

I took a step closer, crowding her against the doorframe. "You aren't a dirty little secret. You could *never* be that," I hissed. She couldn't. My problem wasn't that I was embarrassed of her, it was that I didn't want to let the real world into our little bubble. I didn't want reality to interrupt and ruin what we had.

"Bullshit! You've treated me like that from day one!" she snapped, anger flashing in her gorgeous eyes. "And the fucked up thing is that I've let you! I'm so stupid, so *pathetically* desperate for a goddamned *ounce* of your attention that I let you walk all over me! I keep making excuses because I actually *care* about you, that I've become one of those weak women that I've always despised."

I couldn't stand to hear her talk about herself like that. Self-loathing wasn't even a strong enough word to describe how miserable I felt at the idea that I'd made her feel so bad about herself.

"You aren't weak," I argued, reaching up and taking her face in my hands. "You aren't. And I hate myself for making you feel that way." My forehead dropped against hers and I squeezed my eyes closed. "I care about you, too, Lilly. So goddamn much it physically *hurts*, and I don't know what to do about it. I wish I could be normal for you. I wish I wasn't so fucking broken." Most of all, I wished I could be a man deserving of her.

I moved without thinking, needing to feel her, taste her, lose myself in her completely. Lilly's gasp of surprise when my lips hit hers spurred a longing deep within me. I used her parted lips to my advantage and plunged my tongue inside, craving her with a desperation that boarded on sheer insanity.

But that's how she made me feel.

Absolutely insane for her.

The fight fled from her, and her body melted into mine. I untangled my hands from her hair and lifted her into my arms, basking in the feel of her legs wrapping around my waist as I moved both of us into her apartment, kicking the door closed behind me.

Our lips stayed connected, devouring each other as I carried her through the living room and down the hall into her bedroom. I needed her more than I needed air.

I needed her goodness. I needed her light.

And it made me the most selfish bastard on the face of the earth, but I was going to take every single thing she had to offer.

Lilly

HE WAS DRIVING me out of my mind.

All of my sanity fled the moment Quinn touched me.

Deep down, I knew this was a mistake, that I was only asking for more heartache, but when he said he cared about me, the sincerity in his voice and the earnestness on his face were just too much to deny.

I knew he meant it, but I also knew that the chasm between us was too wide for me to breech on my own. Sex wouldn't solve any of the problems we had, but how do you turn away from a man you love with every fiber of your being?

I wanted to take his pain away, to heal him, fix what he thought was broken. And no matter how many times I told myself that wasn't possible, it never stopped me from trying.

My back hit the mattress and Quinn lifted up just long enough to rid us both of our clothes. His knees hit the bed and the air whooshed from my lungs at the sight of this beautiful man hovering over me. His weight came down on me. His lips crashed against mine in a brutal kiss that drove me wild.

My hands skated across his body, touching every inch of hot, bare flesh that I could reach, committing every valley and rivet of muscle to memory. But it wasn't enough. I needed to feel him inside of me.

I planted my feet into the mattress and lifted my hips seeking the connection I needed so badly.

His cock rested between our bodies, heavy and hard against my stomach, and when he shifted I prayed it was in order to bury himself deep. But he had other things in mind.

In the blink of an eye, he was on his back. I straddled his hips as he gripped my waist with both hands, holding me a few inches above him.

"Ride me. I want to watch you." His voice was husky as he delivered the command. I didn't need to be told twice. Reaching between us, I wrapped my fingers around his cock and lined him up with my entrance before sinking down oh-so-slowly, cherishing the way he stretched me, inch by glorious inch.

My head fell back on a deep moan when he bottomed out inside of me. My nails dug into the skin of his chest as I began to rock my hips back and forth, getting used to the fullness of having him so deep.

Quinn's hands twisted in my hair as I began to ride him, faster and faster with each stroke. He pulled until my head bent down, his gravelly voice demanding, "Look at me. Open your eyes, baby. Let me see you."

I did as he ordered, sucking in a gasp at what I saw reflecting back at me. His green eyes were dark with lust, but there was a warmth in them as he stared up at me in wonder that I felt in my chest.

"Quinn," I breathed, lost to the moment, to the feel of him.

The moment his name left my lips, he sat up, wrapping an arm around me tightly as he kissed me, long, deep, wet. It was as though he couldn't get enough of our connection, like he needed to touch every part of me.

"So good, baby. Always so fucking good. You're unbelievable."

I cried out as my walls began to tighten around him, my release just within reach. I squeezed my eyes shut and began to ride him faster, chasing after that euphoria. "I'm close."

"I know, baby. I feel you. Eyes on me when you come. Give it to me, Lilly." His hips began to lift off the bed, meeting me thrust for thrust, driving himself as deep as he could possibly go.

I opened my eyes and stared straight into his green depths as I drove myself up and down on his thick cock. Something about this was different. Making love with Quinn was always amazing, but there was an intensity to it this time I'd never felt before. His gaze never wavered as he pushed me closer to the edge. It was so consuming that tears began to burn the backs of my eyes as I dove headfirst into the most extraordinary release I'd ever experienced. It wasn't just physical. I felt it on every emotional level possible.

A tear broke free as I cried out his name. He caught it with his lips, and I felt that action down to my soul. His mouth moved to mine just as his cock twitched and he groaned from deep within his throat as he began pouring himself inside of me.

We took our time coming down, and several minutes later, he lifted me off him, softly placing me on the bed before going to the bathroom to get a wet rag to clean me with. He turned out the lights and pulled the covers from beneath me, climbed back in beside me and wrapped me in his embrace.

The last thing I remember before sleep took over was whispering into the dark, "I love you."

Then I was out.

QUINN

. . .

"I LOVE YOU."

Those three beautiful words plunged into my chest like a knife, leaving a searing pain in their wake so excruciating I could barely breathe.

Because I felt the same way.

And I knew I'd just ruined everything. I'd betrayed Addison's memory. I'd betrayed Lilly's trust. I could never be the man to give her everything she deserved. She deserved more than a man with a broken soul.

Actions had consequences. And because of my selfishness we were both going to pay the devastating price.

I had no one to blame but myself.

27

LILLY

I WOKE WITH a shiver as a chill worked its way over me, causing goosebumps to break out across my skin.

The bedroom was still bathed in darkness behind my eyelids, but I could hear the distinct sound of someone moving around. Reaching across the bed, I searched for Quinn's warm body only to come up empty. My eyes popped open at the sound of rustling fabric, and I could just make out Quinn's silhouette in the faint moonlight. Sitting up, I flicked on the bedside lamp flooding the room with soft golden light.

Quinn froze with his jeans halfway up his thighs.

"What are you doing?"

At my question, he came out of his motionless state and finished with his pants, zipping and buttoning before bending back down to snatch his sweater off the floor.

His voice was flat as he replied, "I need to go."

Dread coiled in my belly as I turned to look at the clock. "It's two in the morning, Quinn. Sophia's at a sleepover. Why don't you come back to bed?" I asked, fearing his response. It was like I'd developed a sixth sense when it came to this contrary man. He was a walking, talking contradiction. In the very back of my

209

mind, I finally heard the whispered sound of the other shoe dropping.

He was suddenly devoid of all the emotion that had been bleeding from him just hours before. "I can't. I shouldn't have come here. This was a mistake."

My stomach plummeted. My heart sank. But the one thing I felt above all else was white-hot fury. He was not going to do this to me again.

"Are you fucking kidding me?" I seethed, jumping from the bed and snatching my robe off the back of my bedroom door, using the thin silky fabric as a shield around myself.

His movements were jerky as he yanked his arms through the sleeves of his shirt and pulled it over his head, leaving his hair in disarray.

"I can't do this anymore, Lilly," he sighed, his large frame slumping in defeat. "I can't be the man you deserve. I don't have it in me to give what you want. If you'd have just been happy with the way things were—"

"Oh, I know you're not blaming *me* right now," I cut in, crossing my arms over my chest in order to hold myself together.

He grabbed the back of his neck and turned away from me. "No, I'm not blaming you. This all just got so… goddamned complicated! I don't know what the fuck I'm doing, Lilly. I keep hurting you no matter how hard I try not to."

"Then stop doing it!" I cried, blinking rapidly against the tears that wanted to fall.

"It's not that easy," he stated with a heavy frown.

"Yes, Quinn. It is. I know what happened tonight was intense and scary," I said, pointing toward the bed where he'd made love to me only a handful of hours before. "It was the same for me. But I *saw* it in your eyes. You felt the difference just like I did."

He held my gaze, his lips in a firm, hard line. He couldn't argue, he knew I was right. I closed the gap between us, balling his sweater in my fists. "I love you," I whispered.

"Stop."

"And I know you love me, too. But you're too fucking terrified to admit it." I continued when I got nothing but more silence. "But if you'd just let me help, let me *be here* for you, you'd see how great this could be."

His fingers wrapped around my wrists, pulling my hands away as he took a step back. "You deserve someone better than me."

"I deserve to be with to be with the man I love!" I fought back.

He broke eye contact and studied the ground at his feet for several seconds before saying, "Look, I'm sorry—"

I lost my mind. "Stop saying that!" I yelled at the top of my lungs. "Jesus Christ, Quinn! Do you get off on ripping me apart? Is that what this is? Some sick fucking fantasy where you see how many pieces you can cut from me before there's nothing left?"

"Of course not!"

I ran my fingers through my hair and balled it in my fists. I was teetering dangerously close to the edge of insanity, and it was all his fault. He just kept hurting me over and over. And I kept fucking letting him!

"So this is it." It wasn't a question. I didn't need to ask. Despite what my actions would lead most people to believe, I wasn't stupid, I knew what he was doing. "You're just going to walk away, *again*."

His expression grew devastated as he whispered, "I wish it could be different."

I laughed without an ounce of humor. "And I wish I wasn't in love with such a coward. Looks like neither of us gets what we want."

I stood stiff as a board as he picked up his socks and shoes, tucking them under his arm before giving me one last brief glimpse before he turned for the bedroom door. But I couldn't leave it like that. I had one last thing to say.

"I hope your misery keeps you warm at night." He paused as I continued. "Because I'm so done with this shit. You walk out that door, you don't look back. I won't be your doormat anymore, Quinn. If you'd rather be a pathetic shell of a man for the rest of your life, have at it. I'm done letting you walk all over me."

His head dropped down, and his shoulders rose and fell with a deep breath. "I'm so sorry."

It was too late. I didn't care. "So am I, more than you could possibly know. I'm sorry I ever opened my heart to you. Now get the fuck out."

The echo of my front door opening and closing put the final nail in the coffin that was our relationship.

I didn't sleep for the rest of the night. I spent the next several hours curled up on my couch, staring out the window at nothing. And as the sun finally began to rise over my sleepy mountain town, I picked up my phone and scrolled through my contacts.

As soon as Eliza's groggy voice came through the line, I broke down into tears. Once I was finally able to speak again, I gave her the whole truth about every depressing, heartbreaking thing that had been going on in my life, pouring out every single detail of my time with Quinn. I sobbed, I cussed, I yelled. And she listened to everything I had to say, once again, giving me exactly what I needed.

Even from over five hundred miles away.

28

LILLY

"OH, SWEETIE. WE'VE got to find a way to turn that frown upside down."

I looked up from tracing random patterns on the scarred wooden top of my desk and offered Kyle a pathetic excuse for a smile. He scowled in return. "That's not going to cut it, beautiful."

"Sorry," I offered. I felt bad, honestly. I'd been a pain to be around for the past several weeks. Honestly, I was shocked that Kyle and Samantha hadn't gotten tired of my doom and gloom demeanor yet and kicked me out of my own studio. I was seriously bringing the morale of the place down. Hell, I'd spent Christmas and New Year's moping around my parents' house like someone had just kicked my puppy. They watched on with equal concern, but neither of them pushed, giving me space to come to them if I needed it.

Eventually, on New Year's Day I sat down with my father and told the story once more for him as Mom flittered around the kitchen cooking our traditional New Year's dinner. He offered me a steady shoulder, but kept his opinions of Quinn to himself, telling me he'd said all he needed to say the night of the Winter Showcase; that I was a grownup who was going to travel my own paths, but at the end of the day he'd be there for me no matter what.

"I've just got a lot on my mind," I said to Kyle.

He walked through the doorway and plopped down in the torn leather chair across from my desk. "I'd say. You've got about six feet, three inches, and 22o pound of muscular man on your mind. Yeah, babe. That's a lot."

I rolled my eyes to the ceiling and sat back in exasperation. "What's wrong with me, Kyle? It's been a month. Why am I still hung up on a guy who never really wanted me in the first place?"

His eyes grew sympathetic as he studied me. I was *not* going to cry. I wasn't! I'd cried more than any sane human being thought possible these past few months. I couldn't risk another tear. I'd more than likely die of dehydration.

"Honey bun, that's easy. It's because you love him."

I dropped my head into my hands with a groan. "I do. Damn it. It's so easy to fall *into* love, but fucking impossible to fall out. It's not fair, Kyle!"

"If it's any consolation, he does want you."

I snorted at that. "You're wrong."

Sitting forward in the chair, he propped his elbows on his knees and clasped his hands together. "I'm not. That man was crazy about you, but he's broken, Lil. Undeniably so. I've never seen a man more shattered before, and that's really saying something, seeing as I'm a gay man who was raised in a strict Southern Baptist household. Talk about being shattered."

"I just…" I pulled a deep breath in through my nose and let it out on a heavy, heart-sick sigh. "I wanted to help him. Every time I got close enough to help fix things he'd push me away."

"Oh, sweetheart." His tone was so soft, so full of sympathy that my eyes began to burn. "You can't fix a man like that."

One lone tear broke free and slid down my cheek. Sniffling, I batted it away and looked over at Kyle angrily. "So, what? He's just supposed to walk around living half a life until the day he dies? How is that fair, Kyle? Explain that to me."

Standing from the chair, he made his way around the desk and squatted down so he could wrap his arms around me. "I didn't say that," he whispered. "What I mean is, you can't fix a man like that. But you *can* try to be what he needs in order to make him want to fix himself."

The heaviness of my emotions was too much to bear at the moment, the weight of everything sat on me like bricks. I needed to lighten the tension, so pulling out of Kyle's arms, I gave a small laugh and asked, "So you're like a gay Gandhi now?"

Being a good enough friend to know exactly what I was doing, he gave me the out I was in desperate need of and teased back. "Don't hate on my mad intellectual skills."

I let out a watery laugh and stood up, wrapping my arms around Kyle's trim waist and resting my head on his chest as he returned my hug. Kyle really gave the *best* hugs. "Thanks."

"Anything, honey bun. You know that."

We pulled apart, Kyle heading for the door as I set about locking up the studio for the night. My cellphone rang just as I hit the back stairs to my apartment.

"Hey Mom, what's up?"

"Sweetheart."

Her voice cracked on that one word, the tears so evident in her voice that every fiber in my body froze, my blood running cold.

The hairs on my arm stood on end as I asked the question I dreaded the answer to. "Mom? What's wrong?"

"Honey, I need... I need you to come home. Your father..."

"No," I shook my head frantically as uncontrollable tears broke free. "No. No!"

"I'm so sorry," she said on a pained whisper. "I'm so, so sorry sweetheart."

"Daddy…" I dropped to my knees and sobbed through the line as my heart broke in two.

All it took was one phone call; that was it. One single phone call for my entire world to…

Just stop.

And the worst part was, the one person I wanted to seek comfort in was still so out of reach.

29

QUINN

*J*COULDN'T REMEMBER the last time I'd ever been so mentally and physically exhausted. The warehouse on the outskirts of town had been abandoned for years, and the county had been considering tearing it down for a while now, but with all the junk that had accumulated inside over the years, the goddamned place had gone up like a match.

It had been fully engulfed by the time we got there, and there was no chance any of us were getting inside. Cap had called for a defensive attack as soon as we got on scene, so we spent hours trying to keep it contained so it wouldn't spread to the other buildings around it.

By the time we put the son of a bitch out and got back to the station, it was shift change. We cleaned and restocked the engine and restacked the hose before heading for the showers, and when I finally made it to my truck, I was dead on my feet. I was thankful my mom was getting Sophia to school this morning, because I couldn't imagine anything but going home and collapsing face down in my bed and passing out for the next several hours.

Tossing my duffle bag into the passenger seat, I climbed in, slammed the door, and started the engine, ready to get home. Just as I pulled out of the parking lot, my phone pinged from inside my duffle. Keeping my eyes on the road, I unzipped the bag with one hand and fished around inside. The ping was an alert, letting me know I had a missed call.

I had expected the calls to be from my mom or Sophia, but something in my gut tightened at the sight of that little number 2 next to Lilly's name. We'd barely spoken five words to each other in the month that had passed since I ended things, so seeing that she had called *twice* in the span of just a few hours set me on edge. As I swiped my screen and thumbed to her contacts, I couldn't shake the feeling that something was wrong.

Her phone rang one time before going straight to voicemail and that knot in my stomach began to sour. I hung up and hit redial three more times to the exact same result. Suddenly, the idea of sleep no longer held any appeal. I needed to know where Lilly was, that she was safe.

Turning my truck in the opposite direction of my house, I headed for Main, going faster than the allotted speed limit. As soon as Lilly's dance school came into view, I whipped my truck into the first available space and jumped from the cab as soon as I pulled the key from the ignition.

The blinds were lifted, letting me know the school was open, but the main studio was empty. I shoved through the glass doors at a near run, my eyes scanning over every square inch of the lobby as a startled Kyle looked at me like I'd just grown a second head. "Quinn? Where's the fire, man?"

"Where is she?"

His head cocked to the side as his forehead creased in confusion. The tension in my gut tightened at his silence. "What?"

"Lilly," I snapped, quickly losing patience. "She called me but I was at work..." I dragged my hands through my hair as that feeling of helplessness grew. I knew something wasn't right. "I missed the calls. I tried calling her back this morning, but it's going straight to voicemail. Is she okay? Did something happen?"

A wave of sadness washed over Kyle's face. "She's not here, Quinn. She's in Jackson Hole." At that, my heart stopped, because I knew. "Her father passed away last night."

"Shit," I hissed as I began to pace. Her father had died, the one thing she'd feared for so long had finally happened... and she'd reached out to *me*. And I hadn't been there for her. "Thanks," I muttered quickly, as I turned and bolted out the door. As soon as I got into my truck, I pulled my phone from the cup holder and hit call on the number.

"Quinn?"

"Mom, I need a favor," I spoke quickly as I headed down Main back toward my house. "Do you think you could keep Sophia for a few more days? There's somewhere I need to be."

LILLY

IT WAS LIKE I was living in some sort of haze. Everyone around me was moving and talking, but I could barely make out the shapes and sounds over my own grief. My dad should have been there. He should have been playing host to all the extended family that was currently filling up my parents' house. He was always so good at making everyone feel welcome.

But he wasn't there. And the house wasn't filled with family because they wanted to come for a visit. They were there to help us grieve and say goodbye to the best man I'd ever known.

I wasn't ready.

I didn't want to say goodbye yet. I didn't want to believe he was really gone, that he slipped away in his sleep peacefully. I wanted to climb the stairs and lock myself in my old bedroom so

I could curl up on the bed and cry until there weren't any tears left.

But I couldn't do that. My mother needed me to be the strong one. She'd lost the love of her life, and although she was putting on a brave face, I could see just how much she was hurting. It shone in her eyes like a spotlight. If she crumbled, I needed to be there to pick her back up and hold her together. So I couldn't breakdown. Not yet.

I'd called Eliza on my way to Jackson Hole the night before. She was on her way from Denver and I was thankful for that, even though I'd told her it wasn't necessary. She was pregnant and her husband was in the middle of an undefeated season. She had responsibilities and a life of her own that she needed to handle there, but she refused to hear it. She'd booked a flight and was already on her way from the airport. I couldn't wait to see her, despite the circumstances. She was just the person I needed with me during this time. While I was holding my mother up, Eliza would be at my side, doing the same for me, and even though it made me feel like a burden, I really needed that right now.

"How are you doing, dear?"

I looked from the window, where I'd been standing for the past half hour, looking out at the snow-covered mountains on the horizon. Offering up a small smile that didn't quite reach my eyes, I gave Aunt Jenny the standard response I'd been giving for the past four hours.

"I'm okay. Sad, but okay."

A total lie, but they didn't really need to hear the truth, did they? Everyone was already sad enough.

"Your father was a wonderful man. He will be missed," she whispered as her eyes grew misty, oblivious to the fact I was barely holding myself together. Her intentions were good, it just wasn't the right time for me.

"He was," I somehow managed past the lump in my throat.

"Thank you." Blessedly, my cell phone began ringing in my back pocket at that second, and I used the distraction to end the conversation with my well-meaning aunt. "Excuse me," I started. "I should take this. It's probably Eliza."

I quickly worked my way through the formal living room at the back of the house to the quiet family room at the front before pulling my phone from my pocket. At the sight of Quinn's name on the screen, my heart did something I hadn't even thought possible and cracked *even more*. It was like there was no limit to the amount of suffering one's heart could take.

I sent the call to voicemail just like I had all the others I'd been getting since early this morning. Only this time, once it stopped ringing, I went into my contacts and blocked his number. I'd made a huge mistake last night, calling him. Apparently grief made me do stupid things, because when I got the call from my mother, he'd been the first person I thought of, the first person I called, the first person I wanted with me as my world came to a screeching, crashing halt.

But he didn't answer.

We'd been over for a month, and in that time the only conversations we'd had were about Sophia's dance classes. I'd told him I loved him and he had walked out on me, ending everything in the blink of an eye. Why I thought he could possibly be my rock during the hard times was a mystery. I wasn't going to make the same mistake twice. Quinn made it clear he wanted me out of his life, so I was out.

Sitting on the squashy, overstuffed sectional that took up most of the space in the cozy family room, I lay my head back and curled my legs underneath me, letting the heat from the fire in the fireplace try and penetrate the chill I'd been feeling since I got the phone call the night before.

I tuned out the sounds and voices coming from the back of the house and let my mind wander as I closed my eyes. I just needed a little space for a bit, then I'd go back in to Mom and make sure she was okay.

At some point I must have dozed off, because the sound of the doorbell ringing jolted me awake. I blinked the sleep from my eyes just as the person on the other side of the door began to knock softly. "I got it," I called out, not wanting my mother to have to bother with any more neighbors dropping off casserole dishes.

Placing my hand on the doorknob, I twisted and pulled it opened, prepared to give the well-wisher a smile and move them on, but when my eyes lifted and connected with those familiar sea-green eyes everything in me froze.

"Lilly."

Just when I thought my life couldn't possibly get any worse. The sound of his deep, raspy voice caused every nerve ending in my body to fire. "Quinn." My voice came out just as flat and emotionless as I was feeling. The sight of him was too much. Everything inside of me went numb. It was as though my body shut down as a countermeasure to prevent me from completely losing it, shutting out all emotion. "What are you doing here?"

"I'm so sorry." His face was full of sympathy as he took a step closer. I backed up, but kept my fingers wrapped around the edge of the solid wood door, needing something to hold on to, something that I could place between us with a flick of the wrist. "I didn't see your calls until this morning. There was a fire last night and I—"

I held up my hand to stop him. I didn't doubt he was telling the truth. If I were honest, I hadn't even considered that he was at work when I'd called. But that didn't change anything.

"It doesn't matter. I shouldn't have called you."

His brow furrowed and the frustration flickered in his gaze. "Of course you should have. Your father passed and you were all alone. If I could have, I would have been there for you."

Some of the pain dwindled as anger began to take its place.

"Yeah, well it's not really your place to be there for me, now is it?" I snapped. "I appreciate you coming out here, but now's really not a good time."

I moved to shut the door, but his big, booted foot shot out and stopped it. His voice went soft, so full of pity when he said, "Lilly," that the numbness I had shielded myself with cracked and began to spider like a windshield after being hit by a rock until it finally just gave way. *Oh no. Oh no, no, no.* I was *not* going to cry in front of him. I wasn't! But as I stood there, blinking rapidly and sniffling at the burning in my nose, I knew I was about to lose my battle. And when he reached out and pulled me into his strong arms, the dam burst. "Shhh," he soothed. "It's okay."

As one arm wrapped around my waist, holding me firmly to him, his other hand trailed through my hair. "I've got you," he whispered against the crown of my head. "I'm here, I've got you."

I sobbed into the cotton of his sweater, so overwrought I couldn't find it in me to enjoy his clean, masculine scent. A person could only handle so much heartache until they were swept under the weight of it. And as he offered me his strength and comfort, I let it out and allowed the current to temporarily drag me down.

30

QUINN

SHE LET ME hold her.

Only for a few minutes as her grief overcame her, but it was still a start.

Placing her hands on my chest, she pushed away and wiped the tears from her red-rimmed eyes before inhaling deeply through her nose. "I'm okay now," she spoke, her voice hoarse from crying. "Thanks."

Unable to help myself, I reached out to tuck a wayward strand of hair behind her ear, only to have her jerk her head back out of my reach. "I'm not going anywhere," I told her, tucking my hands into my pockets so I wouldn't feel tempted to reach out again. "I know what it's like to lose someone you love." At the mention of Addy something indecipherable flitted across her face, but it disappeared before I could place it. "You need people around you who care right now. I'm going to be one of those people, Lilly. Because despite what's happened between us, I *do* care about you."

She muttered something under her breath that sounded suspiciously like *yeah, just not enough,* but before I could press her further, another voice from the hallway interrupted.

"Lilly? Is someone at the door?"

We both turned in time to see her mother heading our way. I'd only met her parents once, after the Winter Showcase, and it hadn't been a very good first impression on my part. I'd been struggling with my growing feelings for Lilly, and meeting her parents was too much for me to handle at the time. I'd reverted back to what was familiar to me and acted like a dick.

"Mom." Lilly took a big step back from me as she offered a stilted introduction. "You remember Quinn from the Showcase. He just stopped by to offer his condolences."

I gave her a quick look, understanding exactly what she was up to, it spoke volumes, stating that she wasn't getting rid of me that easily. Extending my hand for her to shake, I squeezed gently and offered, "Mrs. Mathewson. I'm so sorry for your loss."

"Thank you." She smiled politely while her tired eyes shown with the tears she was battling. "And please call me Elizabeth. It was nice of you to come. Would you like to come in? We have plenty of food if you're hungry. The neighbors have been quite generous."

"I wouldn't want to impose—"

"Nonsense." She waved me off. "You wouldn't be imposing at all. The house is full of people anyway, and there's no way I'll ever be able to eat everything in the kitchen. You'd be doing me a favor. I can't let you drive back to Pembrooke on an empty stomach."

I dropped Elizabeth's hand and gave Lilly side-eyes as I said, "I'm actually not going back for a few days. My folks are watching my daughter for me. I rented a room at the Holiday Inn a few miles away. I wanted to be here for Lilly if she needed me."

From the corner of my eye, I could see Lilly's face growing red as Elizabeth pulled in a breath and clasped her hands in front of her. "Oh how sweet! Isn't that sweet, honey?"

Lilly looked like she'd just bitten into a lemon while she ground out, "Yeah. So sweet." It was an inappropriate thought, considering the circumstances, but I couldn't help but want to gloat, knowing I'd just won that round.

"You should stay here," Elizabeth continued. "We have plenty of room. No reason for you to have to pay for a hotel."

"Mom," Lilly cut in. "I'm sure Quinn would feel more comfortable in his own space." She shot me a quick, murderous glare and the knot in my stomach unfurled a bit, seeing that familiar fire in her eyes after how blank they were when I'd first arrived.

"I insist!" Elizabeth kindly patted my shoulder. "Go get your bags, Quinn. Lilly can show you to the guestroom upstairs."

"B-but…" she sputtered as I tried to keep from grinning triumphantly. "What about Eliza? That was supposed to be her room. Where's she supposed to sleep?"

"She can sleep with you, honey. It'll be just like old times when you were kids."

Another wave of sorrow washed over Lilly's face, and I understood exactly what she was thinking. Just like old times, with the exception of one very important person being present. "I'll just go get my stuff," I said in an attempt to pull her from her sad memories.

"I'll help," she offered softly before leading me out the front door.

Once we got outside, I noticed all she had to ward off the cold in the air was a cardigan that she had pulled closed tightly around her. "You shouldn't be out here without a jacket," I started, as I followed her to my truck in the driveway. "It's supposed to start snowing any time now."

"Why are you here?" she asked, ignoring what I just said. "Seriously, Quinn. Don't you think I'm struggling enough already? You have to go and make it harder after—" Her voice broke as another bout of grief worked to consume her. I tried to go to her, but she took a step away, holding one hand out to stop me. In that moment I felt helpless, and it was a feeling I absolutely hated. She was struggling and there was nothing I could do to help her through it. She wouldn't let me.

"I can't do this with you right now," she whispered, wrapping her arms around her waist as if holding herself together. "I need to be here for my mom. I can't afford to lose it."

"And what about you?" I asked, my voice hard. "Who's supposed to be here for you? You can't take all the weight for your mother and not mourn yourself. It's not healthy."

"You think I don't know that?!" she shouted. I could see those whiskey-colored eyes of hers shining with tears before she squeezed them closed and ran both her hands through her hair in agitation. "I can't…" She swallowed convulsively. "I can't do this. I don't know how to do this, Quinn. Everything hurts. I miss my dad. I want him back. I want him to come back, but he's never going to." She sobbed. "And then you show up, and it just hurts to look at you. I can't handle all of this. I need to be strong for Mom, but I feel like I'm drowning!"

I couldn't stay away from her any longer. The distance between us when she was so heartbroken gutted me. Closing the space in two short strides, I wrapped her in my arms and pressed my face against the top of her head.

"I'm sorry," I whispered. "I'm so goddamned sorry. I wish everything could be different. I wish you weren't suffering, but please, please let me be here for you. You need someone who's looking out for you while you look out for your mom. I know you don't want that person to be me, and I know I hurt you, but please let me do this. I can't stand the thought of you dealing with all this shit on your own."

"I have Eliza—" she started to argue, but I broke in before she could finish pushing me away.

"And you'll have me too. Please, Lilly," I begged.

After a few seconds, she sniffled; the muscles in her body loosened and I knew it was time to let her go. She wouldn't allow me to hold her any longer. Dropping my arms, I moved to my truck and grabbed my bag from the back seat.

"You can stay," she said, her voice flat. "You're here, and my mom invited you, so you can stay. You're right. I need all the help I can get to make it through the next few days." I breathed a sigh of relief, but it was short-lived as she continued. "But nothing's changed. You're still the guy who broke my heart a month ago. We aren't friends, Quinn. You're here because I need someone, but that's it. Once we get back to Pembrooke, things go back to the way they've been. Don't try and be a part of my life. Don't try and be my friend. If you can't do that, then you should leave now. Understand?"

It killed me that I couldn't protest, because she was right. Nothing had changed. She'd told me she loved me, and in return, I'd ended our relationship. I still couldn't give her what she needed, what she deserved. I'd had that once already and destroyed it. I didn't deserve it again. The guilt was still there, eating away at my insides, leaving me empty. No matter how much I wanted Lilly, how much she meant to me, I couldn't give her that.

"I understand." I nodded and hooked the strap of my bag over my shoulder, and if it was even possible, her expression grew even sadder. As I followed her up the path to the front door, I couldn't help but think that me being here was only making everything worse on her.

But I couldn't make myself stay away.

To SAY LILLY wasn't coping would have been an understatement. I'd kept a close eye on her the past two days, always at the distance she kept me at. She watched her mother like a hawk, so much so that she was able to anticipate Elizabeth's needs before the words were even spoken. She cleaned, she played gracious hostess to all of her family, and held her mother whenever things got too hard and the poor woman couldn't hold back the tears. Eliza and I accompanied the two of them as they went to make the funeral arrangements, and even then, Lilly put on a brave face, only shedding a handful of tears as she talked to the funeral director.

She was carrying the weight of her own loss *and* everyone else's on her own shoulders, trying her best to take the burden off of an entire family. I kept my mouth closed, but with every minute that ticked by, my worry for her continued to grow. If she kept up at the rate she was going, there was no doubt in my mind that she would eventually have a meltdown.

I knew by the sadness and concern in Eliza's eyes that she saw it too, and felt just as helpless as I did. "She's going to lose it," she whispered to me at one point yesterday.

"Yeah," was all I could say in response.

"I'm afraid she'll do it once I'm back in Denver, that I won't be here to help her."

My gaze traveled down to where her hand rested on the noticeable swell of her belly. "I know she's your best friend, but you can't take on too much stress," I warned, tipping my chin at her baby bump. "Not with that little one cooking inside there."

Eliza smiled and turned her attention from Lilly to me, and my head jerked back in shock at what she said next. "I don't like you very much right now." It wasn't the words that threw me off as much as the tone of her voice. She sounded downright conversational as she told me she didn't like me, not the slightest bit angry. Women—especially pregnant ones—needed to come with a goddamn manual. "I know what was going on with you two," she admitted. "It took a hell of a lot of pushing, but I finally got her to tell me, and I think you're a real asshole."

"I am," I replied, feeling the weight of that admission on my chest. I hated that I hurt Lilly, that I couldn't be the man she deserved. And in the month since I'd ended it, I went to bed most nights wishing things could have been different.

Turning her body in my direction, giving me her full attention, the lightness in Eliza's tone disappeared. "You hurt her, in a way I've never seen Lilly hurt before. And now, when she's struggling with the most painful thing she's ever dealt with, you're standing right here. Why?"

"I..." Taken back by her question, I had to stop and think about my answer, and despite how pathetic it was, the only reply I could come up with was, "I couldn't *not* be here. As soon as I found out, I just got in my truck and started driving."

She nodded like she understood completely. "Well, I might not like you, but I appreciate you looking out for my best friend."

"You're welcome."

Her voice dropped to a low whisper as she added, "But when this is over, you need to leave her alone." At that, I stopped breathing. "You've already made it clear that the two of you aren't going anywhere, so let her go. She's been through enough. She survived you once, but with everything that's happened..." She gave a small wave to encompass Elizabeth's living room and all the people in it. "...don't make her try and survive you a second time. Just... leave her alone."

I knew she was right. I knew that the selfless thing to do would have been to keep my distance and let Lilly move on. There was only one problem.

I wasn't sure that I could.

31

QUINN

THE SERVICE HADN'T officially started yet, so I stood in the chapel as a few family members and close friends milled about, waiting for the doors to open. I kept my gaze firmly on Lilly as she stood at the front of the vestibule, her focus centered on the blown-up pictures of her father that sat on easels between multiple large sprays of flowers. She hadn't moved for several minutes, hadn't said more than a handful of words since waking up that morning.

I felt helpless, wanting nothing more than to take her pain away, but knowing it wasn't my place. I'd given up that right when I ruined us.

"Sweetheart." I turned my head at the sound of my mother's voice and was surprised to see her walking up the aisle, hand-in-hand with Sophia.

"Mom? What are you two doing here?"

She stopped next to me and placed a kiss on my cheek at the same time Sophia wrapped her arms around my waist in a brief, but tight hug. "Soph wanted to come and make sure Ms. Lilly was all right. She wouldn't take no for an answer."

I ruffled my daughter's hair, noticing for the first time that she was quiet, not her usual hyper self. She looked sad as her eyes traveled to where Lilly stood. "Angel, I'm not sure if now's a really good time."

Her sparkling blue eyes came back to me. "Please, Daddy. She's prolly really sad right now. I can make her feel better. I promise I can."

I opened my mouth to argue, even though my daughter's determination warmed my heart, but Mom's hand on my arm stopped me. "Just let her have a few minutes," she said quietly. I nodded and we followed after Sophia, stopping a few feet back as she reached up and gave Lilly's hand a small tug.

"Hi, Ms. Lilly."

Lilly's smile was forced, but she still bent and hugged her. "Well, hey there, Little Miss."

My daughter spoke then. "I'm really sorry about your daddy."

"Thank you. That means a lot to me."

"You know that song you sang to me to chase away my bad dreams?" Lilly's body went visibly stiff as she nodded, and the urge to get to her side and offer comfort shot threw me, but Mom linked her arm through mine and held me back. "Do you... do you think it would work to chase the sad away, too?" Sophia asked, and that one simple question slayed me, slicing to the very core.

Lilly's voice was rough with emotion as she answered, "I don't know, honey."

"Well, Meemaw downloaded it for me so I could learn all the words. I'm really good at it now. Do you maybe want me to sing it to you to see if it helps?"

I heard a soft inhale of breath to my right and turned my head to see Lilly's mom standing there, watching with tears streaming down her cheeks as Eliza held on to her.

I looked back just as Lilly crouched low, resting on her knees in front of Sophia. "I'd like that very much," she whispered. Then Sophia's little voice filled the room as she began to sing "Landslide." Wet hit my eyes just as Lilly's voice joined in on the second chorus. What I was witnessing was so beautiful, so raw. I'd never seen anything like it in my life.

When they finally finished the song, Lilly moved in and held my daughter in the tightest embrace. Sophia just stood there, returning the hug like she knew exactly what Lilly needed in that very moment. It was almost too much to witness. I had to turn away, and when I did, my gaze landed on Elizabeth once again.

Through her tears she smiled and mouthed *thank you*. And once again, I was cut to my core.

LILLY

I COULDN'T SEE the purpose of funerals.

It wasn't that I didn't understand allowing people their chance to grieve the loss of someone they cared about, but if I had it my way, there would be a separate service for family, and another for friends, co-workers, and the like. That way they'd have a chance to say their final good-byes without the immediate family having to deal with countless people saying such banal things as 'I'm sorry for your loss.' Yeah, not as sorry as I am. Or 'Time heals all wounds.' Well can you find me a fucking time machine so I can shoot myself to the point in time where the crushing weight in my chest doesn't hurt so goddamned much? Then, my personal favorite, 'He's in a better place.' I lost count of how many times I wanted to shout in someone's face, asking, "Yeah? How the fuck would you know? You been there?"

Surprisingly enough, Quinn had stayed true to his word. He hadn't left my side the entire day. I might have been walking around in a constant fog, but at least I had him and Eliza to guide my way for me.

"If I have to paste on a fake smile for one more person, I might just lose my mind," I mumbled under my breath once there was a brief lull in the crowd. "My face actually hurts right now." Trying to ease the ache, I opened my mouth wide and worked my jaw around.

"You want us to get you out of here?" Eliza asked, her arm looped through mine as we stood near the front pews of the church. "We can sneak you through the side so you don't have to talk to anyone else. The service is over anyway."

She was right, the only reason we were still hanging around was so everyone in the church could offer their condolences. Since my father requested to be cremated and to have his ashes scattered in the mountains in a place he and my mother had already selected, there wouldn't be a graveside service.

Technically, I could leave if I wanted to, and I *really* wanted to, but as I looked down the length of the pew where my mother stood, talking to the group of people milling about, I knew I needed to stay, if for no other reason than to be there for her.

"I can't leave my mom," I stated, as I plastered another smile on my face when one of my parents' neighbors stepped up in front of me and took my hand.

"It's a sad, sad day. But he's in a better place."

Fuck off! I screamed in my head as my mouth replied, "Thank you, Mr. Whitman."

I'd been teetering on the edge of losing it the entire day, walking a fine rope that seemed to fray with every step I took, and Mr. Whitman's words—despite the well-meaning behind them—threatened to push me over. There suddenly wasn't enough air. I was suffocating, the walls beginning to close in around me, and no one appeared to notice. Well, almost no one.

"We're going," Quinn stated in a firm tone that left no room for argument.

"I can't—" I began to protest, even as a cold sweat broke out on my forehead and my body started to tremble. My heart was beating so hard I was scared it would break through my ribs.

He cut me off. "Eliza can stay with your mother for a bit, make sure she's okay, and explain to her where you've gone. You need fresh air. I'm taking you outside for a bit."

I wanted to cry in relief at the idea of stepping outside the confining room. Feeling just seconds from fainting, I didn't argue as Quinn took me by the elbow and led me from the sanctuary through a side door that led us out of the church completely. The typical frigid winter temperature of Wyoming came as a blessing, and once we got a yard or so away from the building, I bent in half, hands propped on my knees, and pulled the much needed air into my deflated lungs.

"Oh, God," I wheezed. "What the hell was that?"

Quinn's palm came down on my back and he began rubbing soothing circles. "Panic attack. Just slow down, try and control your breathing. It'll pass."

"*That's* what a panic attack feels like?" I asked exasperatedly. "Jesus! I felt like I was dying."

"It'll get better. I promise."

Once my heart rate returned to normal, and the spots in my vision cleared I was able to stand upright. "You've experienced these?" Even with everything that had happened between us, even though I still held a bitter resentment for him, I couldn't help but be concerned, because I wouldn't wish what I'd just suffered through on my worst enemy.

"Yeah. After the… accident." That was all he gave me, but I knew what accident he was talking about. He never spoke about his wife as far as I knew, but everyone in town knew the story of what had happened. A car accident took her life and left Quinn with a long recovery.

It was then that I realized just how much of a sacrifice he'd made for me by coming here, by staying with me the past few days. My voice was thick as I spoke around the painful lump in my throat. "I'm sorry."

He shrugged and stuffed his hands into the pockets of his slacks. "It's all right. Haven't had one in a while now."

"No, that's not what I meant." In all the time we'd spent together, we'd never discussed his wife, his marriage. Hell, even the topic of the wedding ring he still wore was off the table, so saying what I felt I had to at that moment was so much harder than it should have been. "It's selfish, really, but I'm only just now realizing how difficult all of this—" I pointed back at the church, "—must have been for you. And I'm sorry. Not just that you had to deal with a funeral and everything, but for your loss. You never talked about it, and I knew I couldn't truly understand what you went through. I know it's different, losing a father than it is losing a spouse, but I can appreciate how painful it is now. And I just…" I shrugged, feeling helpless. "I'm sorry. I know it's ironic saying that to you when I couldn't stand to hear it from everyone back there a few minutes ago, but it's how I feel."

He looked down at the dark, cracked asphalt of the church parking lot as he rocked back and forth on his heels. I didn't have to see his eyes to know the shutters had dropped back into place. It felt like an eternity, but couldn't have been more than a handful of seconds before he responded, "I don't want to talk about it," he stated with finality. "This… today, isn't about me, it's about you. Let's not discuss—"

"Don't," I snipped, unable to control my turbulent emotions. "I'm not trying to get you to open up, Quinn. It's like beating my head against a brick wall. I know trying to get you to talk to me is a lost cause, believe me," I added sarcastically, because I was mad. No, that wasn't right, I was *pissed*. The past few months had been full of darkness, sadness, and heartache. Quinn had given me a few brief glimpses of light during that time, only to snatch them away from me. Yeah, I was pissed, and standing in the middle of a church parking lot, after saying my final good-bye to my father, the best man I'd ever known, I snapped.

"You made it *perfectly* clear that I'm not enough to help you get past your loss, and I've accepted that. I'm not pushing you right now. Honestly, I've given up. You make trying to help you impossible. But I lost someone I loved with all of my heart today, and I know you've experienced the same thing, and for that I'm sorry. And I'm thankful that you pushed the pain aside long enough to be here for me when I needed someone. So this, right now, it's not me trying to understand what makes you tick. I'm just acknowledging what you've done for me."

"Lilly." When he took a step in my direction, I held my hand up to stop him.

"I'm cold. I should probably go back inside." His mouth opened, but I continued, not letting him get a word in. "And you should probably get back to Pembrooke. You've got your job and Sophia to see to."

I knew he'd argue, and I was proven right when his jaw clenched and he declared, "I'm not leaving you."

Fortunately, I'd reached my limit on pain for the day, so saying what I knew would make him leave couldn't cause me to hurt any more than I already did. "I don't want you here, anymore," I stated flatly. "You've provided what I needed, and it's time for you to go. I *want* you to go, Quinn."

"You don't mean that."

Why? Why did he have to make this so fucking hard? "I do!" I shouted, my voice echoing through the snow-covered trees. "I do mean it! I want you to go. Thank you for all you've done for me, and I'll never be able to repay you, but it's done. We. Are. Done. In every single way possible. I'm staying with my mom for a few more days, and I don't want you there. Please, Quinn, please. Don't make this any harder than it already is. Just leave."

"I want to help you." His ravaged voice cut me to the bone.

"Funny," I laughed without an ounce of humor. "That was all I wanted to do for you. Now maybe you'll understand what I felt every time you gave me a piece of you, only to rip it away again."

I hadn't even noticed I'd been crying until just then. I turned and headed back toward the church, but not before issuing my parting shot. "Go home, Quinn. You would have walked away from me eventually. That's all you're capable of. So do us both a favor and walk away now."

I didn't stick around for a reply. Instead, I let the door between us close for good.

It was the only way I'd survive.

3 2

QUINN

I RIPPED ANOTHER board up and hurled it across the back yard. The fact that I was sweating my ass off even with the light dusting of snow on the ground was a testament to how hard I was pushing myself. After I'd dropped Sophia off at school that morning, I'd come out on my back deck to have a cup of coffee and try to calm my mind by staring out at the amazing view of the mountains that surrounded me.

That hadn't worked.

Three feet out from my back door I stepped on a spot that was starting to rot through. What had started as a simple task of replacing the rotted board had quickly turned into me taking my aggression out and ripping the entire goddamned deck up.

In the middle of fucking winter.

I'd caught a brief glimpse of my neighbor—an old lady who'd lived in the house next door all her life—and didn't miss the look on her face. She thought I was crazy. And as I ripped another piece of wood up, oblivious to the nails that jabbed into my work gloves, I couldn't help but agree with her. I was so hot from working that I'd discarded my jacket twenty minutes ago, leaving me in just my jeans and a long sleeved thermal.

Half my deck now laid in a pile of rubble off to the side. It had been a week and a half since her father's funeral. Three days since Lilly returned home from Jackson Hole, and the only reason I knew that was because Ethan had let it slip that Eliza was staying at her apartment to keep an eye on her. I guess I should have been thankful that they were both back in Pembrooke for the next several months on the tail of Ethan's Super Bowl win, but I couldn't stop thinking that *I* should be the one taking care of her.

I still hadn't seen her. My texts and calls had all gone unanswered. I felt like I was missing a major piece of myself, a piece I needed in order to live. I had no one to blame but myself for the way things had turned out between us, but the worry ate at me until I was so consumed with it I could barely function. I needed to know she was all right. I needed to know she was coping. But I had no right, she'd made that clear.

I reached for another board and ripped with all my might. "Ah! Son of a bitch!" I looked down to see a nail had ripped clean through the sleeve of my shirt. The blood bubbling from the jagged cut on my arm oozed over onto the torn fabric, staining it a dark crimson. Using my teeth, I ripped the gloves off my hand and stomped back into the house, slamming the door behind me.

I jerked the sleeve up my forearm and held it under the faucet at my sink, sucking in a sharp hiss as the water stung the cut. It didn't look like it needed stiches, but I'd definitely need to clean the bastard out really well. Bending low, I grabbed the First Aid kit from under the sink and tore open several alcohol pads. I welcomed the pain that lanced through my arm as I wiped the wound clean. Honestly, the burn was a welcome distraction from the intense ache I'd been living with for the past month. One pain just worked to mask the other.

My cellphone rang from the back pocket of my jeans just as I finished wrapping a piece of gauze around my arm. "What?" I barked into the phone, not bothering to look at the display.

"Uh… Quinn? This is Quinn, right?"

At the unfamiliar man's voice, I pulled the phone from my ear and glanced at the screen to see an unknown number. I brought it back up and answered, "Yeah. This is Quinn."

"Quinn, this is Kyle, from the dance school. I got your number from Lilly's phone. I'm sorry for interrupting, but is there… do you think you could get down here? Soon?"

White-hot fear froze me from the inside out. "What's going on?"

"It's Lilly—" Before he had a chance to finish, I was moving through the kitchen, snatching my keys off the counter as I passed. "I'll be there in ten."

I disconnected the call and rushed out of my house into my truck, telling myself that if it were something really serious, he would have called 911, not me. But whatever was happening was bad enough for him to go through Lilly's phone in order to find my number.

My foot sat so heavy on the accelerator that I cut the time from my house to the studio in half, breaking every single rule of the road in order to get to Lilly.

The brakes screeched as I pulled into a spot right outside the school's doors. The blinds to the studio up front were drawn, but when I hit the main door, it was unlocked. Kyle and the other teacher, Samantha, stood in the lobby, both wearing equally anxious expressions on their faces. I could hear music playing from the first studio, but ignored it as I stomped toward them, demanding, "What's going on?"

Kyle held up his hands to slow me down. "Calm down. She's okay. Well, physically."

That didn't help one fucking bit to soothe my frayed nerves. "Will someone please tell me what the fuck is going on? Where's Lilly? What's the matter?"

Kyle's face was painted with worry, and if I didn't know he was gay that look might have set me off. "She's not doing well," he finally admitted. "She's put on a brave face since she's been back so we wouldn't worry, but we knew it was all an act."

Samantha nodded her head and her eyes shown bright with unshed tears. "We were fine with letting her pretend as long as we thought she was actually getting better. But then this morning…"

"What happened this morning?"

Kyle dropped his head and gave it a small shake before looking back up at me. "Just… come with me." He led me over to the studio door. Stopping at the small window in the door, we stood side by side and looked through the glass at Lilly as she danced, but it wasn't the same. Her body was jerky, not fluid. Her face wasn't at peace. She looked exhausted, but kept on going. Sweat glistened over every inch of her body, her skin flushed red with exertion. I was able to recognize the X Ambassadors song even muffled through the door, and once "Unsteady" came to an end it started all over again.

"She's been at it since we showed up around seven this morning," Kyle said, pulling me from the sight before me. "Same song over and over. Sam and I have come in here to try and get her to stop, but it's like she's a zombie. She won't even stop for water." I looked into his eyes and saw nothing but sadness. "We didn't know what else to do. She can't push herself like this. Physically, it's not good for her, but she won't listen to us. I actually tried to shut the music off and she nearly bit my head off. She's not our Lilly right now. It's like she's trapped in her own head and refuses to come out."

I turned back to the window just as she attempted to execute a leap. I'd seen her do the same jump before, only this time she barely caught any air. She looked like she was seconds away from collapsing.

I put my hand to the knob and gave it a twist, glancing at Kyle over my shoulder as I pushed the door open. "Thanks for calling me. Let me see what I can do." He nodded right before the door closed behind me.

Her eyes were closed as I moved a few feet into the room, rested my shoulders against the wall and just watched, trying to think of any way to get Lilly to stop. I hadn't noticed the dark circles under her eyes, or how sunken her cheeks looked from the window, but now that I was standing closer it was obvious that Lilly had lost weight... weight that her already slight frame couldn't afford to lose.

I'd been right to worry. She wasn't taking care of herself. She wasn't okay. And just as I'd feared, it looked like she was in the middle of a breakdown. The only thing I could do to help was be there when it finally hit her full force.

I didn't have to wait long.

As soon as the man started singing to his father about trying to fight when he felt like flying she lifted up on the ball of one foot. Her body began to turn, and her leg extended out to her side. But before she could make the turn completely, her ankle gave and she fell to the floor in a crumpled heap. Rushing from my spot at the wall, I hit my knees only inches from her and lifted my hands to move the hair from her face.

"Baby," I whispered, running my hands down her limbs to make sure she wasn't hurt. "Are you okay?"

Her head came up and tears skirted down her cheeks in a quick rush. "Quinn." Her voice broke on that one word, and I knew she'd finally reached the tipping point. "I miss him so much." Then her body folded in on itself as deep, ravaged, gut-wrenching sobs tore from her. I sat on the floor and wrapped my arms around her, pulling her trembling frame into my lap and holding on tightly.

"It's okay," I breathed into her ear, as I rocked us back and forth. "Let it out, baby. I've got you. Just get it all out."

Her body shuddered and shook violently as each anguished

cry broke free, shattering a piece of me with every one. I don't know how long we sat there on the cold, slick floor of the dance studio before the tremors started to lessen. The sobs had finally quieted, but in their place, silent tears continued to fall, soaking through the front of my shirt.

At one point Kyle had peeked through the door, finding us sitting on the floor in the middle of the room, and went over to stop the music before exiting once again. It felt like an eternity had passed before she finally cried herself to sleep in my arms in the silent room. When I felt it was safe to move, I stood from the ground with Lilly in my arms and carried her out of the studio. She didn't wake, too physically and emotionally exhausted. She simply burrowed into my neck and let out a stuttered sigh.

"Her apartment unlocked?" I asked Kyle and Sam. Kyle grabbed a set of keys off the front desk and led me through the back of the school to the interior stairs. He went up before me, unlocking the door and held it open so I could carry Lilly across the threshold undisturbed. He followed through the apartment and into her bedroom, his worried eyes resting on her as I lay her down in her bed.

"Thanks for coming. I can stay with her until she wakes up."

"I've got it," I rasped. There was no way in Hell I was leaving her. Not now, not after she'd just cried her sorrows out on my chest. I was staying, whether she wanted me to or not. I needed to be with her just as badly as she needed a shoulder to lean on. And now that I'd seen her, I couldn't walk away. I was determined to be that shoulder for her as long as she'd allow it.

Kyle gave me a hesitant look. "You sure?"

"Positive. I'm not leaving. You can either stay here with me, or you can go down and handle Lilly's classes for her."

He looked from me to her and back again. "I'll go down to help Sam. You know where to find us if you need anything."

I toed off my boots and set my keys and cellphone on Lilly's bedside table, offering a polite, "Thanks," just before climbing on top of the mattress next to her and pulled her body against mine.

Seconds later the sound of the front door opening and shutting echoed through the apartment. I finally had Lilly back in my arms.

I just wish it had been under better circumstances.

33

LILLY

I FELT LIKE I'd been hit by a truck.

My eyes burned, my throat was sore, and my entire body ached every time I took a breath. I couldn't remember the last time every muscle in my body hurt so bad.

The sky outside my bedroom window was dark. The only light in my room was what poured through my bedroom door. My bedside clock showed it was a quarter to seven, and I rolled to my back and tried to remember what had happened that day, why I was still in bed.

A clang sounded from somewhere inside my apartment as I was trying to pick through the pieces of my fuzzy memory, and suddenly I remembered. It all came back to me like a movie playing on a screen, like I was just an observer and hadn't been the one to actually live through the breakdown.

I remembered waking up with a pain in my chest so acute I couldn't breathe. I remembered walking down to the studio in a fog, desperate to escape the reality that my father was gone. I remember losing it, falling to the ground as my sobs choked me, only to have Quinn scoop me up and hold me, attempting to offer me comfort as the weight of everything that had been happening came crashing down on me.

What sounded like pots banging together pulled me from my head and back into the present. I stood from my bed and slowly crept into the hall, my sore body protesting every step. I stopped on a dime at the sight that greeted me. I'd expected to find Eliza as soon as I stepped from the hallway into the living and kitchen area, but that wasn't who was standing at my kitchen stove.

"Hey, sweetheart. How are you feeling?"

I let my eyes drink in the sight of Quinn as he turned back to the skillet resting on one of the burners. Using one of the spatulas Eliza had left behind for me, he flipped the pancakes before cutting off the heat and sliding the perfectly round pancakes onto a waiting plate.

"How long was I asleep?" God, I barely recognized my own voice. It sounded and felt like I'd been gargling with rocks.

"About eight hours."

Oh damn, I'd slept the entire day away. Pushing that realization to the side, I asked, "What are you doing here?"

He turned and walked toward the small kitchenette table, setting the plate down next to a bottle of syrup and a glass of water that were already in place. "I wanted to make sure you had something to eat when you woke up."

It was then that I noticed the bandage wrapped around his forearm. The sleeve of his shirt was rolled up, but that did nothing to hide the bloodstains on the cotton. "Oh my God." Without giving it any thought, I rushed to his side and grabbed his arm, lifting it for closer inspection. "What happened?" I could see the faint red from where blood had seeped through the gauze bandage, but it appeared to be old. "Are you okay?"

He took his arm from my hold and lifted his hand, tucking pieces of my hair behind my ear. "I'm fine. This is nothing. I cut it on a nail when I was fixing my deck."

"Do you need stitches?"

His lips tipped in a soft smile as he stared into my eyes, and as the silence around us grew heavy, I realized just how much I'd missed him. "Don't worry about me," he spoke softly, placing his hand at the small of my back to lead me to the table. "Let me take care of you right now, yeah?" He pulled out the chair and waved for me to sit. I did so and looked down at the food in front of me.

His kindness was too much. If I hadn't cried myself to the point of dehydration earlier, I probably would have morphed into a blubbering mess. Luckily, my tear ducts were no longer producing. "Th-thank you," I rasped. "But you didn't have to do all this."

"I wanted to," he spoke so earnestly, so sincerely. The look on his face made my stomach flip. He looked like it was taking everything in him not to touch me. I knew the feeling. However, after everything we'd been through—everything he *put* me through—I just didn't have the strength for it. I was done in every way possible. After today's meltdown, I knew I needed to reserve what little energy I had left into healing *myself*. No matter how badly I wanted to, I just couldn't heal Quinn. It was time I took care of me for a change.

I blinked rapidly, my eyes so dry they itched. "Quinn, I..." I had to swallow past the thickness in my throat. "I think you should go."

He grabbed the back of the chair next to me and slid it across the floor until it was only inches away. Once he sat, he rested his elbows on his knees and took both of my hands in his. "Lilly, I'm not leaving. After what I saw in that studio, it's clear you need someone to look after you for a while. I'm going to do that. You shouldn't be alone."

I slid my fingers from his grip and sat tall in my chair. In the past, I might have caved to the beautiful concern written all over his handsome face, but I couldn't do that anymore. For my own peace of mind, I needed a clean break. "If that's what you really think, then I'll call Eliza. But you can't stay here. I need you to go."

I could see the determination in his eyes. I knew that look as well as I knew all of his others. He was setting in for a battle. "Baby, you lost it in front of me, Kyle, and Samantha. They were worried about you. Hell, *I* was worried about you. I'm not leaving here until I'm convinced you're okay."

Yep, he was geared up to fight me. Only, this time it wasn't going to work. The damage he'd done, coupled with the loss of my dad made it impossible for me to get past the animosity brewing in the pit of my stomach. "I know, Quinn, believe me. I lived through it." I replied sarcastically. "I appreciate your concern. But I don't *want* you here. Don't you get that?"

"Baby—"

With that one word, I snapped. "Stop!" I shouted. I stood so fast the chair behind me crashed to the floor. Quinn followed suit and reached for me, but I managed to sidestep his hold. "Don't call me that. And don't touch me."

He held his arms out in surrender, but that didn't stop him from slowly moving toward me. With each step he took, I took one backward. "Okay," he said quietly. "All right, I'm sorry. I don't want to upset you right now, Lilly. But you're not all okay. Can't you see that? You need someone to take care of you."

"I know I'm not okay!" I bit out. "I know that, all right? I know it'll take a lot of work, and I'll probably have more days like today, but the difference between me and you is, I know I'll eventually move past it, because, unlike *you*, I can't imagine walking through the rest of my life with this pain in my chest." I balled my fist up and hit the spot right above my heart for emphasis, and at my words Quinn's entire body locked up and quit advancing. I thought I had cried myself dry, but the sudden dampness on my cheeks proved me wrong. I reached up to brush the tears away only to have more fall in their place.

"You can't take care of me, Quinn," I continued, my voice as ravaged as my heart. "How can you expect to help me through my loss when you're still holding on to your own? You're so consumed with the past that you can't see what's been right in front of you." I threw my hands out and gave a humorless, slightly hysterical laugh. "Please, explain to me how you think you can fix me when you can't even fix yourself. Jesus, Quinn. Do you realize you've never even *talked* about her? She's the mother of your daughter and you've never told me about her! You kept everything about you locked up so tight I never stood a chance, did I?" Reality suddenly slammed into me with the strength of a sledgehammer. I felt like such a fool. "All this time," I whispered. "All this time I've been falling in love with you, and you knew... you *knew* you'd never be able to love me back, didn't you? And you just *let me* fall deeper anyway."

I expected the shutters I'd grown so familiar with to fall over his expression. Instead, a look of pure anguish spread across his features. "I'm sorry," he whispered. The words sounded like they were ripped from his throat. "I'm so fucking, sorry, Lilly. I never meant to hurt you."

I sniffled and pointlessly brushed more tears away. "But you did. Over and over again. I can't do it anymore, Quinn."

It was like my words were too heavy for him to carry. His knees buckled and he fell to the couch, his head in his hands as he repeated, "I'm so fucking sorry." I stood silent for several seconds as he ran his fingers through his hair. Even disheveled, even hurting, he was still the most beautiful man I'd ever seen. "I don't... I don't know how to let her go."

If there had been any pieces of my heart left intact, they would have broken right then and there. I couldn't allow him to continue to hurt me, but I also couldn't stand to see him suffering. Dropping to my knees in front of him, I took both of his hands and held tightly. "That's not what I wanted. I'd never ask you to let her go, Quinn. She's a part of you and always will be. She gave you Sophia. There's beauty in that. I'd never expect you to let that go. I didn't want to replace Addison. I wasn't trying to take her place. I just wanted a place of my own in your and Sophia's lives."

His green eyes began to glisten and grow red, and I knew he felt the finality of what was between us just as strongly as I did. What we had was officially coming to an end, we both knew it, and that killed, but it was time for us to stop torturing each other.

"You can't fix me, Quinn. And I can't fix you, no matter how badly either of us wants it. We both need to heal, and we can't do that as long as the other is holding us back."

His eyes squeezed shut and he shook his head like he was trying to dispel my words. When he finally opened them again, I felt the agony reflected in the jade depth down to my very soul. "What are you saying?"

I pulled in a deep, fortifying breath and finally said what I needed to say. "We aren't good for each other."

He shook his head again. His fingers clenched around mine to the point of pain. "That's not true," he objected desperately.

"It is," I whispered. "It is, Quinn. And it tears me apart to admit that, because I love you *so much*. But we can't keep doing this to each other. I need to get past losing my father, and you need to learn to cope with your past. I tried... I tried so hard to be what you needed, to help you see you didn't have to live like this, but I can't do it anymore. I'm sorry."

I finally let go of his hands and stood tall, moving away from the man who had my heart. It felt like an eternity, but what I'd said finally began to penetrate, and Quinn got to his feet, looking down at me like the thought of leaving gutted him. "I wish things were different, Lilly. You have no idea how badly I wish that."

I offered him a sad, watery smile. "I think I have some idea, because I wished that, too."

He moved to the front door, his hand resting on the knob as he looked back over his shoulder one last time. "I know you don't want to hear it, and you probably won't believe me, but I do care about you… more than I've cared about anyone in a very long time."

I shrugged as a fresh wave of tears rolled down my cheeks. "I wish that was enough."

He nodded his head, turned the doorknob, and pulled it open. "You know I want the absolute best for you, right?"

"I do. And I want the same exact thing for you. Take care of yourself, Quinn."

His shoulders slumped as he stepped across the threshold. His back remained to me as he whispered, "You do the same, baby." And with that, he was gone. The snick of the door closing behind him rang out like a gunshot.

It was done.

I wanted to curl into a ball and let life pass me by, but I couldn't. It would hurt, but I'd put one foot in front of the other and, eventually, I'd move on with my life, just like I told him I would.

I only hoped he'd learn to do the same.

QUINN

*I*T HAD BEEN two weeks since Lilly cut me out of her life, and I grew more and more miserable every day. She wouldn't even look at me when I stopped by the school to pick up or drop off Sophia.

I'd gotten to the point where I was thankful to be on shift at the firehouse. At least I couldn't fixate on Lilly when I was in the middle of fighting a fire. Things were slow at the station, today. Normally, I would have been happy for the down time, using it to catch up on sleep. But it seemed like every time I closed my eyes, the dream of the car crash came back, only this time, when I looked over into the passenger seat, it wasn't my Addy that I saw there.

It was Lilly. And she was wearing the same heart-broken expression on her face that she had the day I went to the studio and saw her completely shatter.

I felt like I was losing my mind, being pulled in two directions. There was the part of me that felt unworthy of her love. I hadn't been able to protect my wife three years ago. Hell, if not for me, she'd still be alive. I didn't deserve another chance at love after failing so completely with Addison. Then there was the part of me that rebelled at the thought of letting Lilly go, which led to guilt at the thought of betraying my wife.

Not that it mattered, because she was finished. No matter how badly I wanted to hold on to the small piece of goodness Lilly offered, the soft ray of light in my dark world, I'd hurt her too much. She was done. And for the second time in my life, I'd lost the best thing that had ever happened to me.

I was a mess, and beating the hell out of the punching bag in the weight room of the fire department wasn't helping like it usually would.

"You good there, Mallick?"

I looked over to find Tony watching me from his place on the weight bench. He was probably the closest thing I had to a friend within the department. Tony was about ten years older than me and had been with PFD for about fifteen years. I liked him, he was a decent guy, which was why I hadn't minded picking up a shift for him a while back. I knew he was good to return the favor.

"Yeah," I breathed heavily. "I'm good."

He regarded me skeptically. "You sure? Because you look like you're trying to drive your arm right through that bag. Won't be much use in a fire if you snap a bone working out."

Wrapping my arms around the bag to hold it steady, I dropped my forehead against it and worked to get my breathing under control before finally admitting, "It's Lilly. I don't know what the fuck I'm doing, man. I'm going crazy."

"What about her?" he asked, raising an eyebrow. "I thought you guys broke up."

"I don't even know if you can call what happened a breakup since we were barely together to begin with." And if I hadn't thought it was possible to feel worse than I already did, admitting that out loud just proved I was wrong.

"I'm not sure I'm following."

I sighed and moved from the bag, ripping the tape from my knuckles before grabbing my water bottle and downing several long gulps. "We were together... we spent our free time with each other, we were sleeping together, but there wasn't a label, you know? I just... I couldn't put a name on it when it came to that." Running my hands through my sweat-soaked hair, I dropped onto the bench across from him. "I cared about her... still fucking do, more than I should. But she said she loved me and I freaked. Ended whatever it was we had. Then her dad died and I couldn't bring myself to stay away. She needed someone to lean on." I paused as the memory of her breaking down gutted me. "I wanted to be that person for her."

"So be that guy," Tony answered with a shrug, like it was the easiest thing in the world. And I guess it was, for a family man like him. Tony had a wife who adored him and two little kids. To him it probably seemed as simple as breathing.

"It's not that simple. I've got Sophia to think about." It was a bullshit excuse, even I knew that. I dropped my head and studied my hands, the gold of my wedding band glinted in the overhead lights. "I can't be the guy Lilly needs."

"And what is it you think she needs?" he asked after several seconds of silence.

"A forever guy," I replied honestly. "I can't be that. I'm too fucking broken. I had forever once, and I lost it. She deserves better than being the woman I call when I start feeling lonely. She deserves a guy who'll worship the fucking ground she walks on." Even as I said it, the thought of her with another man made me damn near murderous. How fucked up was that?

"That what you want?" At his question, my eyes darted from my ring to Tony. "You want her to find some other guy? You think that'll make what you're dealing with right now easier?"

"Fuck no," I growled in response, without thinking. It was purely instinctual.

"So, let me get this straight." Tony leaned forward and rested his elbows on his knees as he studied me. "For the first time since your wife passed, you finally found a girl who caught your eye. Not only that, but you actually *liked* being with her."

I nodded, wondering where he was going with all this.

"So things start to develop between you two, and when she tells you she loves you, you freak, feel guilty because of Addy, and bail. But when something in her life knocked her down, you wanted to be the one she leaned on to get through the hard times, because despite feeling like you're cheating on the memory of your dead wife, you still want this girl. How am I doing so far?"

"Uncannily accurate," I grumbled and waited for him to finish his come-to-Jesus speech.

"Because you love her."

At that, I froze. It wasn't a question, it was a statement, and judging by the look on Tony's face, he felt pretty damn confident in it. As he should, because he was right. I was in love with Lilly. I'd known for a while now, but the realization did nothing to ease the turmoil rolling around inside of me.

"I do," I finally admitted out loud for the first time. "But I shouldn't. It's not right."

The look on his face was one I hadn't expected. I thought I'd have confused him, thrown him for a loop, but what I saw when I looked at him was understanding. He seemed to get it, which surprised to hell out of me.

And when he finally spoke, and revealed the truth behind that understanding in his eyes, I was floored. "You know, Sarah's not my first wife."

"What?"

He nodded as a wave of sadness passed over his face. "Yeah. I was married once before, right out of high school. She was…" he trailed off, seemingly lost in thought. "She was my everything. Never thought I'd have something like that with anyone else. Connie was *it* for me."

My stomach dropped as I asked, "What happened?"

The smile he gave me was full of pain. "Two years into our marriage, she got pregnant. Didn't think I could be any fucking happier than when I saw those two pink lines, man." He laughed lightheartedly at the memory, and I found myself smiling along with him. And then the memory appeared to turn bad, because the happiness disappeared as he continued. "It was a rough pregnancy, but we were just so excited to finally meet our baby that we didn't let it get to us, you know?"

"I know," I said softly.

"She was already in her ninth month when she woke up bleeding one night. I rushed her to the hospital, but the placenta had torn, and she was bleeding so goddamned much..." He stopped for a while and breathed deeply, dropping his head in an attempt to compose himself. It took a few minutes, but I let him be, gave him the silence he needed to get himself to a better place. When he was ready to finish his story, he looked up. "I lost them both that night. My wife and my son."

"Christ," I breathed as my chest squeezed to an almost painful level. "Tony, fuck, I'm so sorry, man."

I couldn't imagine going through the same loss Tony had. If it hadn't been for Sophia, I don't think I would have made it. But he lost *both* of them. The fact that he was able to move on from that spoke to the character of the man, and I had an entirely new level of respect for him. "I didn't tell you my story because I wanted you to feel sorry for me. I told you because I get it. I know what you're struggling with right now, Quinn. When I first met Sarah, I couldn't imagine giving her that piece of myself that had belonged to Connie. It felt wrong. I felt like I was betraying her for falling for another woman. So I get what you're going through.

"But having been in your shoes, I have a perspective on the situation that you can't see yet. And if telling my story can help you move past this, I want to do that. I was just as broken as you are now, but falling for Sarah when I was at my lowest was the smartest fucking thing I've ever done. After I lost Connie and our son, I was barely living. I didn't want to feel for Sarah the way I did, but she'd gotten under my skin. She burrowed deep and wouldn't let go." He gave a little chuckle before going on. "She saw the pain I was in and she wanted to help me. It didn't start out as something romantic, it was just her wanting to be a friend."

Christ, what he was saying was so much like what I'd gone through with Lilly. There'd been an attraction between us from the start, but it took a while for us to come to terms and act on it. We'd gotten to know each other on a totally different level first. We became friends. *Best* friends. She'd been what I hadn't even realized I needed.

"That friendship grew into something else, and that scared the shit out of me," Tony expressed. "I was where you are now. I fucked it up and almost lost her for good. But it took doing that for me to open my eyes and realize something. Loving Sarah didn't mean what I had with Connie was any less important. Connie was everything I needed back then. I became an adult with her, learned responsibility, learned what it meant to be a real man and put someone else's needs and wants above my own. She helped me grow into the man that was worthy of a woman like Sarah. She gave me exactly what I needed when I had her, and being with her taught me how to give Sarah exactly what she needs now. I don't think I'd be where I am today without the lessons I learned with Connie.

"Some people aren't lucky enough to find the love I had with Connie once in their lives. I was lucky enough to find that *twice*. How can that possibly be bad? If what you feel for Lilly is even a fraction of what I felt when I met Sarah, you need to grab hold of that, brother. Because I can promise you, Addy would want you to be happy. She'd want you to find a good woman who can take care of you and Sophia. If that woman is Lilly, don't fuck it up and lose it because you're scared. Every goddamned thing that matters in life is scary. Nothing worth having ever came easy. You and I learned that the hard way. But falling in love a second time doesn't mean you're devaluing the memory of your wife. It just means you're one lucky bastard. Take all those lessons Addy taught you in the past and be the man Lilly needs today and every day in the future."

I felt like I'd just taken a fist to the gut. It hurt to breathe as I admitted, "I think I might be too late on that, man. I hurt her. I fucking hurt her too many times. She's done with me." Christ, saying that out loud burned something fierce.

"She's not done, Quinn."

I looked over at him, my heart aching with each beat in my chest. "She is. She told me we weren't good for each other."

Tony stood and gave my shoulder a pat. "Then be good for her, man. She's still here. She's alive and breathing, and as long as that's the case, it's never done. Be the kind of man that's good for her. Pull out all the stops to get that second chance, and I swear, it'll be worth all the blood, sweat, and tears you put into it."

I was thankful when he headed out of the weight room. I needed time to process everything he'd just said, and I wasn't sure I could do that in the company of others. It took an hour for the wakeup call to fully penetrate. By the time a call came in for a small kitchen fire, and I was pulled from my inner musings, the battle that had been raging inside me for months suddenly seemed to disappear. I felt a sense of calm I hadn't experiences in years. Finally, I knew what I had to do.

I had to be the man Lilly needed.

When we got back to the firehouse, I found Tony in the locker room. "Hey, I need a favor."

He secured the towel around his hips and gave me a knowing grin. "Yeah? With what?"

"Think you can cover my next shift for me?"

That grin on his face grew into a full-blown smile as he answered, "I got you, brother. Go do what you need to do."

I fully intended to do exactly that. I just hoped I could fix the damage done from trying to hold her at arms-length for so long, because I finally accepted that I couldn't imagine a life without Lilly in it.

And I prayed that she felt the same.

QUINN

Y PALMS WERE sweating, the skin on the back of my neck tingling, as I made my way up the familiar walkway toward the front door. It had taken two weeks since my talk with Tony to set my plan into motion, but now that I was finally here, standing outside a house I'd come to know so well, I was second-guessing my decision.

I had no doubt they didn't want to see me. They probably didn't want to hear a word I had to say, but if I had any hope in fixing this deep, bottomless hole inside of me, if I had any hope of fixing myself and getting Lilly back, I needed to do this.

I closed my eyes and pulled in a deep calming breath. On an exhale, I reached out and pressed the doorbell, listening to the faint chimes echoing through the solid wood door.

The door opened and her eyes grew wide with shock. "Quinn. This is a surprise."

"Janice," I tipped my chin down. "How are you? I'm sorry to just drop by like this."

"Is everything all right? Is Sophia okay?" She fidgeted nervously with the necklace she'd worn every day since Addison and I gave it to her as a birthday present. The locket held a picture of Addy as a baby on one side, and a picture of Sophia an hour after she was born on the other.

"Sophia's fine, she's with my parents." I swallowed around the mass in my throat and asked, "Is Garrett home?"

She didn't look any less confused as she stepped to the side to let me in. "Yes, of course. Come in. I'll get him for you."

"I actually need to speak to both of you. If that's all right." Janice led me into the living room. It looked exactly the same all these years later, and memories of all the happy times I'd spent here as part of my wife's family assaulted my senses. I hadn't been back to this house, back to Seattle, since I uprooted mine and Sophia's lives and headed to Pembrooke. Being back here, surrounded by pictures of Addy was both painful and comforting all at the same time. It had taken a lot for me to not let the pain of the memories debilitate me, and I still had so much work to do but, thanks to the therapist I'd started seeing three times a week, I was learning to remember the good times I had with my wife, and tried to look beyond the guilt.

I didn't want to let the past consume me anymore. And in order to do that, I needed to face this one particular obstacle. The biggest one I'd had yet.

"I'm not going to lie, Quinn. You're kind of scaring me right now. It's not like you to just show up here. Are you sure you're okay?"

I offered a small smile to the woman I'd once loved like a second mother. To be honest, that love was still there, but I'd buried it under so much grief and despair, I'd forgotten how good it felt. "I'm trying to be," I offered softly.

Something about that statement seemed to hit Janice, and she jerked back a step. Then, slowly, her eyes tearful, she nodded her head. "I'll just go get Garrett," she whispered, and disappeared down the hall.

As I waited, I made my way over to the mantle above the fireplace, studying the pictures I hadn't seen in ages. I stopped when I came to one that made my heart squeeze in my chest.

Reaching out, I picked up a photo of Addy and me at our wedding reception, bringing it closer to my face. God, we were so happy. I remembered it like it was yesterday. We were in the middle of our first dance as husband and wife. Everyone was watching as we moved across the floor, our heads bowed together as we whispered to each other, lost in our own little bubble. Halfway through the song, Addy gave me a playful smile and asked if I wanted to sneak any of the bottles of booze from the bar out under her skirts when the reception was over. I'd pulled back with a surprised laugh. She'd joined in seconds later, and the photographer captured the moment on camera.

After losing her, I'd forgotten what it was like to be that happy. I'd grown so accustomed to carrying my sorrow with me, I couldn't remember what it was like to have my shoulders free of that miserable weight.

"If I remember correctly, you two stole away with about a thousand bucks of top-shelf booze in Addy's dress that night." My head jerked up at the sound of Garrett's voice. I hadn't even realized I was smiling, really and truly smiling, until I felt it slide from my face at the sight of him. I set the picture back on the mantle and turned to face my father-in-law. "Hello, Garrett."

He tipped his head at me. "Quinn. What can we do for you, son?"

Son. Christ. I took a step back in shock at his casual use of that word. *Son.* I hadn't heard that in so long. Hadn't deserved it.

I cleared my throat, hoping to dislodge the emotions welling up inside of it. "Can we... can we sit? There are some things I'd like to say to you and Janice."

He nodded, and he and his wife sat side by side on the sofa. I took the chair across from them, resting my elbows on my knees and wringing my hands together as I tried to recall the speech I had planned out for this very moment. But the words escaped me. I couldn't even remember where to start.

"Fuck," I hissed, raking my hands through my hair in frustration. "I don't know how to do this," I said, more to myself than to them.

"Do what, exactly?" Garrett asked, pulling me out of my head.

I looked between him and Janice as nerves started to take over, and I began to rock back and forth in the chair. "Apologize," I finally answered. "I came here to apologize to both of you, but nothing I can think to say is good enough. I want to tell you how sorry I am, but now that I'm here I'm fucking it all up."

Janice's forehead wrinkled in confusion. "Apologize to us for what, Quinn?"

I could hear the anguish in my own voice as I finally admitted, "Apologize for taking your daughter away from you. I'm so goddamned sorry for putting you through so much pain. I've wanted to say this to you for three and a half years, but I was too much of a fucking coward."

"You..." Janice trailed off and a lone tear breached her eyes and traveled down her cheek. She visibly struggled to find the words, but Garrett didn't have the same problem.

"You think we blame you for Addy's death?"

"It was my fault," I rasped, losing the tenuous hold I had on my emotions. I hadn't cried in years, not since I lost her, but now, sitting in front of two people who'd both earned my love and respect... well, it was all too much, and I felt the wet hit my eyes before I could do anything about it. "It's my fault. If I'd have been paying better attention—"

"It was an accident!" Garrett boomed. He stood from the couch and began pacing in agitation. "Jesus Christ, son. It was a goddamned accident. Is this what you've been thinking all these years? That we blame you for losing Addy?"

My gut clenched in discomfort. "You could barely look at me..."

"Because I was hurting. Christ, Quinn. No parent should ever have to bury their child. But I never, not once, blamed you for what happened that night."

I turned my wide eyes on Janice to see she was silently crying, her hand over her mouth. "Oh, Quinn, honey. How could you possibly think that?"

"Because it's the truth!" I shouted, shooting up from the chair. "You both know it, that's why neither of you spoke hardly a word to me before I left. You know it's true!"

Garrett's voice was suddenly so much lower when he stepped into my space. "Yes, I hardly spoke a word to you, except to fight with you when you informed us you were leaving, but not because I blamed you. Because I was pissed. We lost our daughter that night, our only child. No parent should ever have to feel that pain. But Janice and I were so goddamned thankful that you'd made it out alive. It was the only thing that got us through that time. But then you took yourself away from us, too. We didn't just lose Addy that night, Quinn. We lost you as well. And that pissed me off. Maybe I should have handled it better, son, but I didn't know what else to do.

"You wore your grief around your neck like a noose. There was no pulling you out of it. Every day you slipped further and further away, and goddamn it, I resented you for that. I was mad you shut us out. Because you're *my son*." His own tears broke free and made tracks down his face as he put his hands on my shoulders and squeezed, giving me a slight shake. "You've been a part of this family since the first time Addy brought you home. You always will be. I'm so sorry we've let this go on for so long, that we led you to believe you carried the blame. That stops now, son. Right this goddamned minute, you hear me?"

I let the tears run, unchecked as he pulled me into a crushing embrace. When we separated, Janice was right there for a hug of her own. She wept into the fabric of my shirt as I held her tightly.

"We love you, Quinn," she whispered against my chest before taking a step back and wiping at her eyes.

My voice was ragged as I said, "I love you too. Both of you, and I'm sorry I put you guys through this." I cleared my throat again and shook my head. "I don't know how to let go of the guilt. I miss her every fucking day. It kills me a little more every time I think about her, but I can't let her go," I rasped. "I can't let her go," I repeated on a whisper.

"Who said you had to?" Janice asked quietly. "You'll never be able to let her go completely. You had a life together, you two made a beautiful child. But that doesn't mean you can't be happy. It doesn't mean you can't move on." She cupped my cheeks in her soft hands. "Honey, you can't stay stagnant like this, it's not right. She wouldn't want to see you so miserable. You have to move on, sweetheart."

My throat burned like fire as I asked, "How? How do I move on?"

She sniffled and her fingers clenched against my skin. "You start by forgiving yourself. If you can't do that on your own, let me and Garrett help you, please."

I took her wrists in my hands, not to remove them, but to absorb more of her touch. "I want to try," I whispered.

Janice smiled so brightly her eyes glittered, just like Addison's used to do. Her hands fell and she moved back to sit on the couch. Garrett joined her and wrapped an arm around his wife's shoulder. I followed suit and sat in the chair. "Do you know I heard you laugh—really laugh—at Sophia's birthday party for the first time in three and half years? That woman, Lilly? She whispered something to you and for just a second, you forgot to feel miserable and you let go."

I let out a little chuckle. "You're a lot more intuitive than I'd like."

"Don't feel bad for falling for her, son," Garrett chimed in, surprising me that he'd noticed as well. "She was a beautiful woman, and for a brief flash, she seemed to make you happy. Addy would want you to be happy."

I rubbed my hands against the stubble on my jaw and admitted, out loud for the very first time, something I'd known in my gut and my heart for months. "I love her."

"Then we're happy for you," Garrett said. "And we'd love a chance to get to know her."

"Is she helping you?" Janice asked. "Is she the reason you're finally here?"

That familiar shame came back in full force. "Not for the reasons you're thinking. I hurt her... *badly.* I want to make it right, but I knew I couldn't do that until I talked to you. I couldn't make an attempt to move on unless I fixed things between us."

Garrett leaned forward and clasped his hands between his thighs. "Well, son, if she's enough of a woman to make you want to let go of the past, then she already has my vote."

"Mine too," Janice added.

I hadn't realized it until they both said it, but that was exactly what I needed to hear. Their words, offered with so much sincerity, meant absolutely everything to me.

"HEY, SWEETHEART," I muttered as I brushed the snow from the cold stone that read:

Addison Mallick.
Beloved wife, mother, and daughter.

"I'm sorry it's taken me so long to visit. I've been a real asshole the past three and a half years. But you probably already knew that, huh?"

I smiled as I traced her name with the tip of my index finger. "It's taken me a long time to do a lot of things, honey, but I'm finally starting to heal everything I broke after you died." My voice dropped to barely above a whisper as I continued to talk to my wife. "I met someone. I didn't mean for it to happen. Hell, I didn't *want* it to happen for the longest time. But she got under my skin.

"I think you'd really like her. She's great with Sophia. She gives everything she has to the people she cares about, and she loves 'Landslide.'" I chuckled as I rested on my haunches. "She even taught that song to our daughter to help chase away bad dreams. How's that for coincidence?"

My palm flattened against the chilled marble, and I had to close my eyes and bow my head as I allowed my feelings to course through me. "I'll always love you sweetheart. Always. You'll have a piece of my heart until I take my last breath. But I think it's time I give another piece to Lilly. You'll be a part of me for the rest of my life, Addy. I'll make sure Sophia knows what an amazing woman her mother was, and how much we loved each other, but it was time for me to start moving on. I hope you're okay with that. I think you would be, but that doesn't make this any easier."

Looking down at my left hand, I toyed with the gold band that sat around my ring finger. *Time to move on*, I thought. That meant finally taking this off. My heart ached as I slipped the ring off my finger, but it wasn't the same debilitating ache I'd suffered with for years. It was more bittersweet. The end of one thing and the beginning of something new. Maybe one day, when she was old enough, I'd give the ring to Sophia as a way to remember her mother. I'd put it on a chain so she could wear it around her neck as a constant reminder that her mother was loved whole-heartedly. Sophia would love that.

Bringing the ring to my lips, I placed a kiss on the cold metal before sliding it into my front pocket.

I inhaled through my nose, blowing out slowly between my lips as I stood from the ground. "You gave me absolutely everything I needed when I had you. You taught me how to be a better man, a man worthy of the love of two of the best women I've ever had the privilege of knowing. Thank you for giving me that, honey. I hope I was able to give you the same thing."

Kissing my fingertips, I bent and placed the right over her name. "I'll be back again, I promise. I love you, Addy. Always."

I stood tall and turned back toward my rental car. Just as I lifted my head, something from the corner of my eye caught my attention. I turned my head just as the sun peaked out from behind the dreary gray clouds that always hung over the Seattle sky, and a rainbow formed, its colors pale but clear as day against the gray backdrop.

My lips spread into a smile that reached all the way to my eyes, and I kept my gaze on that rainbow as I made my way back to the car. There wasn't a doubt in my mind what that meant. Addy was happy for me. And that was her way of telling me I'd given her everything she needed.

QUINN

*ne month later*

I TURNED FROM the stove and slid a plate of pancakes in front of Sophia. She didn't bother lifting her head from her hand as she reached for her fork.

"Why the long face, Angel?"

She shrugged her shoulders and stuffed a huge bite of pancake in her mouth without answering. "Sophia."

She finally brought her eyes to mine and let out a dramatic sigh. "I miss Miss Lilly."

I lifted one of my eyebrows as I bent to rest my elbows on the island in front of her. "You see her all the time in dance class, honey."

"Yeah, but that's not the same," she insisted. "I miss her coming here for dinner and hanging out with us. I miss her making you laugh really hard."

"I laugh all the time, sweetheart."

She gave me a sarcastic scowl that only a seven-year old girl could pull off. "Not like you do with Miss Lilly."

I let out a small sigh of defeat. "You really miss her being around, huh?"

Her look screamed *duh*. "And she's sad like, *all the time*."

My back snapped straight and I frowned down at my daughter. "What do you mean?"

She shrugged again. "I dunno, like, she's just sad. She doesn't look happy like she used to. And sometimes, when I hug her, she looks like she wants to cry. It makes *me* sad. I want her to be happy, and I want you to laugh at her funny jokes."

I knew the feeling. Each day without her had dragged into the next at a snail's pace. I missed her so much it hurt, but I knew I couldn't try to win her back if I hadn't fixed myself first. So I had to give it time, no matter how fucking much I hated it. My actions meant more to her than my words, I needed to prove I was the man she deserved.

And I was trying.

There were still subtle reminders of Addy around the house, but that was more for Sophia's benefit than anything else. My wedding ring was sitting tucked away in a drawer, waiting for my daughter to be old enough to have it. The picture that used to rest on my bedside table now sat in a box on my closet shelf. I didn't get rid of anything, but it was packed away, ready and waiting to be pulled out when the time came to tell Sophia stories about her mother.

My therapist said I was making progress, and I walked out of each session feeling like I'd shed a bit more of that guilt I'd been carrying. For the first time in years I felt better, almost happy.

Almost.

Because I didn't think I could be fully and totally happy until I had Lilly back. But I was closer than I had been.

And I felt like the time had finally come.

"Hey Angel?" I called, taking Sophia's attention back from her pancakes.

"Yeah, Daddy?"

"What would you say if Miss Lilly started coming around here a lot more often?"

Her face broke out in a huge smile. "That'd be *awesome!*"

That was what I'd thought. I nodded my head, more determined than ever to take this final leap. It wasn't just for me, it was for Sophia, too. Me and my daughter *both* needed Lilly in our lives.

I needed to make a grand gesture.

And I knew exactly how I was going to do it. But I was going to need help.

Lilly

"God, I feel like I have to pee again."

I cut a look at Eliza as she hopped from foot to foot, her hands holding her belly. She looked about ready to pop.

"Then go pee," I told her. "I don't know why you're back here anyway. You have a nice, comfortable seat in the audience."

She shrugged her shoulders and continued her pregnant pee dance. "The show hasn't even started yet, and I've never been back stage before. I was curious. Isn't this where all the action's supposed to happen?"

I giggled and turned fully to face my best friend. "It's the Spring Showcase, Eliza. Not a Broadway production. These are just kids, it's not like there'll be much action."

I could have sworn I heard her mutter, "You never know," under her breath, but before I could question it, Ethan came hustling up to us. "Did I miss it?"

"Not yet," Eliza answered, turning her head so he could place a kiss on her lips.

"Miss what?" I asked in completely bewilderment. "What are you guys talking about?"

"Nothing!" Ethan grinned widely before changing the subject. "Did Eliza tell you the good news?"

"What good news?"

"We're moving back!" she squeaked excitedly, clapping her hands together.

My mouth dropped open and my eyes nearly bugged out of my head. "What? When? *How?*"

"Ethan's retiring."

I looked up at him, surprised to see he didn't look upset about it in the least. "But... you're only like, thirty!"

He shrugged like it was no big deal. "Yeah, but my knee hasn't been the same since the injury."

I gave him a skeptical look. "You just won the Super Bowl. I'd say your knee's doing pretty damn good."

"Yeah, but better to get out while I'm on top, right?" His hand traveled down to his wife's belly. "Plus, when this little guy—"

"Or girl!" Eliza jumped in.

"Comes along, we want to raise him, *or her*, here around family. It's already a done deal. And Noah hooked me up with a coaching job at the high school."

I would have worried he wasn't happy—football had been his dream since he was a kid—but he looked so damn excited at the thought of starting his family here in Pembrooke, that I couldn't help but feel overjoyed.

"So, I'm getting my best friend back, full time?"

"Yes!" Eliza yelped.

We both squealed and hugged each other tightly. The past several months had been so depressing that getting news like this filled me with a much-needed warmth.

"What's happening?" Kyle asked as he and Samantha came rushing our way. "Did we miss it?"

What the hell was wrong with everyone? "What are you guys talking about? What's there to miss?" Each of them gave me a different brand of a secretive smile, and I could have sworn they'd been huffing fumes. Was everyone around me losing their minds?

"Hi, honey."

I spun around, my forehead wrinkling in confusion. "Mom? What are you doing back here?"

She waved me off. "Oh, I just wanted to come and wish you luck."

I looked around the group of people surrounding me. "Seriously, what's up with everyone? The show's starting in fifteen minutes. You two," I pointed at Kyle and Samantha, "should be getting the kids ready. And you guys," I waved my hand at Mom, Eliza, and Ethan, "should be in your seats."

"The kids are ready and raring to go," Kyle said, giving me a wink. No one moved from our little huddle.

I opened my mouth to speak up when a familiar little voice shouted out, "Miss Lilly!"

My head whipped around and down as Sophia came rushing at me, wrapping her arms and me and squeezing tight. "Hey, Little Miss," I smiled down at her. "What are you doing? You should be getting ready."

She looked at me with that beaming smile I loved so much. "I got a surprise!"

I hefted her up and rested her on my hip. "Yeah? I *love* surprises. What is it?"

"Look!" she shouted, pointing in the direction of the stairs at the side of the stage that led down into the already packed auditorium. All the air rushed from my lungs as Quinn made his way toward us. He wore another suit that only accentuated his perfect body and in his right hand was a massive bouquet of the most perfect red roses.

Seeing him walking in my direction was a massive blow to my system. Sure, it had been impossible to completely evade him in such a small town, especially with me being his daughter's dance teacher. But I'd done everything I could the past few months to avoid eye contact, and we hadn't spoken a word to each other since my meltdown after my father's funeral.

He stopped just close enough for me to smell the intoxicating scent of his cologne, and with that familiar scent came a wave of memories of our time together that had me battling back tears. I'd put in so much work the past few months to move past all the sadness. I thought I'd finally gotten past the uncontrollable crying fits, but here, now, I was dangerously close to bursting into ugly sobs.

"Quinn," I said on an expelled breath.

"Hey, baby." Then he smiled. *Smiled.* All the way to his eyes, and the beauty of it hit me square in the stomach. I'd never seen anything so amazing in all my life.

"What... what are you doing here?"

He scooped Sophia up with his free arm and gently placed her feet on the floor before lifting the roses. "I wanted to give you these."

I moved on autopilot, taking the flowers from his hand as I stuttered, "Th-thank you. They're, um, they're beautiful."

His right hand came up and caressed my cheek, the pad of his thumb trailing along my cheekbone to my temple. Just that simple touch was like an electric jolt. "Not nearly as beautiful as you."

What was happening? Was I dreaming? That was the only logical explanation for the baffling turn my day had suddenly taken.

"I don't," I stumbled over my words, as his green eyes held

mine captive. His gorgeous *smiling* green eyes. "I don't know what's happening right now," I whispered.

He took one step closer, both of his hands cupping the sides of my neck as his fingers threaded through my hair. "What's happening is I've been a fucking idiot."

"Language, son!" At the unexpected female voice, I tipped my head to the side and noticed, for the first time, that Quinn's parents were standing right behind him... and beside them were Addison's.

Quinn's hands shifted my face back so I was looking up at him. "I've been an idiot," he amended. "I've missed you so much, Lilly. And I couldn't wait another day to see you."

I put pressure on his hands, needing to break the connection between us. I couldn't handle it. It was too much. My poor, battered heart couldn't possibly take another beating. "I don't—"

"I'm in love with you," he spoke, loud and firm, and I froze in place, my eyes going wide as my jaw dropped. "I love you, baby. I have for a long time. But I needed to work on letting go of my past before I could come back for you. I needed to prove to you that I'm the kind of man who deserves you."

I couldn't process what he was saying. After having my heart broken so completely, I didn't trust my own ears, so instead of saying what my heart was screaming for me to say, that I loved him too, I leaned in and spit out the first words that came to mind.

"Quinn, everyone's watching," I whispered, as my gaze darted around our captivated audience. "They can hear you."

He chuckled lightly as his hands gave me a squeeze. "I know, baby. I asked them to be here."

I reared back as far as I could with his hold on me. "What? Why?"

"Because if there's one thing I learned in everything I put you through, it's that my actions speak louder than my words. I couldn't just tell you I loved you. I had to show you."

His hands unwound from my hair and reached down, taking the roses from my hand and passing them off to Kyle so he could grip my own. I lowered my gaze and sucked in an audible breath that what I saw.

Or, more to the point, what I didn't.

His ring was gone.

"Lilly," he said, pulling my attention back to his face. "You aren't my dirty little secret. I'm not ashamed to be with you, I never was. I just had to learn how to let go of my past before I could give you exactly what you needed. But I'm ready to do that now. I love you with everything I am. And I'm asking… no, I'm *begging* you to give me another chance, because I can't imagine my life without you in it."

Damn it. I was crying again. In front of everybody. But I couldn't find it in me to care. "You really love me?"

He smiled that smile that took my breath away. "Since the first time you set your kitchen on fire."

I threw my head back and laughed, loudly and from deep within my belly. When I finally looked back at him, his eyes were on my dimple. He lifted our joined hands and ran the tip of his finger across it. "God I've missed seeing this."

The warmth in my chest spread through my entire body, blanketing me in happiness. "I love you too," I rasped, as more tears spilled from my eyes.

A loud, hiccupping sob cut through the moment, drawing my and Quinn's attention away from each other.

"Sorry," Eliza blubbered when we all looked at her. She waved her hands in front of her face like she was trying to stop crying. "Sorry. It's just so beautiful." She burst into another round of sobs as her face pinched up. "Oh god, these pregnancy hormones are the *worst*!"

Ethan wrapped an arm around her shoulders and drew her in so her front was pressed to his side. He buried her face in his chest and he waved at us. "Carry on."

Quinn and I both laughed as we faced each other once again. "So," he asked, using his grip on my hands to pull me flush against him. "Does this mean you'll take me back?"

I nodded wildly, and gave him a watery smile. "Yes."

He dropped his head back and declared, "Thank Christ!" to the ceiling.

"Yay!" Sophia shouted. "Miss Lilly's gonna be Daddy's girl-friend! I want a little sister for Christmas!"

I burst into another peal of laughter, only for Quinn to cut it off with a toe-curling kiss. I wrapped my arms around his neck and stood on my tiptoes to kiss him back with the exact same enthusiasm. It was by far the best moment of my life. I never wanted it to end.

Unfortunately, Kyle had to clear his throat and ruin it. "Sorry to break up this happily ever after, folks. But we've got a show to put on."

"Oh God! I completely forgot!" I cried, jumping from Quinn's embrace to turn and shout across the backstage area. "Five minutes, guys! Everyone get in place for the opening number!" The kids who'd been scattered all around started rushing to get into place.

Sophia's arms around me pulled my gaze downward. "Love you, Miss Lilly." Oh God, I couldn't take much more goodness or I was going to be just as emotional as Eliza. But that didn't stop me from squatting down and wrapping her in a tight hug. "I love you too, Little Miss." She struggled from my hold and squealed excitedly before rushing off to take her position. There was very little she loved more than being the center of attention on that stage, and I couldn't wait to watch her dance. It was quickly becoming one of my very favorite things.

Mom came up to my side and placed a kiss on my cheek. "You happy, honey?"

I leaned in for a hug. "So happy, Mom."

We pulled apart and she gave my cheek a soft pat. "Then that's all that matters." Then she turned and made her way to her seat.

"I'll just take this hot mess to our seats," Ethan said, guiding a still crying Eliza from the back stage.

Quinn's parents stepped in front of us, and Mrs. Mallick offered a genuine, "Welcome to the family." I got an arm squeeze from Quinn's dad before they, too, headed for the audience.

That left me and Quinn with his late wife's parents. I didn't know how to act, what to say to them, but I soon discovered that it didn't matter. Quinn's father-in-law slapped him on the shoulder like a proud father, and offered him a, "Good work, son."

Janice's eyes were full of happy tears as she smiled up at me. "I'm really looking forward to getting to know you."

"I'm looking forward to that, too," I whispered.

"Well, I guess we'll see you two after the show," she added, then the two of them made their way from the back stage.

I felt Quinn's arms wrap around my waist, and I turned to look up at him. "Are you going to go find your seat?"

He bent and pressed another kiss against my mouth. "No fucking way," he muttered softly against my lips. "Now that I've got you in my arms, I'm never letting go. I'll watch from back here. With you."

I sighed happily and melted into his embrace. "I love you, Quinn."

"I love you too, Lilly. And I'm going to spend the rest of my life showing you just how much."

Oh yeah. Definitely the best moment of my life.

And somewhere deep inside, I knew my father was looking down on us, happily. Because he knew his baby girl had found exactly what she deserved.

LILLY

I'D BEEN ON cloud nine all evening. As promised, Quinn stayed with me backstage for the entire program, only letting me go when I needed to flit around to help students get ready for their numbers. As soon as I was finished, he rejoined me, and we watched the kids dance while wrapped around each other.

Once the show was over, he'd asked if I would stay at his place for the night. Sophia was going to dinner with Addison's parents, then staying with them at their hotel for the night.

Alone time with Quinn after he confessed in front of all our family and friends that he loved me? Yes, please!

We walked through his front door, and I made my way into his living room, kicking off my heels as I went before dropping my purse in the recliner. I turned back and looked over my shoulder as I plopped down on the couch. Quinn was resting against the wall, his arms crossed over his chest, that gorgeous full smile on his face as he watched me.

"Do you still have *Vikings* on your DVR? I kind of got hooked on that show when I babysat Sophia that one time."

He chuckled and moved further into the living room. "I do. But first, there's something I want to show you. Will you let me?"

His question caught me off guard. "Of course."

"Wait here." He leaned down to the couch and kissed my lips before heading off in the direction of the hallway. He returned a minute later, carrying a cardboard box in his hand. "I want you to see this," he said, as he took a seat next to me, setting the box on the coffee table in front of us. "I need you to see that I want you in every single part of my life. And in order to do that, I need to open up, talk to you about my past."

My heart was in my throat and tears began to well up, clogging my throat and making me unable to speak.

"This is Addison, my wife," he spoke quietly, removing the lid off the box and pulling the picture out that I knew used to sit on his nightstand. He'd moved that, too. God, he was killing me.

I took the picture that he handed to me and looked down at it. Feeling myself smile at the sight of his own radiating out from the photo.

"I met her my first year of college after I moved to Seattle. We got married shortly after we graduated. She was…" A variety of emotion flitted across his face.

I rested my hand on his thigh and gave it a gentle squeeze, trying to offer comfort. "Quinn, you don't have to do this."

When he looked back at me, his eyes were shining brightly. "I want to." His voice was hoarse. "It's sad, and I still miss her all the time, but it doesn't hurt like it used to." He pulled in a long breath and I waited, giving him time as he composed himself.

Eventually, he continued, taking a different picture from the box and studying it as he spoke. "She was amazing. A great wife and mother, a fabulous daughter. There wasn't a single person she met who didn't instantly fall in love with her." He turned his head and gave me his eyes. "You would have really liked her."

"I have no doubt," I whispered. "She sounds wonderful. And

she helped to make you the man you are today. That takes someone truly amazing."

His smile touched his eyes as he leaned into me, touching his forehead to mine. "And she really would have liked you."

At that, I lost the strength to hold back the tears and let one… two… three slide down my cheeks. But these were different. For the first time in months, I was crying because I was well and truly happy. "I hope she would."

"I know it," he replied earnestly. "Lilly, I want… I want to keep Addy's spirit alive here, for Sophia's sake. I want her to know her mother. She was so little when she died. I—"

I reached up and pressed two fingers against his lips, silencing him mid-sentence. "For you and Sophia both," I told him. "I don't want her memory to be a bad one for you. Sophia deserves to know her mother, and you deserve to remember the woman you loved with all your heart. It's tragic how she was taken away from you, but we don't have to let it stay that way.

"She's an important part of both of you. That should never change. I wouldn't want it to."

"You mean that?"

"With all my heart, honey. I never want you to feel like you have to choose between the two of us. You gave her a part of you years ago." I rested my palm flat against his chest, staring down at it as I said, "I'm not going to try and steal it back. That's hers always. But I'm lucky, because there's another part that's just for me."

"God, I love you," he rumbled, his lips moving against mine as he asked, "You believe me, right?"

I gave him a small nod. "I do. And I love you, too."

"Thank you," he breathed against my skin. "Thank you for giving me another chance, for believing in me, for loving me."

"You're welcome," I smiled, giving him that dimple I knew he loved so much. "And thank you for fighting so hard to be the man I deserve."

"Always, baby. Now, about *Vikings*…"

"Yeah?" I asked on a soft moan as his lips skated across my jaw and down the throbbing vein in my neck.

"It's going to have to wait. Because I'm taking you to bed, right now."

I giggled and wrapped my arms around his neck. "You won't get any argument from me."

EPILOGUE

QUINN

hanksgiving

I TOOK IN the view of the chaos happening through the glass French doors that led inside as I stood on the back deck of my new house. Well, mine and Lilly's, seeing as she agreed to marry me when I proposed a few months back, and didn't put up much of a fight when I told her we were buying a house and moving in together.

I brought the bottle of beer to my lips and chuckled as the screams of children getting into God only knew what echoed from somewhere inside. We had a full house this year, and I couldn't be happier about it, but that didn't mean I didn't need an escape—a few minutes of peace and quiet to break through the pandemonium that came with hosting Thanksgiving with everyone you knew and loved.

Garrett and Janice had flown in from Seattle to spend the long weekend with us. Eliza and Ethan where here with their baby girl, Avery, and their own families. That included Ethan's sister Harlow and her husband Noah, and Eliza's father Derrick and stepmother Chloe, along with both of their brood of rugrats. We had a full house. Lilly's mother had commandeered our kitchen right alongside my mom, Eliza, and Janice. Garrett, Noah, Ethan, and Garrett had set up in front of the TV in our massive family room to watch the football game, and Chloe and Harlow were busy trying to keep the kids in check. From the sounds of something breaking inside, they weren't doing all that good of a job.

But I couldn't seem to care that my house was being torn apart, because I had everyone I loved right here under one roof. There was nothing but goodness and light in my life lately. I turned to face the snow-topped mountains that surrounded our little town in such beauty, thinking how thankful I was.

I was lucky enough to wake up each morning and get to make pancakes for the two most amazing women in my life. It couldn't possibly get any better than that.

The sound of the door opening and closing had me turning to look over my shoulder. The sight of Lilly joining me on the deck had a smile stretching clear across my face, and just like every time since the Spring Showcase, Lilly sucked in a breath at the sight of it. She'd told me not long after that the sight of my smile reaching my eyes was the most beautiful thing she'd ever seen.

I turned as she made her way in my direction. "What are you doing out here all by yourself?" she asked, as she fitted her chest to mine.

"Enjoying the quiet," I answered, wrapping her in my arms. She nuzzled into my chest and let out a content sigh. "What about you? What brings you out here?"

"They kicked me out of the kitchen," she grumbled, making me burst into laughter.

"You should have known better, baby." I chuckled, as she gave me a playful smack.

"Yeah, well. I thought I had veto power since it is *my* kitchen."

I smiled against her hair and asked, "You tell Jan and Garrett we're flying out the day after Christmas?"

"Yeah." She giggled. "I thought Janice was going to burst into tears. She's already making an itinerary."

"She likes hosting family," I told her, remembering how much she used to love it when Addy and I would pack Sophie up and come to stay with them for a few days, even though we lived in the same city. Janice was a natural-born hostess.

"Then I'm more than happy to give her that," Lilly whispered. My girl, always giving so much of herself. Luckily, now she was surrounded by people who gave her the very same.

We settled into silence, just holding on to each other, happy to live in the moment.

"You know, I've been thinking," she said a few minutes later, her voice all soft and happy.

"Oh yeah, what about?"

"I think we should change the wedding date."

I lifted my head and she tipped hers up to look into my frowning face. "If you think I'm pushing the wedding date back, you've lost your fucking mind." We'd fought when she informed me she wanted to wait until the following summer to get married. I'd wanted to make her my wife the moment she had my ring on her finger, but she refused to rush, saying a wedding took months to plan.

I'd finally caved, but I wasn't necessarily happy about it. Lilly was mine, but I wanted her tied to me in every way possible.

She smiled, giving me that dimple that drove me crazy. "I was thinking more along the lines of pushing it up."

My brows shot up in confusion. "What?"

"Yeah," she shrugged. "I mean, I wouldn't want to walk down the aisle big and pregnant, now would I?"

Every muscle in my body locked tight as my arms squeezed around her waist. "What?" I repeated on a ragged breath.

"I'm pregnant," she said so softly I barely heard it.

"Are you joking with me right now?"

She shook her head and giggled as my heart expanded in my chest. "No shit. You're really pregnant?"

"No shit," she confirmed. "I'm really pregnant."

I grabbed her hand and jerked her across the deck and back into the house, shouting, "Sophia!" as I pulled her through the kitchen and into the family room. The women saw my frantic motion and quickly followed after us. "Sophia!"

"What?" she shouted back, as she came around the corner.

"You're going to be a sister, baby!"

She screamed loud enough to burst an ear drum before launching herself at Lilly and me. I scooped her up and wrapped both of my girls in a bone-crushing embrace as everyone around us hooted and cheered with excitement.

"So I take it you're happy?" Lilly giggled, giving me that dimple.

I put my lips against hers as I answered, "Every time I think I couldn't possibly get any happier, you prove me wrong."

"I love you, Quinn," she breathed.

"I love you too, baby."

"And I love that I'm gonna have a baby sister!" Sophia yelled, making everyone burst into laughter.

Oh yeah. Nothing but goodness and light in my life.

And it just kept getting better.

The End
keep reading for an excerpt from PLAYING FOR KEEPS

ENJOY AN EXCERPT FROM PLAYING FOR KEEPS

The Pembrooke series is returning with another amazing story soon! One thing you have to know about me is that I love putting little Easter eggs in my stories to connect them together. Playing for Keeps introduces the next character in my Pembrooke series. Enjoy the excerpt below!

Chapter 1

Charlotte

Sunlight shone through the open blinds of my window, illuminating my figure in a warm, golden glow as I stood in front of the full-length mirror and stared at my reflection.

Happiness and sunshine were a contradiction to the emotions swirling inside of me as I took stock of the litany of scars that peppered my face and body. Wounds that had healed but left reminders behind in the form of physical imperfections. Most specifically, the pink puckered scar on my abdomen a couple inches above and to the right of my belly button. There was another that cut right through the arch of my left eyebrow that I could fortunately cover up whenever I filled my brows in, and another that slashed across my right cheekbone. Then there was the thin silvery line that angled across the bridge of my nose—a bridge that was no longer straight as an arrow thanks to having been broken.

The scars might have been months old, but if I paid them close enough attention like I was doing right then, I could still feel the burn of the skin opening up when each of the wounds had been created.

As it usually did whenever I started to really study myself, my vision began to grow fuzzy, and I found myself getting lost inside my own head.

There were some people in the world who led charmed lives. Most others were happy to live ordinary lives, filled with ups and downs, happy times and sad.

Then there are those like me.

I wasn't one of the fortunate few who led a charmed life. Hell, I wasn't even lucky enough to be one of the majority. More times than not, I'd have given anything to be blissfully ordinary.

The downs I lived through were nearly constant. Each day felt like a tumble even lower than the one before. Ugliness followed me around like a putrid black cloud everywhere I went. For every good day I experienced, there were countless bad ones that followed. For every happy moment, guaranteed sadness would follow in its wake.

It was a crushing weight I couldn't get out from under no matter how hard I tried, but I must have been a glutton for punishment because no matter how many times I got knocked down, I always forced myself back up. No matter how many bad days I experienced, I couldn't let go of that microscopic glimmer of hope that things might get better. Even though they *never* did.

Most people would have learned their lesson and given up hope for a turnaround, accepting the bad and learning to live with it, letting it taint them and turn them into something or someone else altogether. But despite my hard exterior, at my center I was still a soft, gooey optimist.

And it was that optimism that had gotten me into so much damn trouble.

In my attempt to pull myself out of the gutter, I'd blinded myself to the wolf in sheep's clothing. I'd hitched my wagon to a man I thought was a knight in shining armor. Turned out, just like every single man who'd come in and out of my life, he was a monster.

Malachi Black had the looks and the smooth charm that made me believe he was something he wasn't: namely, a good and moral person. I was far from the first woman he'd fooled, but *I* should have known better. I'd had more than my fair share of scumbags and users and criminals filter in and out of my life; I should have been able to spot the threat he was from miles away. But I'd been seduced by a set of dimples, an easy smile, and firm, hot muscles.

If only all criminals were as ugly on the outside as they were on the inside. However, that wasn't the case with Malachi. He had the sexy looks that belonged on the cover of a magazine.

By the time I realized the man didn't have a single decent bone in his body, it was too late. I wasn't just stuck, I was trapped, held prisoner in a life I'd willingly walked into with rose-colored glasses affixed to my face.

He might have been arrested a while back and locked up for a *very* long time, but the black mark he'd left on my soul remained, and by letting him into my life, I'd let in another monster as well. One that was arguably worse because he hid his evil behind a shiny badge and a uniform.

If Malachi Black was a blight on humanity, Officer Greg Cormack had been the devil incarnate.

In a long line of mistakes, getting tied up with those two men was the one I regretted the most. The penance I tried to pay in an attempt and make things right had nearly cost me my life—literally. Yet it still didn't feel like enough. The mess I'd tangled myself in had cost one good man his life and put countless others in danger, and I wasn't sure if there was enough atonement in the world to fix the damage I'd been a party to.

I was ripped from my depressing thoughts by the ding of my cellphone. I dropped my T-shirt, covering the scar left behind from that unforgiving bullet that tore through my abdomen and moved to grab my phone off the bedside table and check the text that had just come through.

Hayden: *Just a warning, Micah said if you try to cancel on dinner tonight, he'll come over there and drag you here by your hair. Don't forget to bring wine. Love you!*

If you had told me a year ago, or hell, even six months ago, that I would be best friends with a woman like Hayden Young, I'd have laughed in your face. Given what we'd both lived through, I was certain she'd want nothing to do with me, that I would have been a reminder of a nightmare she wanted to forget. But the strange bond that resulted from a shared trauma was something Hayden had insisted on cultivating, not running from.

Before we met, I'd been working as an informant for a detective by the name of Micah Langford. I'd wanted to help him and his partner, Leo Drake, take down Cormack and the other dirty cops and criminals he had working for him after he'd stepped in to take over Malachi Black's drug operation when Malachi had gone to prison. Hayden and Micah had been dating at the time, and to say our first meeting had been an unfortunate one would have been putting it mildly.

Hayden was one of the good people who'd gotten hurt in my tangled mess. Cormack had abducted her as a way to get back at Micah for coming after him, and I'd been shot trying to save her.

She'd been forced to kill him while I'd lain bleeding on that dirty floor in a desolate cabin in the middle of nowhere, and I worried constantly that having to do that was going to scar her in a very profound way.

I'd tried pushing both her and Micah away after everything was said and done, thinking they were better off without me around, but no matter how much I fought it, they refused to let me slip away quietly, all but forcing me into the fold of their lives. I'd gone from having no one to being an extension of their family.

I had dinner at their house once a week, saw Hayden and my ever-widening circle of friends for lunch or coffee at least twice a month, and she'd even asked me to be a bridesmaid in her wedding when Micah popped the question a couple months ago.

I shot off a quick reply, letting her know I was just about to head her way and started across my studio apartment toward the front door.

The place was the size of a matchbox but the whitewashed brick walls and view of the foothills and mountains that surrounded the valley from pretty much every window made the lack of space totally worth it.

I grabbed my purse from the kitchen counter and headed out.

Just as I shoved my key into the lock, the door across the hall from mine opened, and my neighbor's curler-bedecked head popped out.

Deloris Weatherby was at least eighty years old—and that was being generous—cantankerous as hell, nosey, and a bit—*a lot*—dramatic. Most of the other tenants in the building found her salty and suspicious nature annoying, but I saw a lonely old lady who was just trying to connect with people the only way she really knew how.

"Hey, Ms. Weatherby," I said with a wave of my hand.

Her eyes were cartoonishly small behind her Coke-bottle glasses as she looked right then left down the hallway. "Oh good. It's just you. I heard a door and worried it might be a burglar."

"No burglar. Just me," I assured her.

"I thought they'd finally come for my Precious Moments figurines. I have one of the biggest collections in the state, you know. It tends to make people jealous."

Oh, I did know. She'd told me about her extensive collection countless times. She'd even invited me over for lemonade once and spent two hours showing them off, giving me a very detailed history of when and where she'd gotten every tiny statue.

"Don't worry, Ms. Weatherby, your collection is safe. No burglars in sight."

"Well, that's a relief." With her knickknacks no longer under threat, she let out a relieved sigh and pulled the door open farther, revealing her brightly colored muumuu and fuzzy house slippers. "I just made a fresh pitcher of lemonade if you want to come in for a glass."

A sense of panic washed over me. Even with those crazy thick glasses, the woman was still blind as a bat, so she couldn't tell the difference between salt and sugar. It was something I'd discovered the hard way.

"I'd love to Ms. W, but I'm actually heading out. Maybe another time?"

She gave me a suspicious look. "You aren't going out carousing, are you? Young people these days. Always carousing." She pointed a gnarled, arthritic finger in my face. "That'll get you in trouble. You could pick up some good-for-nothing lowlife, and next thing you know, he's breaking into your building, stealing all the neighbors' most valuable possessions so he can pawn 'em to pay for his crank! It could happen. I just saw it on *Dateline*. All her neighbors were robbed blind! And the police never found her body," she added, almost as an afterthought.

"I'm not carousing," I promised. "Just having dinner with some friends."

One of her bushy white eyebrows hiked high on her wrinkled forehead. "At a bar?"

"At their house."

"And these friends . . . are they the criminal types?"

"One owns a flower shop and the other is a cop."

That seemed to finally placate her. "Well . . . all right then." That finger came back into my line of sight. "But if someone offers you a funny-looking cigarette, you say no. Understand? It could be *the weed*. And you make sure you watch them pour your drinks. I saw a show where a woman was on vacation and someone slipped something in her drink, and she woke up in a bathtub full of ice missing her liver."

Sweet Jesus.

I began backing away slowly toward the elevators, reminding myself to have a talk with my little old neighbor about all those crime shows she watched when I had the time. "You got it, Ms. W. Tell you what, I'll pour all my own drinks. How's that sound?"

"They could still have put something in the bottle, but I guess that'll just have to do. I'll keep a lookout. If you don't come home by morning, I'll call the police to start a manhunt."

"Sounds good. See you later, Ms. Weatherby."

After a quick stop at the store—because I had indeed forgotten the wine—I pulled up in front of Hayden and Micah's house. I made my way through the jungle of plants and flowers that made up their front yard and knocked on the front door.

It flew open a second later, and I nearly went deaf from the frequency of the high-pitched shriek. Hayden's daughter from her first marriage, Ivy, began to jump up and down in her little glittery pink biker boots. Her long curly red hair was a wild mess of tangles down her back and shoulders, and her neon pink tutu and skull leggings were covered in dirt, probably from playing in the garden in the backyard.

"Charlie! You're here!"

"Hey there, munchkin. How's it going?"

"It *was* good," she stated crestfallenly, "but then Mommy told me I couldn't have five dollars to get ice cream at school tomorrow." Her cheerful demeanor fell in an instant. Her eyes went big and began to water while her chin began to quiver. "Do you think *you* could give me five dollars?"

I gave my head a shake and tried my hardest not to laugh. "Uh-uh, girly. I know what you're playing at, and it's not gonna work."

Hayden's voice sounded from inside the house just seconds before she appeared in the entryway. "Ivy Young. What have I told you about using *The Look*."

Ivy dropped her head back and huffed dramatically. "I can only do it to Mike, 'cause he's a sucker."

Hayden beamed, proud as hell of her little girl's capability to manipulate her soon-to-be stepfather. "That's right. Now go wash up. We'll be eating soon." Ivy went skipping off, the five dollars all but forgotten.

"Look at you, raising your girl right."

"Thanks. I think so." She pulled me into a quick hug before taking the bottle of wine and waving me inside.

"That Charlie?" Micah called from the kitchen. "I heard the door. Is she here?"

We turned the corner into the kitchen and I spotted him with his hip propped casually against the counter, an open beer in his hand. He gave me a blank look.

"Yeah, I'm here."

"Well, would you look at that? She *is* alive," he stated sarcastically. "I was starting to wonder since I haven't heard from you in *forever*."

When it came to me, Micah had a tendency to be a bit overprotective. And by *a bit* I meant it was so over the top it bordered on downright intrusive at times.

It had started when I was working with him and Leo to take down Officer Cormack and only got worse after I was hurt. No matter how many times I told him it wasn't his fault, he still blamed himself for the fact I'd been tortured and shot. As time progressed and I healed, our relationship morphed into one where he began to look at me not as a responsibility but almost as a little sister. It was kind of sweet . . . when he wasn't being a royal pain in my ass.

"I just saw you three days ago," I said with a roll of my eyes. "Don't be so dramatic."

"I'm not being dramatic," he grumbled. "All I'm saying is you could maybe call once in a while. For all I knew, you could've been lyin' dead in a ditch somewhere."

I felt my lips pull up in a smile, something I hadn't done a whole lot of in my life until recently. "That's the very definition of being dramatic, Micah."

"Whatever," he continued to pout.

I moved to him and lifted up on my toes, placing a kiss against his cheek. "I'll call more often. Promise." He was being totally ridiculous, I knew that, but if a little more effort on my part was all it took to put him at ease, I'd do it. I owed him more than I could ever say. He'd saved me in more ways than one. He proved there actually were people in this world who were trustworthy, he'd given me a family and a place where I felt like I belonged, and I'd forever be in his debt for that.

"That's all I ask." His arm came around my shoulders, and he gave me a slight squeeze before putting me in a playful headlock. "Now let's eat. All that worrying really worked up an appetite."

CLICK HERE TO KEEP READING

She's a romantic at heart.

Chloe Delaney had three very specific wishes, growing up. She wished to stay settled in the small mountain town of Pembrooke, where she grew up, to one day be her own boss, and to fall in love with a man who would be willing to go to the ends of the earth for her. With her roots firmly planted in Pembrooke's soil and her bakery, Sinful Sweets, thriving, two of her wishes have already come true. When a handsome single father moves to town, she's certain she's found the man to fill the role of wish number three. The only problem is, you can't force a frog to turn into a prince.

He isn't the Prince Charming type.

When Derrick Anderson moved from Jackson Hole to the small town of Pembrooke, he did it determined to wipe the slate clean. After eight years spent trapped in a miserable marriage, he's made a vow to never take the plunge again. He wants to be untethered, not tangled up in the strings that come with a committed relationship. He has his daughter, his career, and an ex-wife hell bent on making his life unbearable. His plate is already full. The only problem is, he didn't have a plan in place to protect his heart from her.

Neither of them were prepared for the course their lives would take. But once a rollercoaster begins to move, you can't just climb off, now can you?

The only thing they can do is strap in, hold on tight, and enjoy the ride.

She knew what it was like to feel unwanted.

At an early age Eliza Anderson learned a very hard lesson. Sometimes the people who are supposed to love you the most are the ones that cause you the most pain. She learned to guard herself, hesitating to let anyone close for fear of feeling that rejection all over again. Then Ethan came into her life, and what had started as a simple childhood crush morphed into a friendship she eventually came to cherish above all else. He was her safe place. Her rock. A shoulder she could lean on. Until he ripped it all away.

He knew what it was like to feel like an outsider.

Ethan Prewitt grew up learning that you couldn't always trust the people you loved the most to be there. That sense of security he craved had always alluded him, leaving him to feel like an interloper in his own home. He dreamed of escaping the small town of Pembrooke and building a life where he didn't have to depend on anyone but himself. What he never expected was for his friendship with Eliza to grow into something that meant everything to him.

Mistakes were made. Hearts were broken. But now Ethan's home and he's determined to make it right. It was time for their relationship to come full circle.

Because what they had was once in a lifetime.

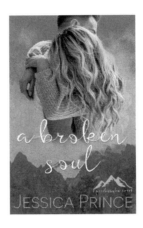

He's terrified of loving her.

Quinn Mallick already had his happily-ever-after, and in the blink of an eye it was ripped away from him. Now he's content to walk through the rest of his life carrying the weight of that guilt on his shoulders. He's convinced he doesn't deserve a second chance. But when the town's beautiful dance teacher turns her sights on him he finds himself questioning everything.

She's terrified of losing him.

Lilly Mathewson's once quiet, predictable life has been turned on its head. Feeling alone and adrift, she finds her comfort in the most unexpected of places. Falling for the town widower was never part of the plan, but there is just something about the temperamental man she can't seem to let go of.

What started as two grieving people leaning on each other has quickly turned into something neither of them expected. Lilly is ready to take the next step, but how do you move forward when the man you love refuses to let go of the past?

Especially when the only hope they have of healing their broken souls is if they do it together.

ABOUT THE AUTHOR

Born and raised around Houston, Jessica is a self proclaimed caffeine addict, connoisseur of inexpensive wine, and the worst driver in the state of Texas. In addition to being all of these things, she's first and foremost a wife and mom.

Growing up, she shared her mom and grandmother's love of reading. But where they leaned toward murder mysteries, Jessica was obsessed with all things romance.

When she's not nose deep in her next manuscript, you can usually find her with her kindle in hand.

Connect with Jessica now
Website: www.authorjessicaprince.com
Jessica's Princesses Reader Group
Newsletter
Instagram
Facebook

Twitter

authorjessicaprince@gmail.com

Made in the USA
Middletown, DE
13 August 2023

36604808R00184